AN ANGEL OVER THE AIRWAVES

Books by Dayle Schear

Dare to Be Different (Autobiography)
The Psychic Within (True Psychic Stories)
Believe (Spiritual Fable)
Tarot for Beginners (Book & Video)
An Angel Over the Airwaves 2006

AN ANGEL
OVER
THE AIRWAVES

A Novel by
Dayle Schear

Blue Dolphin Publishing

Published by Blue Dolphin Publishing, Inc.
P. O. Box 8, Nevada City, California 95959
Orders 1 800 643-0765
http://www.bluedolphinpublishing.com

ISBN: 1-57733-182-6

First printing, March 2006

Library of Congress Cataloging-in-Publication Data

Schear, Dayle.
    An angel over the airwaves : a novel / Dayle Schear.
        p. cm.
    ISBN 1-57733-182-6 (pbk. : alk. paper)
    1. Angels—Fiction. 2. Talk shows—Fiction. 3. New York
(N.Y.)—Fiction. I. Title.

    PS3569.C476A83 2006
    813'.54—dc22

                                                    2005037374

Cover Design by Stephany Hurkos, www.stephanyhurkos.com

Printed in the United States of America
5   4   3   2   1

This Book Is Dedicated
To All My Special Souls
In Heaven

For the wonderful souls in my life
who have recently passed,
I dedicate this to you.

Aunt Molly, 96 years of life;
Aunt Esther from New Jersey;
Johnny, forever and always;
Phil, you taught me how to live.

Acknowledgments

I wish to thank the following people for their encouragement, help and inspiration:

First and foremost, my husband Blythe—sometimes my teacher and mentor, and my best friend. I thank you, Blythe, for putting up with me all these years.

Karin, I'm proud to call you a friend. Karin and I collaborated on **An Angel over the Airwaves** for well over five years before it was written. She encouraged me to write Annie's story in book form. I call her my "idea fairy." Whenever I was lost in writer's land, I picked up the phone and Karin always had a great story to tell me about the adventures of our character Annie. Thank you, Karin, for always being there for me in more ways than one.

I want to thank everyone at Harrah's Bill's Casino in Lake Tahoe where I appeared for almost two years. John, Bobbi, Tim—what a great inspiration you all were. Without the down time at Bill's Casino, I would have never thought of writing again. Tim, thanks for your wonderful encouragement and for your inspiration.

Stephany Hurkos, what a wonderful person you are. I have been so privileged to know you and your kindness. Thank you for staying up late and listening to me as I read my chapters aloud to you. What are friends for?

Rose, thank you so much for being there for me always; I love you from the bottom of my heart. Thanks for encouraging me and telling me how proud you were that I was writing my book.

Andrea, thank you for being there for me, no matter what time, day or week I would emerge out of my writer's room, sometimes lost in my own house, sometimes bewildered. You were always there for me. When I needed just a line for my book—we writers call it a bridge line—somehow, some way, you always found the answer. Thank you from the deepest depth of my soul and its journey from my heart.

Special thanks also to my editor, Maybelle Boyd. I remember placing the call to Maybelle after many years and telling her I was writing another book.

"But I'm retired," she said.

"Well, Maybelle, not for long; I need you, only you." She came through. I really didn't want to write without her. She has the uncanny gift of letting me be me. There are no words to thank someone who has given you so much.

In Hawaii, we call it the Aloha spirit, which Maybelle certainly has. For without this very special editor—once teacher, writer, and playwright—this book would have never been written.

THANK YOU!

And now, Ladies and Gentlemen, read on; for Annie, **An Angel over the Airwaves,** is waiting to be read.

Some of the people who appear in this book
may be represented as composite characters.
The characters are fictitious.
Any similarities are merely by chance.

Chapter 1

The story I'm about to tell you is based on a spiritual tale.
It's been passed on through Heaven by a mere whisper
as long as I can remember.
Never in my wildest dreams would I have ever imagined
I would play a part in this grand, heavenly scheme of things,
but here I am.

My name is Gabriel. The tale that I tell you may change
your way of thinking about Heaven forever.

This story is amazingly delightful. You see, it all started one Sunday morning as I was doing my routine rounds in Heaven. I suddenly remembered I hadn't checked upon my favorite little one yet: Annie.

Annie is an angel; not just any angel, mind you. Annie was made in Heaven. She's special. I personally sent Annie down to Earth on a very special mission. She was to help guide the lost souls of Earth while giving them insight.

I would always check on her now and then. I was well overdue.

Peering down from Heaven wasn't an easy task, you know; but what I saw this time made my eyes flutter and my wings flap.

Annie was getting married, right in the middle of Central Park, New York. I watched as she recited her wedding vows.

She stopped at her fiancé's side. They turned and embraced each other with their eyes. There was a gentle smile on her face as they exchanged their wedding vows. The minister pronounced them man and wife.

Man and wife, for goodness' sake. Hello, down there! Is anybody listening? Annie's an angel! Hello.

Not only was Annie getting married against all Heavenly rules, she was marrying a mortal man. I mean, these things are uncalled for. I didn't know what to do. I was shocked, to say the least.

Oh! I might add the wedding really was very lovely.

There she was, all dressed in white. She was beautiful, if I must say so myself. Brandon, her new husband, was a handsome, charismatic gentleman. However, that's beside the point.

Suddenly, a shot rang out. Chaos set in. Annie slumped to the floor, shot by Brandon's ex-lover.

Brandon sat on the floor, holding Annie's limp body in his lap as blood dripped from her chest. He held her closely and rocked her from side to side in his arms, as he strained to speak through his tears. He pleaded, "Annie, Annie, don't leave me! Please don't leave me. I love you so much."

He cried, "Oh, God! Why me? I love her so. I finally found her— the one woman in the world who taught me how to love." He held Annie in his arms so tightly.

Annie looked up gently at Brandon. With the last of her gasping breath she whispered, "Look into my eyes; remember me. Please, Brandon, remember me."

Then, I watched Annie's frail little soul as it floated out of her body and from her new husband's arms while she made her way back home to Heaven.

I was taken aback when I next found her sitting in a chair, deeply engrossed in a book, thumbing endlessly through the pages.

The book she was reading—*The Transition of Life on Earth into Heaven*—explained it all, but Annie had refused to believe the words and their meaning. It was her guide book, the Book of Life.

I noticed her blonde curly hair hid her slim, demure body as she read. She glanced upward; her beautiful blue eyes fixed on the clocks that dangle where a wall would be, one clock reading Earth time, the other clock reading Heaven time.

Time is so slow here, especially when it is meaningless. She sighed to herself and continued to read.

I slowly approached Annie. Clearing my throat, I tapped her gently on her right shoulder.

"Annie, sorry to startle you," I said.

Annie glanced upward; she was not surprised or amused. "Gabriel, my guardian angel." She smiled. "You always appear when I fall off my guided path. Quite the man you are today, so distinguished and refined," she said.

"Annie, Annie, what am I going to do with you? The guidebook you're reading hasn't changed. You know the rules inside and out." I spoke firmly. "Annie, you broke the rules."

Annie sighed heavily again. She looked at me with her big blue eyes, then lowered her gaze. "I know."

I placed my hands on her shoulder in a fatherly way. "Annie, I just don't know what to do with you anymore. What are you looking for in that book?"

"A loophole." Annie smiled and looked up at me.

"I love Brandon. You have to help me. I promise, this time things will be different. I know in my heart Brandon and I are supposed to be together. That's why I have been reading my guide book." She thumbed endlessly through the chapters. "There must be something about Brandon and me in here. I just know it's in here somewhere. Brandon and I were supposed to be together; what went wrong?" she asked.

"I went wrong. I watched every move you made on Earth. I plucked your sweet little soul back to Heaven. You really messed up, Annie. The rule book states angels are not allowed to get involved with mortals."

I shook my finger at her. "Annie, Annie, Annie. What am I going to do with you? Now you have really done it. When are you going to learn? I keep sending you down to Earth to help guide people and you keep falling in love." I shook my head. "You see, Annie, it's not about loving someone that's wrong. It's your obsession with Brandon. Then you go and marry the guy. Annie, you're one of my most gifted angels. You're the best angel I have when you get things right. I just don't know what to do anymore."

I was momentarily lost for words. I tried again.

"On Earth you can observe. You can help. You can even manipulate a situation for the good of all; but Annie, you're not supposed to fall in love and, by the way, marriage to a mortal is not allowed." I sighed. "When are you going to learn?" I thrust my arms outward.

"The love that you have for Brandon—it's co-dependent love addiction. You're obsessed, young lady. What am I going to do with you?" I sighed in exasperation.

Annie smiled. "Maybe Brandon is my soul mate. Gabriel, please come here; check my guidebook with me. Maybe if we look together we can find something in the guidebook that will explain this."

"I don't think that is going to happen. Annie, you're one of my most gifted angels. But I have noticed lately you have developed too many human tendencies."

Annie cried, "I want to go back to Earth. I want to be with Brandon. I promise this time I'll do anything you want, as long as I can be with him." She pleaded her case.

"Annie, you must do nothing," I said. "You must let things happen the way they are supposed to. Remember, your mission on Earth is to help many souls. We want to diminish their pain as much as possible."

"I promise I will do whatever it takes; just send me back to Earth, please." Annie spoke from her heart with all the enthusiasm an angel could muster.

It was heart-rending, to say the least.

So I paced back and forth thinking. "Ah! This gives me an idea." I rubbed my chin vigorously. "There's only one way I'll send you back to Earth."

"How? Tell me how." Annie stared intently at me.

I smiled. "I'll send you back to Earth if you can find a way to help **one thousand souls.** I mean **really** help guide them on their path, give them insight, so when they're ready to enter Heaven's gate they won't be so clueless. I mean, really interject and help." I was very serious.

Annie jumped out of her chair eagerly with her hands open, her palms facing upward. "Gabriel, how am I going to do that?" she asked.

"That's up to you, Little Angel," I said knowingly.

Annie was demanding. "Gabriel, will I ever find Brandon?"

"Only if you abide by the rules I give you. If you break just one rule, then you will never see Brandon again." I was stern.

I motioned to Annie with my index finger. "Annie, come here. Sit next to me. I happen to have a copy of today's *New York Times*. Let's look at the apartments for rent and to share. I don't want you all by yourself; God only knows what would happen if I leave you alone." I glanced upward.

Annie pointed to an ad that struck her fancy. "Look, Gabriel, this ad is really interesting."

The ad read as follows: **Young man looking for roommate to share big apartment. Park Avenue. Must be clean and open to all kinds of friends coming over. Non-smoker. Rent $1500 per month. Call 212-555-5252.** "This looks good." Annie looked up at me.

"No, Annie, I think not," I said.

"Why not?"

"Annie, he's a man. You know all the trouble you have with men."

Annie shrugged her shoulders.

"Here we go! This ad is perfect." **Soho, New York City. Roommate wanted, single female preferred. Artistic in nature. Non-smoker. Loft, 2-bedroom apt to share. Must be spiritual. $1600 per month. Call early morning 212-555-2999. 419 West Broadway.** "What do you think, Annie?"

"Perfect. Now, what do I do, Gabriel?"

"Well, let's see now. I will give you enough money until you can get a job and rent that great new apartment in Soho. Annie, you will have to work."

I raised my hand over Annie's head and snapped my fingers.

Annie was now dressed in work clothes, ready to find a job and an apartment. Annie turned around slowly for me.

"Well, look at you," I said. "You're wearing a pretty black and white polka-dot sundress. Black shoes to match. The heels are not spiked—you know how clumsy you can be at times—and, might I add, your purse is stunning."

"Gabriel, how do I look?"

"Go look for yourself, Annie."

Annie paused momentarily in front of a mirror. "Wow! I look just perfect. I know I will find Brandon now." She spoke confidently.

"Annie, now remember, this is not about finding Brandon. This is about helping **one thousand souls.** Your life will be very different now. I'm counting on you to do this on your own. This is a test. If you really love him, you will do as I say.

"If, by chance, you run into Brandon or try to find him, he will not recognize you. You will always look the same, but the way Brandon perceives you will be different.

"He will notice some of your old tendencies. He will feel like he has met you before, or even as though the two of you had known each other in a different life. He will feel very comfortable around you.

"The two of you will share a lot of things. However, he will know you are not his Annie that died in his arms—the Annie he loved so very deeply. Brandon will feel emotions and feelings for you, but in a very different way.

"Annie, I can't stress firmly enough that, if you try to meet him, it would be a major mistake. It could create major karmic problems for Brandon as well as for you.

"Things will happen with Brandon when they are supposed to and especially when they are meant to be. You can't change this or even mess with this outcome."

My speech was long but effective. Annie listened to every word and nodded.

"Gabriel, had I known Brandon before?" she asked.

I hesitated and looked down. "Yes, Annie, you had met Brandon once before, in a different life."

"What went wrong? What did I do?"

"Annie, the both of you never got it right. It has to be right in order for it to be true love and not addiction. Brandon is your Twin Soul, not just your soul mate. He is the part of you that you have been searching for. It's just like a big jigsaw puzzle; when you find the missing part, it all fits.

"You are being given one more chance to get it right. If you fail, you will never see Brandon again. So don't intervene." My lecture was over.

Annie's eyes were cast downward; she felt a little ashamed. "I won't. I promise."

So I sent Annie back down to Earth.

New York City

Chapter 2

With suitcase in hand, Annie found herself in a taxicab in New York City. She heard the loud chatter of the city, horns honking, people shouting. While holding a newspaper in her left hand, she fumbled about, trying to smooth out her new polka-dot dress with her right hand.

"Where to, Lady?" the cab driver asked.

Annie was startled. "Huh?"

"Where to, Lady? I don't have all day. Where do you want me to take you?"

"Oh!" She held up the New York Times and read aloud, "419 West Broadway, please. The Soho district."

The taxi driver squeezed his way into traffic. He turned up his radio to drown out all the noise from outside.

Annie was spacing out while taking in the sights of NYC again, trying to remember all the wonderful times she had with Brandon.

Suddenly, the radio's blaring interrupted her thoughts. She heard a wild, zany DJ's voice coming through the speakers of the cab.

"Good Morning, New York City! This is Roll-over-with-Rob-in-the-Morning on 92.3 FM.

"Caller, you're live on the air with Rob. What's your beef about NYC today?"

Annie found this show rather interesting. People were calling in live on the radio. She was aware that Rob was trying to give them advice. Annie asked the cab driver to turn up the radio a notch; she found this show fascinating.

"Who is this guy?" she asked.

"I guess you're not from New York, Lady. Roll-over-with-Rob is the number one DJ in Manhattan. Everyone who is anyone listens to this guy. He seems to know a lot. When we want to know about a traffic jam, we listen. When something important is happening in New York, we listen. His talk show is cool. I'd better pay attention to the road. Be my guest; listen and learn."

Annie did just that. She listened and learned. He had a lot of listeners calling in. Mainly, they debated issues of the world…current events. Annie felt drawn to the sound of his voice. There was something familiar about him, something she couldn't quite put her finger on.

An idea crossed her mind. "Maybe if I called the station I could convince them to put me on the air," she told herself. "I could help people. This could be my way of helping one thousand souls in New York City." She jotted down the call letters of the radio station; after she was settled in her new apartment, this would be first on the list of things to do.

The taxi screeched to a halt. "Here we are."

"Thanks." Annie paid the driver.

The taxi driver drove off into traffic and Annie was left by herself. She double-checked the address of the apartment building: 419 West Broadway. "Well, this is it."

Annie looked around and studied the area. She noticed the apartment building was a brick brownstone building with seven tiny steps leading to the entrance. To the left of the building was the local cleaner. That was good for Annie, since she was always spilling something on herself. To the right was a Chinese restaurant. The area didn't look half bad. It was somewhat clean. Annie started up the stairs when she suddenly remembered she was supposed to call first about the apartment.

She opened her purse, looking for a cell phone. There it was. "Gabriel thinks of everything," she thought, "and what he doesn't think of he manifests. Oh, he must be having a grand time in Heaven watching me." Annie dialed the number.

"Hello."

"Yes, I'm calling about the room for rent. My name is Annie and I seem to be in front of your apartment building. Is the room still available?" she asked.

"Yes, it is. I'll buzz you in. Come to the fifth floor, apartment eight. I'll be waiting and, by the way, Annie, my name is Kate."

Annie walked into the apartment building, checking out everything on her way up to the fifth floor. There was an elevator, but she decided to walk. The building was very clean. She was pleased so far.

Annie knocked gently on the door. Kate answered. "Hi, Annie, come on in." Annie smiled and shook her hand.

Kate showed Annie around. Kate was very demure, a tall, thin blonde with straight shoulder-length hair, blue eyes and lots and lots of energy to match Annie's.

"Annie, this is the kitchen, small but cozy. We have all the appliances that you need. Everything comes with the apartment. It's spacious. Look up there; we have a loft that serves as my office and you're welcome to use it as well."

Annie climbed the stairs to the loft. Down the hall there were two bathrooms and two bedrooms.

"There's your room. I do hope you like it," Kate said.

"Kate, this place is amazing. All the photographs of very unusual people as well as their cultures. Do I detect a hint of Peruvian?" Annie turned toward Kate.

Kate nodded.

Annie gushed, "I just love the animal pictures, especially the lions and elephants of Africa. To make it interesting, to say the least, I notice the skyline of New York in the midst of all this. I especially love the rock stars' photos. Your photos tell a wonderful story. You are very versatile.

"I love all your photos. The placement in the hall of each photo is uncanny.

"The windows are so artsy. How the sun's rays capture the colors in your stained glass window and shed light upon the apartment, might I interject, is just heavenly. I also noticed that every room is painted a different color to coordinate with the photos." Annie was exhilarated.

"Annie, I'm a photographer by trade. I mainly photograph rock stars, animals and the city. It's quite an interesting job. I freelance a lot, as well. I do travel a lot. So there are many weeks you will have the apartment all to yourself. And what do you do?" Kate questioned Annie.

Annie had to think fast. She didn't want to let on that she was an angel yet; she hardly knew Kate. That information would be well saved for a later date. She had to figure out a way of landing this apartment without really lying.

"Kate, right now my father is supporting me. I have plenty of money. I plan to land a job in radio; that is my goal. I would love to have my own talk show and help people in a spiritual way. I just love this apartment." Annie smiled.

Kate thought Annie was so darling; she was mesmerized by her. She noticed the twinkle in her eyes. She felt that Annie and she would get along just great. And besides, Kate needed the money right now; she was pressed for cash. You might say she was in a little bit of a dry spell.

"Okay, Annie, you can move in."

Annie handed Kate the rent money and Kate gave Annie the key to the apartment.

"We will have plenty of time to get to know each other, Annie. If I can help you in any way, just ask," she said.

"I will, Kate. I have all I need for now."

Ordinarily, Kate would have checked her out, but something in her head said this would work itself out. She knew they would adjust to each other.

She also knew that they would end up friends forever. In Kate's spiritual fairyland mind, everything was happening the way it was supposed to, not merely by chance. Kate really believed this. She believed in giving people a break. She believed in trusting. Annie was special and she just knew it.

Annie slept well the first night in her room, until the alarm clock startled her. She hurried to get dressed and then made her way down the stairs to put on a pot of coffee. Kate was nowhere to be found. Kate must have left early.

Annie turned on the radio and, lo and behold, there he was, Roll-over-with-Rob-in-the-Morning. This was a sign, she thought. "This is it! This is the way I can help thousands of people."

She looked up the phone number in the directory for 92.3 FM and dialed the number.

"Good morning; 92.3 FM. How may I help you?" the voice on the other end of the phone said.

"Hi, my name is Annie. Whom can I speak to about getting on the radio with Rob?"

"Well, John is our program director. Would you like to speak to him?"

"Yes," Annie replied sweetly.

After a short pause a male voice said, "Hello, this is John. What can I do for you?"

"Hi, John. My name is Annie and I'm an angel. I was listening to your talk show and I found it most interesting. Is there a possibility that I can be on the radio with Rob and help people?" she said.

"An angel!" John shouted.

"Yes, John, I'm an angel; I know I can help your listeners."

"Well, Annie, I thought I'd heard it all. Hold on, please."

John put Annie on hold and turned to Rob, who was on commercial break. "Hey, Rob, we have a lady on the phone that wants to be on your show."

"And? What else is new?"

"She says she's an angel," John snickered.

"Is she crazy or what?" Rob asked.

"She sounds for real. I think she really believes it. Rob, you've had psychics on your show before. What's the difference between having a psychic or an angel?" John paused to consider his own question. "I don't know. It's up to you, pal; it's your show." John waited for Rob to respond.

Rob gave John a sly look. "I have an idea. Have this lady meet us for lunch 12 noon at the Stage Deli. If it works, why not? We've had everything else on air. I need to check her out. Could be interesting, you know. **An Angel over the Airwaves** would be great for ratings."

John reached for the phone. "Annie, Rob and I would like to meet you. Can you meet us at noon at the Stage Deli? By the way, what do you look like?"

"I'm blonde, blue eyes, medium height. But don't worry, I'll find you. I saw your ad in the Yellow Pages; I know what Rob looks like. I'll see you there at noon."

Annie had to decide what to wear; she needed to make a great impression. Since her wardrobe was slim and right out of a suitcase, she decided to wear her cute polka dot outfit again; at least it matched. There would be more time for shopping when she landed this job.

Annie was ready to go. She scooted out of the apartment, huffing and puffing down five flights of stairs to hail a cab.

She checked her watch. It was so unique. Her watch read Earth time as well as Heaven time. (There is a difference of 30 minutes, you know. Heaven allows for delays so it can fix things before they happen.) Earth time: 11:30 a.m. She needed to hurry.

"Taxi!" she shouted, waving her arm vigorously.

A taxi screeched to the curb. "Where to, Lady?"

"The Stage Deli and please hurry."

Earth time: 12 noon; right on the dot. Annie loved being punctual.

She walked into the crowded Deli. All eyes turned in her direction. And why not? Annie had a glow about her. She scanned the room until she saw Rob. She recognized him from the picture in the Yellow Page ad. She walked over to their table. John's and Rob's eyes were fixed upon her.

"Hi, I'm Annie."

Rob and John gestured for her to sit down. "Hi, Annie, I'm Rob and this is John, my program director. I hear you want to be on my show. By the way, here's a menu. Order whatever you want."

Rob was mesmerized by Annie; not only was she pretty, but also her glow of energy was not from this world and he knew it.

Annie stared at Rob. He was about 45, very good looking with well-proportioned features. Tall, nicely built. Salt and pepper hair that fell gently over his forehead. She loved his moustache. But most of all, there was gentleness in his eyes.

Annie suddenly remembered what I had lectured her about. She must not fall in love. She was on a mission.

John, the program director, was medium built and a little on the chunky side. He was about 43, slightly balding. His eyes were gentle and soft.

Rob asked Annie to tell him a little bit about herself. While Annie was speaking, Rob was finding it hard to finish his lunch. He found her so fascinating, so unique.

He interrupted her. "Annie, it really doesn't matter if you are an angel or not. I've made up my mind. I feel this would be so good for ratings. I mean, no one has ever had an angel on his show. I would be honored. I have but one question, though... Why me? Why choose my show?"

"Rob, I was sent down to Earth with a mission. I'm supposed to help one thousand people on earth. I mean really help them. I believe your show was chosen for me because you have the most listeners," she said.

"Well, I can't argue with that," he chuckled.

John was very observant throughout the whole conversation. He didn't know what to make of this. He hardly spoke.

Rob thought for a moment. Then he said, "Okay, Annie, I've made my decision. Why don't you come down to the station tomorrow; I'll put you on the air for a test run. We'll see how many people call in and how many people you can help. Besides, I need a boost for my karma. Isn't that what you would call this? Karma boost."

Annie nodded. "Yes, Rob, for whenever you help someone, it's recorded in Heaven."

"Okay, Annie. See you tomorrow at about 7:00 a.m."

Annie finished her coffee and off she went.

John looked at Rob. "What did you just do? You hired an angel. I don't believe any of this. I don't believe she's an angel," John argued.

"John, it really doesn't matter what you believe, does it? It's my show. I'm going to give the kid a chance. In fact, I'm going to do everything in my power to make her mega-famous. It doesn't matter if she thinks she's an angel. All that matters is that she helps people. We'll get to the bottom of why she thinks she's an angel, eventually." Rob continued to eat.

"You're smitten with her," John said jokingly.

Rob turned away.

"You find her attractive." John smiled.

"And your point is…?"

"I get it," John answered.

Rob spoke firmly. "And you know what else, John? She may cost me a lot of money, but she's going to make the station a lot of money.

"I'm going to put up billboards all over New York City: **An Angel over the Airwaves.** She will fly into everyone's dreams. Annie will become a household name when I'm through with her. I can see the dollar signs, John; trust me."

"Rob, that's not all you see, my friend." John rolled his eyes upward.

Friday morning, 7:00 A.M. Annie arrived at the radio station ready to go on air.

Rob motioned to Annie to sit next to him. "John will give you a headset so you can listen to the callers. Then just speak naturally and they'll hear you. I'll interview you first, and we'll get all of New York familiar with who you are and why you're here."

"Okay." Annie sat on the chair next to Rob.

"Good morning, New York City," said Rob in his husky radio voice. "We are broadcasting live. This is Roll-over-with-Rob-in-the-Morning and I have a special, unique guest this morning. Her name is Annie. She claims she is an angel…an angel sent from Heaven to help all the people of New York. What do you think of that, New York?" Rob paused, then addressed Annie.

"Annie, before we get started, tell me a little about yourself."

"Well, Rob, I was born an angel. You might say I was made in Heaven." She giggled.

"I see, Annie. Do you really expect me to believe that you're an angel? I mean, we have intelligent listeners out there. What's your mission on Earth?" Rob pretended to take Annie very seriously while playing the devil's advocate.

"Rob, my mission on Earth is to help and guide one thousand souls. What better place than your radio station?"

"Well, I can't argue with that," Rob said cockily. "Tell us a little bit about Heaven. I mean, what is it like up there? When we die, is that where everyone goes?"

"Heaven is a very special place, Rob. All souls who pass go to Heaven's gate, then to a holding station modeled after the planet

Earth. "Whether they are let into Heaven is another story." Annie shrugged. "That all depends on the life you have led on Earth and the many lives you have lived before, lifetime after lifetime."

"Whoa! Did you say lives we have led before? Such as in, Past Lives?"

"Yes, Rob, everything we do in this lifetime and all other lifetimes affects where we go when we get to Heaven's holding station. You know about karma? It's how we progress in each lifetime that determines our ultimate place in Heaven." Annie tried hard to sound light-hearted.

"Annie, can you tell me something about me...since you have access to Heaven and Earth?"

Annie stared very deeply into Rob's eyes; she saw the depth of his soul.

"You want me to tell you something about you?"

"Yes," he replied smugly. "Don't hold back. I have nothing to hide."

"Okay." Annie closed her eyes momentarily. "Rob, I see when you were about thirteen years old, you had a dog named Albert."

"That's true. Go on."

"Do you remember the time your house burnt down to the ground?" she asked.

"Yes," Rob answered softly.

"You and your family were going to visit your Aunt Mary. You refused to go because she didn't like dogs. Your family persuaded your Aunt Mary to accept Albert. So off you went with your family to West New York, New Jersey, to visit your aunt for the day.

"Later that evening after the long drive home, when you reached your house, it was burnt to the ground. If you had never left your house, you and your dog Albert would have died in that raging electrical fire. Am I correct?" she asked.

"Yeah! Albert lived twelve more years. He was the best dog I ever had. Boy, do I miss him." Rob snapped back to reality. "How did you know that?"

"And Rob, you know what else? I saw Albert in Heaven and he wanted me to tell you that he misses you, too."

Rob choked up and hurriedly said to his listeners, "It's time for a commercial break. We'll be right back."

He turned back to Annie and, frowning, said, "I'm sorry. I don't understand any of this. I don't even know how you knew about the fire."

John jumped in. "Rob, maybe she read about it in the paper."

Rob shook his head. "John, no one knows about this besides my family, and they're all dead. It was never in the paper. For God's sake, man, I was only thirteen years old." Rob tried to compose himself.

John held up a finger for quiet. "3, 2, 1, we're back on air."

"This is Roll-over-with-Rob-in-the-Morning and my special guest is Annie, our angel. Annie, either you're a great mentalist or some sort of psychic. I don't know. Or maybe you are an angel. Our phone lines are all lit up. Do you want to take a few phone calls and help the people of New York?"

"Yes, Rob. That's why I'm here."

"Did you hear that, New York? We have an angel over our airwaves." Rob called out, "Annie, you're live on the air with Sandy."

"Hi, Sandy. I'm Annie. How can I help you?"

"Well, Annie, I wanted to say I believe in angels."

"Sandy, let me focus on your voice. Ah, Sandy, your son Robert just passed away in a car accident. You wonder if the accident was his fault."

"Yes, Annie," Sandy sobbed.

"You couldn't have stopped your son on that day or any other day. I know you felt something bad would happen to him, Sandy. You'll have to believe me; he would not have listened to you."

Annie read Sandy's mind. "No, Sandy, this accident wasn't your fault. There was an on-coming car that hit your son head-on. No, Sandy, he didn't suffer. It was his time to go. He's now in Heaven with his brother Josh who died at birth." Annie asked, "Was that what you wanted to know?"

"Yes," Sandy cried. Thank you, Annie, and may God bless you." Sandy hung up, feeling somewhat relieved.

Rob was amazed and quiet; in fact, the whole studio staff was quiet.

Rob finally said, "Annie, we're out of time for today. We have to get back to paying the bills. Would you like to come back tomorrow? I'm sure our listeners would be delighted."

"Yes, I would; I have nine hundred ninety-nine more souls to help, Rob." Annie winked.

Meanwhile, all over New York while driving in their cars, people were listening to Annie, An Angel over the Airwaves.

Rob jumped in. "Thank you, New York. I know this is very unprecedented for our show, but I felt when I met this young lady that she was someone special. Now I know she is. We just might make her a regular feature on our show. Let's hear from our listeners. Please call in if you want more of Annie on our show. John, my program director, will take your calls." Rob chuckled.

Rob delegated a commercial break while he spoke to Annie.

"Annie, I will be off air in fifteen minutes. I know a quiet Italian place down the street; let's go there for lunch. I have a lot of questions I need to ask you before I put you back on air. Understand, little darling, I will be putting my reputation on the line for you. I need to know everything about you. Okay?"

"Yes, Rob."

So Annie and Rob walked over to Louie's Italian Restaurant about four blocks away. This time Rob went without John; he needed to be alone with Annie.

Rob's head was murky and spinning, to say the least. He had so many questions he wanted answered about Annie, he didn't know which way to turn. He felt he could turn into a babbling idiot at times.

When they reached the restaurant, Rob was greeted by the owner.

"Hello, Mr. Rob, and who is this?"

"Annie."

A Little about Brandon

Chapter 3

"Well, hello, Miss Annie." The owner nodded. "Rob, it's been a long time, my friend; I'm honored. I just happen to have your favorite booth available. Why don't you follow me?"

The restaurant's decor was simple and lovely. Checkered tablecloths covered the tables; candles flickered throughout and low-hanging lamps cast soft shadows on the walls. Gentle music in the background filled the room. The atmosphere was sensual but meaningful for Rob.

Rob was single now, after a very long marriage to his high school sweetheart. This year was a turning point for him. His wife had wanted more and left him for someone else. Rob never got over her. This had been their favorite restaurant. Until Annie, Rob had never taken anyone else to Louie's place.

As Annie and Rob sat close to one another, the owner couldn't help but notice and wonder.

Rob turned toward Annie, the look on his face serious. "Annie, I have so many questions. Just tell me what you are doing in New York, and why you are here? I need to know everything. I don't know if I believe in this angel bit, but I need answers. The press will hound you soon, and we need to be on the same page."

"Okay, Rob. I'll tell you my story briefly. First of all, I **am** an angel. I know that may be hard for you to believe, but over the course of time I will more than prove this to you. I have a guardian angel named Gabriel who watches over me. He even tells me in my head what to eat for breakfast."

"He does? Excuse me for asking, but what do you mean 'you were made in heaven'? Are all angels made in heaven?"

"No, Rob. Gabriel explained to me that I was special. My mother was from Earth. She married my father, who later died in the war.

18

My mother, who was pregnant with me when she lost him, died in childbirth of complications. Gabriel plucked me from my mother's womb as she was giving birth, so you might say I was born in Heaven, for that's all I know. Heaven is my home."

"Have you ever met your mother or father?" he asked.

"No, it's not allowed. Gabriel felt if I met them that my mission on Earth would falter. Gabriel raised me himself. He really was more than a father to me.

"They have strict rules in Heaven, especially when it comes to helping people on Earth. Rob, somehow I have not been doing so well down here. Gabriel gets very angry with me. You see, every time I come to Earth I fall in love with someone rather than help him."

"What? Explain, please." Rob stared intently at Annie. He didn't know how much more of this he could take. This whole story sounded contrived; however, her sincerity was overwhelming.

"For example, do you know the name Brandon Turner?" Annie asked.

Rob nodded. "Yes, I do. He's a huge television star; he's on in the late evenings every night. Everyone knows who he is. Why?"

"Well, do you remember a few months back he was getting married, and when the minister pronounced them man and wife, his bride was shot dead?"

"Yes."

"Well, that was me," Annie said proudly. "I was Brandon's wife. My soul went to Heaven and Gabriel was fuming at me the whole time."

Rob was drinking some water while listening to this story and he literally choked and started to cough out loud. Several waiters ran to his side.

"Are you all right, Sir?"

"Yes!" Rob waved them away and turned back to Annie. "THAT WAS YOU? Everyone around the world knows that story. They say Brandon has never recovered. He believes in his heart that he will find that special love again. So he hasn't stopped looking for her. That is so sad, Annie. Why did that happen?" Rob asked between coughs.

"Well, I'll tell you," Annie said with a sigh. "When I first met Brandon, I was on a mission to help several people on Earth. I stumbled upon his television show in New York by mere chance, as you might call it.

"I twisted my ankle outside his studio. Brandon had just come out of a restaurant on his way to his show when he noticed I was hurt. He ordered some people to take me into his dressing room so they could tend to my ankle.

"It was then our eyes locked and we knew we were supposed to be together. You see, Rob, once in a while that veil comes down, and you can see the person you have been with lifetime after lifetime. And that was the case with Brandon and me. We fell madly in love again. We spent day and night together for several months. Then Brandon asked me to marry him. I said yes."

Rob was eating his sandwich at a very fast pace, engrossed in Annie's story. True or not, she had him at this point.

"But Annie, I've seen pictures of Brandon's wife. You do look a little like her and her name was Annie as well, but is there any proof of all this or did you read this in a magazine?"

"No, Rob, you'll have to believe me; it's called blind faith. I'll tell you about our wedding day; then, maybe you will understand," she said.

"That evening Brandon was extremely dapper in his tux, even with his tie undone. He stared at me with intense longing. I felt his desire to be with me every time I looked into his eyes.

"Of course, I was a picture-book bride as well. I had daisies in my hair and wore an elegant satin dress and fairytale slippers. The wedding was so beautiful. All our friends were there."

Rob listened intently.

"Somewhere in the distance, I was told, a figure lurked by the punchbowl, moving closer to us.

"Brandon sneaked a quick kiss from me while the minister was performing the wedding ceremony. Then the minister said, 'I now pronounce you man and wife.' He slowly closed the Bible as Brandon swept me into his arms and planted the most passionate kiss on my lips.

"The figure loomed closer and closer; then, the woman slowly pulled a gun out of her black beaded Prada purse. Her hand trembled.

She locked her left arm onto her right elbow to steady her aim. She pointed the revolver straight at me while the guests were applauding Brandon and me with tears of joy.

"Just as Brandon and I turned to face the crowd of well-wishers, two shots rang out. Total chaos and pandemonium set in. There was screaming, running, and panic. I dropped to the ground, confused and in much pain. My beautiful gown was soaked with blood. I had been shot in the chest.

"I could hear Brandon gasp in disbelief. He fell to his knees and lifted me into his arms.

"Brandon pleaded, 'Annie, Annie! Don't leave me. I love you so much.'

"Rob, it took every ounce of my strength to speak as Brandon was holding me." Annie hung her head as she continued her story.

"I looked deeply into his eyes and whispered, 'I love you. Look into my eyes. Please remember me.' My voice faded.

"Brandon held me tightly to his chest while rocking me. He cried like a baby. At that moment Brandon realized I was gone. He collapsed on my body in unspeakable horror. The pain of it all pulsed through him in waves. Brandon cried loudly, 'She's gone! My Annie is gone.'

"I remember hovering over my dead body, watching Brandon while he held me. I heard voices shouting. Then I felt my spirit move slowly upwards toward Heaven. A rainbow of colors led me to the bright shining light above.

"One of the guests heard a gun drop to the ground. A woman shouted, 'Someone call the police. Hurry, call the police!'

"The murderer was a tall model. She fled into the crowd and was caught by a group of people who slammed her to the ground.

"She screamed, 'Brandon, I still love you! Now will you come back to me?'

"Off in the distance a woman shouted, 'My God, it's Brandon's ex- lover Vi.'"

Annie paused to catch her breath.

"So, Rob, that is my story. And that was the short version."

"Good God, girl, did Brandon ever know you were an angel?" Rob asked.

"I told him, but he didn't believe me. Just like you. So, when I went back to Heaven, I really got lectured by Gabriel. I pleaded with him to let me come back to Earth.

"Gabriel told me the only way I would be allowed to return is if I could learn to help one thousand souls, and that's where you come in. I chose your show to do it. That way I will be allowed to meet up with Brandon again if everything goes well. You see, Rob, I love him so. I never stopped loving him," Annie said.

"So why don't you just go down to his show and hook up with him again? Then you could prove to Brandon you really are an angel," Rob stated.

Annie shook her head. "Well, it's not that easy. I have to help one thousand souls first. I am forbidden to meet up with Brandon. Gabriel told me I have to let things unfold without manipulating them, or I will never see Brandon again. Ever!"

"I think I got it, Annie. I need time to mull this over right now. It's a whole lot of information that I need to process. I need time."

"Rob, I wonder what Brandon is doing now. If only I knew, it would make my life a lot easier while I help these people on your show."

Rob shrugged.

Annie and Rob continued eating, but there was very little conversation going on. Rob decided to file all of this in the back burner of his brain. He had so many ideas about Annie. Rob wondered if the whole story could be true. It was mind boggling.

Rob decided to change the subject. "Annie, I have an idea. I'm going to help you. God knows, I don't know why. But I'm going to help you with your mission. I feel compelled for some reason. Maybe there is a future book in all this for me. I don't know. All I ask of you is to keep me informed every step of the way. I will take notes."

"Okay, Rob."

"Tomorrow, you'll be back on my show. You will continue to help people on the air. I'll help you keep track of this. I will also get the art department to put up several billboards all over the city of New York. This should help your quest, and we will see what happens." Rob was brainstorming.

"Rob, I can't thank you enough. If there is anything I can do for you, I will. You will let me know, won't you?"

"Oh, yes, I will, Annie. Thanks for the lunch. I'll see you tomorrow."

"I'll be there bright and early, Rob. Thank you." Annie smiled.

Off she went to hail a cab. She needed to go back to her apartment and organize things. She couldn't be wearing the same dress again. It was time for her to unpack.

On the way, Annie wondered about Brandon. She knew he was the heartbeat of this century, tall and slim, mega-rich and famous. In his early forties, Brandon was **king** of the late night television talk show circuit. She wondered if he was with anyone now. She also wondered if Brandon ever thought about her.

The taxi screeched to a halt right in front of her apartment building. Back to reality.

Annie raced up the stairs, let herself into the apartment, and found Kate working in her office.

"Hi, Kate."

"Hi, Annie. Hey, Annie, I was driving around town running some errands when I turned on the radio and thought I heard your voice. Did you get a job on the radio?" Kate asked.

"Yes, that was me," Annie cutely answered.

"Whoa! How did that happen?"

"I called the radio station and asked to speak to the program director. I told him I was an angel and they put me on the air. They wanted something unique and they got it."

"Annie, I'm so happy for you. You found what you were looking for. I only heard a little bit on the radio while I was driving. I have to tune in to your show so I can hear more. By the way, tomorrow I'll be leaving on a photo shoot in Chicago for about a week. Will you be okay here alone?"

Annie smiled. "I'll be just fine. I need to get my work clothes in order and I really need to unpack. I have lots to do, Kate. Have a great trip."

Annie was about to go to her room when a strange feeling overwhelmed her. She found herself unsettled in her mind. She was swept away by emotions. Annie felt sad. She tried to figure out what was wrong. Then it came to her...Brandon. She felt him. "Kate, I need to get away for a little while," she said.

"Are you okay?"

"I'll be fine. I'll be back in a little while. I'm going out."

Annie hailed a taxi. "Central Park, please."

She remembered that when times were draining, she had always felt better in Central Park. Brandon and Annie had taken such wonderful walks through the park. She needed to think for a while. She couldn't stop thinking of Brandon.

"Here we are, lady, Central Park."

Annie got out of the cab and started to walk. It was autumn in New York and the leaves were changing colors from green to orange to yellow. The wind was blowing gently.

She stopped at the merry-go-round and watched as the children went round and round on their horses. Then, she found a park bench and sat for what seemed an eternity.

There was an ice skating rink off in the distance. Oh, if she could only be with Brandon again; they loved to ice skate. They would hold each other's hands and skate round and round as if time stood still. She wondered what Brandon was doing now.

Brandon was in his five-bedroom penthouse, an exquisite Park Avenue apartment with a fantastic view of Central Park. Dressed only in boxer shorts, he rummaged through the clothes in his closet, trying to decide what to wear for his big night on the town with his new girlfriend, Ali. He mechanically picked out a shirt to wear.

The phone rang; it was Ali.

"Hi, Brandon, so where are we going tonight? What do I wear? And what time will the limo pick me up?" she asked.

Brandon was very cordial. "I'll pick you up at 7:00 P.M.; we have reservations for 8:00 P.M. Dress sexy and sheer. We're going to an art gallery opening in Soho. Don't eat anything; there will be food and plenty of drinks at the party. See you soon, Darling." He hung up and continued to search for something to wear.

Ali was 28 years old, a Texas beauty queen and a model for "Victoria's Secret." Other than the fact that she was tall, there was nothing real about her. Her body had been nipped, tucked and enhanced from top to bottom. For this occasion she would wear a sheer dress that left nothing to the imagination.

Brandon was ready to rock and roll. He bolted for his limo. He was handsomely dressed in a white silk shirt, black pants, and a matching black Armani jacket.

At Ali's apartment Brandon checked his watch. "We'd better hurry," he urged. "We're running late. Ali, you should know how I hate to be late for anything."

Once inside the limo, Ali snuggled up to Brandon and gave him a light kiss on the lips. He smiled. "You look stunning, my dear," he said. Just the way Brandon wanted her.

They arrived at the party, which happened to be two blocks away from where Annie lived.

There were paintings by several local artists that hung in a huge warehouse high atop the second floor of the Soho gallery.

False kisses graced the air. All the beautiful people were there: models and rock stars high on themselves and high on each other.

Brandon and Ali mingled for about an hour or so before Brandon started to feel uncomfortable and bored. He grabbed Ali and whispered in her ear, "Let's get out of here; my place, now." He walked out quickly and Ali followed.

When they arrived at Brandon's apartment, he made Ali a martini and had one as well. Before they had finished their drinks, Brandon grabbed Ali and began tearing at her clothes. She responded by tearing at his clothes; they landed on the satin sheets of his bed. He was filled with passion; it had been a while since he made passionate love to anyone since Annie. Brandon and Ali had sex all night long.

Hours later Ali glanced over at Brandon. He was staring at the ceiling.

"Brandon, is there anything wrong?" she asked.

"No. Would you get me a glass of orange juice?"

"Sure."

On the way to the fridge Ali noticed a picture on the mantle of Annie and Brandon embracing each other.

When she returned to the bedroom with the orange juice, she said, "Brandon, I noticed in the hall there's a picture of you with a very pretty lady. Who is she?"

Brandon felt very uncomfortable talking about Annie, and his response was abrupt. "Hey, kid, it's been a fun time for you and me. It's time for you to go now." Brandon got out of bed and gulped down his juice. He looked around for Ali's clothes and tossed them to her; he couldn't get her out of his apartment fast enough.

Ali was confused. "What's wrong with you? I just asked a question."

"I don't want to answer. Time to go. I'll call you a cab." Brandon did just that. Brandon didn't want to think anymore. He handed Ali money for the cab. "And don't ever ask me again about that picture!" he shouted. He walked her to the cab.

Brandon told the driver to take her wherever she wanted to go.

Ali shouted out the window, "It's true what they say about you!"

Brandon slammed the door and walked as fast as he could back to his apartment. He slumped on the edge of his bed, put his hands to his face and shook uncontrollably. He tried to hold back his tears.

"Annie, if you can hear me… I miss you so much, it hurts." Brandon cried and drank himself to sleep.

A Little about Rob

Chapter 4

Annie sat alone on her park bench. As she gazed off into the distance, little did she know Brandon and she were having the exact same thought at the exact same time.

Annie looked upward and cried out, "Brandon, can you hear me? God, I miss you so much, it hurts."

Reluctantly, Annie went home. She walked briskly for a while before she tired and then spotted a cab, which drove her home to her apartment. She neatly unpacked her clothes while getting ready for tomorrow's show with Rob.

In another part of the city Rob and John were having dinner at a restaurant near the studio.

John asked, "Well, Rob, how was your lunch with Annie? Did you find out what you needed to know?"

"Yes, and more than I wanted to know. Of course, this will be an on-going situation. I'll have regular lunches with her. I need to find out an enormous amount of information; Annie just gave me a small taste. I want more time with her."

"Well, did she convince you she was an angel?" John smirked while looking up at the ceiling.

Rob moved closer to John. "You know, John, it's not about Annie being an angel. I could care less. It's about her making **me** and the station money." Rob tried very hard to persuade John about this matter; he didn't want his feelings to show.

"You know how badly I need the money now. I'm still supporting my ex-wife and two kids. I have to put them through college. John, I love them and miss them. You know that."

Rob started to reminisce about his ex. "Hope you don't mind, pal; I need to get this out." John was all ears; he knew Rob needed to talk.

"I remember when I first met Jan. We met at NYC-PS 52 High School. Jan was a beautiful, petite redhead and a cheerleader. I was a tall drink of water.

"I figured a girl like that would never go for a guy like me. We were kids. I fell for her like a ton of bricks, and all it took was just one look and I knew I would marry her some day." Rob looked over at John to make sure he was listening. And he was.

Rob continued. "Shortly thereafter we dated for about six months. We never left each other's side. I was such a happy guy. I believed then, as I do now, that Jan was my true soul mate—there would be no other."

John continued to sip his coffee while he listened to Rob's speech, a speech he had heard at least twenty times before. He knew that Rob had to get this out of his system again. So he always listened. John might have been bizarre, but he was a good friend to Rob.

"When we married, it was great. All our families got together; we all managed to get along very well, to say the least. Years sped by.

"When I look back on it now, it seems as though Jan and I didn't have enough quality time together. I'll tell you, my friend, when you find the ONE, I mean THE ONE, don't ever let her go." Rob stared right into John's eyes.

"To this day I don't know what went wrong. I noticed last year our sex life started to dwindle. Jan would say NO more often. There were times I pleaded with her. But you know, John, as hard as it was, I never cheated. I figured she was going through something and would eventually get over it.

"So I put in long hard hours at the station. Every evening I came home later and later just so I wouldn't have to deal with the sex thing. I would go straight to bed. We grew further and further apart.

"Jan's life was full. She had the kids and the dogs. She always managed to keep herself busy. Jan had a full life without me."

John asked the question he had asked so many times before: "Rob, didn't you try to talk to her? I mean, maybe she was going through that menopause thing. Didn't you ask her to go speak to a shrink?"

Rob replied, as he had so often before: "I did, but she didn't want any part of it. So things got worse. Then one day when I came home, Jan said she wanted to talk. I remember this as if it were yesterday. We sat in the kitchen; it was at that moment Jan said she was unhappy. She wanted a divorce.

"The look I gave her. I was shocked. I told her I knew we were having problems, but I didn't think they were that bad. I asked her if we could try to fix this. She said NO; her mind was made up. She felt in the eighteen years that we were together a lot of that time was wasted. She wanted to find out who she really was.

"She had been thinking about this for a long time. She looked me in the eyes and said, 'Rob, it's over. I've outgrown you. I would appreciate it if you left.' Jan turned away. John, she never really spoke to me after that.

"It was about six months later that I found out Jan was involved with someone else. She is still with the guy, who isn't half the man I am. I just don't get it." Rob stared blankly at the floor.

"Hey, man. Don't let it get to you. These things happen." John reached out.

"I know, buddy. But it still hurts so much."

John tried to cheer Rob by sharing his own story with him. "Rob, take me, for instance. I'm a happily divorced man. I get all the chicks I want. My wife left me three years ago. I couldn't have been happier. Of course, my enormous sex drive for different kinds of women was my downfall. But, Rob, I'm happy. I think.

"That's why I'm having a hard time with this Annie chick. I mean, she is so… pretty. If she weren't a so-called angel, I would give her a whirl myself." John chuckled.

"Don't go there. Don't even consider it, pal." The look on Rob's face was priceless.

"Don't worry. I understand. She's yours. You're going to make her famous. I got it." John winked and did a thumbs-up.

Rob smiled. "You got it. Well, let's go over tomorrow's schedule. What do we have planned?"

"They way I see it, tomorrow is tight. We have lots of weather and traffic reports and we have so many commercials. I don't know how I'm going to fit Annie in." John frowned.

"Oh, you'll fit her in. I want her to take only a few calls—just a few. I want the listeners to crave more and more of her. I want her to be special. Unique. I'm going to build her up slowly and leave them wanting more of her. John, I have so many ideas running in my head. There is so much we can do with her." Rob was on a high.

"I got the picture, Rob. By the way, I had several calls today from the press. They want to interview her. What do you think?"

Rob shook his head emphatically. "No, she must remain a mystery. I will not allow her to speak to the press. She will not be allowed to go on television. We must keep her away from everyone for a while.

"All I want are several billboards placed around town in key positions. Washington Square, Times Square, on buses, on taxis, in the subway, you know." Rob slapped the table excitedly.

"And where do we get the money for all this?" John asked.

"Don't worry about it. I'll talk to Tony, the owner of our station, and explain how we need funds for this project. When I'm through with him, he'll see where I'm coming from; and if I'm right, this will pay off in a BIG way."

"And if you're wrong, pal, then what?"

"I won't be wrong, John."

"Why is that?"

Rob stood up. He towered over John. "I just won't be wrong. Get it? I'm never wrong; I've never failed this station. One way or another I will make this happen. And you know what, John? I really don't care how. I don't care when. I don't care how long this will take. I promise you one thing—it will happen, buddy, and you want to know why?" he said.

"Why?"

"Because Annie is an angel." Rob grinned from ear to ear as if to say "I know something you don't."

"Oh, boy! Let's go. See you tomorrow." John and Rob left the restaurant.

The next morning, back at Annie's apartment, the alarm clock blared. Annie jumped out of her warm bed and into the shower. She couldn't wait for her new day to begin. "Maybe I will help ten people today," she thought aloud. She sang and scampered around the apartment.

It was 8 A.M. when Annie arrived at the radio station. Rob introduced her. "You're live on the radio with Annie, Our Angel over the Airwaves. John, who is our next caller?"

"Rob, I have Lyndy on the line for Annie. Go ahead, caller."

"Hi, Annie, my boyfriend just passed away. I'm having haunting dreams about him. What does it all mean?" Lyndy asked.

"Lyndy, sometimes when we miss someone that much we tend to draw them ever so close to us. That's what you are doing, young lady. You are the one who is willing his visitations. The harder you think of him, the more he can feel you; so he appeared to you in your dreams.

"You must understand they have work to do in Heaven. Your boyfriend has been reviewing his life. He is learning how he could have lived his life better. He's being taught about other choices that could have made his life more rewarding, such as helping others, instead of his being self-centered and always thinking about himself.

"I get it, Annie."

"Lyndy, wait a minute. I see something else. I'm being told from above, keep your eyes open for a new man who is coming into your life soon. He has slightly graying hair, blue eyes. You will meet him at Borders Book Store. Trust me on this. There will be a similarity between your boyfriend who passed and the new gentleman you will meet. Remember his eyes, for the soul never dies. His eyes will draw you to him."

"Thank you, Annie," the caller responded gratefully. "I will call you when this happens."

Rob shouted, "Well, it's time for a commercial break!" John cut away.

John commented to Rob, "I've never seen these phones lit up like this. It's amazing."

"Yes, John, and Annie is amazing." Rob smiled in her direction. He wanted to give her as much confidence as he could.

Annie twitched and moved about in her chair self-consciously. She felt Rob looking right through her.

In another part of New York Brandon was sitting in his elaborate dressing room, viewing five different television stations. The make-up girl rushed to apply his make-up. She had a script in her hand; she was listening to Roll-over-with-Rob-in-the-Morning.

Brandon had an early shoot that morning. He was to be on a daytime morning talk show to promote The Brandon Turner Show.

The make-up artist Tracy shouted, "I don't believe this!"

Brandon responded, "What don't you believe?"

"Rob, the radio DJ, has an angel on his show and she's giving advice to the listeners."

"What—an angel, such as with wings?" Brandon swiveled around in his chair.

"Listen to this." Tracy turned up the radio so Brandon could hear.

Brandon sat up and stared at the radio. There was something in Annie's voice that touched him very deeply.

Brandon refused to believe what he was hearing on the radio. "Tracy, do you know what Annie looks like?"

"No."

"There's something unique about her. I know… I'll change my voice and call the radio station and ask her a question." So, the prankster that he was, Brandon dialed the number. He got a busy signal no matter how many times he dialed.

Brandon got out of his chair and paced the floor of the spacious dressing room. "This is ridiculous! I think we should have her on our show. Tracy, do something. I want that girl, Angel, whatever, on my talk show this evening. Drop everything you're doing and find someone on my staff to call Rob," Brandon said wildly.

Back at the studio Annie was answering call after call. She literally was stunning the city. They were amazed at her wisdom. Many drivers pulled off the road so they could listen to An Angel over the Airwaves.

"Hey, Rob, I have Brandon Turner on the phone. He wants to talk to you."

Thank goodness, Annie was busy helping a listener and never heard what John had said.

"John, tell Brandon I'll call him back. I'm on air now."

"Sorry, Brandon, we are jamming. Rob is real busy. He'll call you back after the show."

"Yes, but, but…," Brandon stammered. Then, with resignation, he said, "Okay."

Rob said, "Well, Annie, you did amazingly well today. You helped a lot of people. Will you join us again tomorrow?"

"Yes, Rob, I will."

The show ended. Rob needed to get Annie out of the room. He told John to take Annie to their favorite coffee place across the street. "John, now it's your turn to ask her questions; and hurry—I don't have much time today. After a quick bite to eat I have to create some new commercials. I have a full schedule today and so do you." Rob motioned to John to get Annie out of the building. He then dialed Brandon's phone number.

"Hey, Brandon, Rob here. What can I do for you, Pal?"

"Hi, Rob. That angel you have on the air… is she for real?" Brandon asked.

"For my money, she is," Rob chuckled.

"Well, I want her on my show tonight. I'd like to interview her. This would be great for your show as well."

Rob had to be really careful here. He didn't want to piss Brandon off. Brandon could make him or break him. He quickly thought of a way out.

"Brandon, this has been only the third time we've had Annie on the show. I'm in the middle of testing her. I want to see how well she does. I think we should wait a little bit longer. I promise you will be the first person to have her on your show. I have some major work to do with her. Brandon, the timing is off. You understand, buddy?"

Brandon knew he had no choice but to agree. "Rob, I understand. I also understand I am dying to meet her. Is she pretty?"

"So-so." Rob skirted the issue. "Please understand, you will be the first when I get this new show together. You know what I mean."

"I understand. You know me. When I want something, I get it. That's just me, Brandon Turner. Rob, I'll honor your promise; whenever she is ready, let me know. I'm a man of little patience, but I will make room for her." Brandon hung up the phone somewhat loudly in Rob's ear.

Whoa! Rob couldn't imagine how he got out of that one. Rob had run circles around Brandon. He remembered what Annie had told him: they were not supposed to meet till she helped 1000 souls. He wondered what they would do to her in Heaven if she messed up again. Rob raced over to the restaurant to join John and Annie.

The day was a little overcast. The sun peeked through the window where they were having lunch. There was Sam behind the bar;

he was in constant motion. Autographed pictures of famous people in the usual eight-by-ten format lined the wall where they were sitting. Brandon's picture was extremely visible. Annie was seated with her back to the picture and she really never noticed Brandon staring at her from the picture. Rob thanked the lucky stars for that one.

There were crowds of people waiting to be let into the restaurant. A tall, skinny gay waiter with red-blond flaming hair approached the group. His name-tag read Elle.

Elle approached John. "Hey, boyfriend, what's up? Who's your girl toy?"

"Annie."

"So, Barbie, where's Ken?" Elle giggled.

"Huh?" Annie turned to Rob. "I don't get it."

"Neither do, I, sweetie. Just ignore."

Elle rambled on, telling John his latest story. He waved his hand quite daintily.

"Girl, did I have a night last night. I saw the most beautiful man that ever graced this planet. He doesn't know it yet, but he's mine."

John belly-laughed.

Rob asked, "What happens when he finds out?"

"Well, all I can say is… A girl should never kiss and tell." Elle turned and swayed his hips.

With pen in hand, Elle asked, "Can I take your usual order, fellows, or will there be a change of venue?"

"The same!" they shouted in unison.

Rob took a little offense at Elle's performance, but John loved it. John thought Elle was so witty. He knew he was acting up because he wanted to show off and be on the radio. John tried several times to explain that to Rob, but Rob never bought into it.

Elle danced his way into the kitchen.

John turned to Annie. "Can I ask you something about this angel business?"

"Sure," she replied.

"Do we all have guardian angels?" John was curious.

"Yes, John," Annie sighed. "It's a fact. And did you know that all angels have missions, just like people on Earth? We are all here on

Earth to save souls and we must do it without interfering in people's lives."

"How can you help without interfering? I mean, for example, hypothetically, you see a guy who's going to get into a car wreck. Then you see him dying in this wreck. What do you do?"

Rob nodded. "That's a good one, John."

"Well!" Annie paused for just a moment before answering. "I would whisper in his ear. If he were paying attention, he might take another path. That's how important it is to trust our intuition. Or I might look on the road to see if there was a glass or a nail so he could get a flat before the wreck occurred. If none of that worked and he still got into the accident, then it was meant to be. You get it?"

"Well, sort of." John rubbed the back of his neck. "You mean, if I don't pay attention to my inner voice, I could die?"

"Only if you are meant to; if your time is up on Earth. We all have an expiration date. When it's up, it's up." Annie smiled. "You see, John, I'm here to shed light on each person I touch. I'm supposed to guide them to their destiny."

Rob jumped in, extremely curious. "What about free will, Annie?"

"Ah, Rob, that's another story. We have very little free will; just a little, an itsy bitsy. Most of our life events, I mean the major events in our lives, are predestined."

"Oh, come on now. Are you telling us we are all actors in some play on Earth? We don't have a choice in the matter?" Rob asked cynically.

"Yes and no."

"What does that mean—yes or no—which is it?" Rob was annoyed at not getting a straight answer.

"We give each person enough information to see the light. We sometimes show them their path very clearly, and once we show it to them, it's up to them to act upon it in the proper manner. It's like a test, Rob."

"Well, let me see if I can get this straight," Rob said, trying to analyze what Annie was saying.

"Let's say, for instance, I'm about to catch a plane to California. The plane is destined to crash. No matter what, it's meant to be; but

I, Rob, don't know this. However, while I'm getting dressed, I look into the mirror and get a weird bad feeling. I start to get nervous, so I pace from room to room. I try to figure out what's wrong. I still don't get it. I jump in my car. The closer I get to the plane, the more violently ill I feel. Then, what do I do, Annie?"

Annie was very matter-of-fact. "Rob, that's where I come in. You examine your feelings. Don't listen to your logic that says you must take that plane for your meeting. Listen to your inner voice—the inner voice that has been telling you something is about to go very wrong. That was emphatically why you were feeling ill. **Take the next plane.** It's that simple.

"If more people were to listen to their feelings or inner voice, fewer accidents, as you would call them, would occur. In my book there are no accidents. We, as angels, come down to Earth to guide and protect you in one form or another. I'm here to put that little voice right back into your head. Then I have to step out of the way and hope you get the message.

"Rob, John, listen to me. It's like I'm sending you a fax. Sometimes you receive it, sometimes you don't. All I'm asking for you guys to do is to listen to that voice in your head. Then make the proper decision and act upon it. Got it?"

"Sort of." John looked at Rob and they both shrugged their shoulders.

Annie shook her head as well, wondering how she could break through to these guys.

Then John asked, "Annie, how do you choose who you're going to help?"

"My Angel Gabriel chooses. He's the head angel, you know. He always tells me my mission and I do whatever he wants—sometimes, when I don't mess up. If I do things right with my work in helping people, I will advance to the next angel level. However, sometimes I just don't get it right. I have the tendency to forget things, as well. Remember, I'm still earning my wings." Annie giggled.

Rob stood up from the table and looked directly at Annie. "What do you mean 'mess up'? If we can't trust an angel, who can we trust?" Rob sat down again and waited for her to answer.

"To be honest with you guys," Annie looked shyly at Rob and John, "I have this human frailty condition."

John interjected, "Is it catching?"

Annie ignored John and continued. "You see, whenever I'm on Earth, I naturally bond with whomever I'm helping. I become human. I feel for them so deeply, sometimes I fall in love with them. This distracts me from helping them. Then I start thinking on the same level as they do, and I make the wrong decisions as well."

"Oh, boy!" John shook his head and pushed back his chair. "Well, Rob, I think I've heard enough for today. She's all yours. Annie, it was a pleasure. I have to go back to the studio." John gathered his things, shaking his head the whole time and mumbling to himself.

"Did I say something wrong, Rob?" Annie asked.

"No, I got it," Rob replied. "I have to watch over you to make sure you don't mess up. I have to keep you away from Brandon, until you hit your mark of one thousand souls." Rob looked upward towards Heaven and shouted, "Why me? Why me? What did I do to deserve this?"

Stunned by Rob's reaction, Annie said, "I'm sorry, Rob; I'll do better."

Rob got up from the table. "Annie, I'll see you tomorrow." He said, while pointing his finger at her, "Stay out of trouble." He turned and left.

Annie sipped her coffee slowly. She spaced out while thinking of Brandon again.

It turned out that Brandon was only a few blocks away from Annie. A doorman greeted Brandon as he walked into Sardi's Bar and Restaurant. Sardi's was known for its low lights and soft upbeat music. Plush red-velvet carpet lined the floor. Brandon headed for the bar toward the right of the entrance.

Charlie the bartender was a **huge** fan of Brandon's. Charlie had gray hair and wore a white shirt and red vest. The red vest hid his funny little pot belly, but nothing could have taken away from his heavy New York accent.

"Hey, Brandon, what will it be?"

"Vodka on the rocks, Charlie. And make it a double."

"That bad, Brandon?"

"Yup."

"Brandon, you look under the weather. Do you want to talk about it?"

Charlie stood in front of Brandon at the bar. Brandon leaned a little closer. "Charlie, I don't know. I had this date last night with a beautiful model. You know the one, Ali; her face is on every magazine cover. Nice girl."

"I know the one," Charlie replied.

"Well, we just got through making love, you know, and she spotted Annie's picture on my dresser in the hall. Then she started asking me questions about her. I lost my temper. I went crazy.

"I flashed back, remembering Annie and all the fun we had. Everything flooded my memory. I still love her so much, Charlie. There are times I feel like she's in this room or down the block."

"Get a grip," said Charlie with some concern. "Brandon, have you ever spoken to a shrink about this?"

"No, I can't. If I did and I was caught, it would be all over the trade papers. My life wouldn't be my own. Hit me again, Charlie.

"I miss her. All those memories of how we first met. How naïve she was. How perfect Annie was. I finally found her, the love of my life, and she's dead. I can't believe it. Then, to top it off, I was listening to that radio show Roll-over-with-Rob-in-the-Morning…you know the one."

Charlie nodded.

"I heard a lady on the air. Her name was Annie. Her voice was so similar to my Annie's. I called Rob to get her on my show. But he's stalling. I have this strange feeling that this Annie could take my pain away."

"Brandon, get it together. Your Annie's dead. No one can replace her. Get a grip, guy."

"You want to hear something strange?"

Charlie nodded again.

"When I held Annie in my arms just before she died, she said to me, 'Remember me. Remember my eyes. Promise me.' I promised her.

"I mean, I'm not a huge fan of supernatural stuff, you know. But there was something in this lady's voice on the radio. If I didn't know Annie was dead, I would say that was her. I can't shake it. I have to meet her." Brandon held up his empty glass. "Charlie, another drink."

"Slow it down, pal. Brandon, I've known you for fifteen years. I've never seen you this shaken by anyone."

Charlie wiped the bar glasses with a towel while talking to Brandon. "Brandon, I remember the time you were doing your local television show right next door. You were striving for fame. You were going through a divorce at that time. Then CBS signed you for your own talk show. Man, you were happy. I mean, Brandon, you've worked so hard for your fame. Ten years, man. You have it all, fame and riches. What more do you want?"

"Love, Charlie. I just want someone to love me for who I am." Brandon laid his head on the bar. Charlie motioned for someone to take Brandon home.

Radio and More

Chapter 5

Annie left the coffee shop and made her way home. She stopped at several new fashion boutiques in the neighborhood. Time went by fast that evening. She was wondering when she and Kate would have time to spend together.

She went back over the day and hoped she didn't offend John. She would make it up to him in the morning. Time passed quickly, and before she knew it she was back at the radio station with Rob and John.

"You're live on the air with Annie, our Angel over the Airwaves. And your name?" John asked.

"My name is Tom. Can I speak to Annie? I'm the engineer on the train for Penn Station. I'm the one who gets you to where you need to go." Tom chuckled a little; he was proud to boot. "Yup, that's me."

Rob interjected, "So you're an engineer on our rail system. You know, I always wanted that job as a kid—I mean, I used to play with my Lionel train set. Boy, that was fun. Is your job just as fun, Tom?"

"Yup."

John quipped, "There you go again, Rob. That gentleman called in to speak with Annie. Why don't you let him talk? Rob, you have to share." Then, in a whispered aside to Rob, he added, "I mean, Annie has a mission here; we don't want to mess up her timing. She needs to help 980 more people."

"Okay."

Annie stared off into the distance. She had a very clear vision and she could hear Tom's voice. She was disturbed. She saw Tom running his train as usual. The number of people flashed across her mind: **252.** She saw the lights and other trains passing in the opposite direction off in the distance. She saw Tom asking Paul, his assistant, to watch his train while he took a quick jaunt to the men's room. Annie shook her head in disbelief.

"Oh, my!" Annie blurted out. "Tom, YOU MUST NOT LEAVE YOUR TRAIN POST FOR ANY REASON TOMORROW. THERE IS DANGER. I SEE EXTREME DANGER."

Rob asked, "Annie, what do you see?" He was a bit edgy asking her to continue; he wasn't sure he wanted to know. But he hesitantly told her, "Go ahead, tell Tom."

Without hesitation Annie said, "Tom, I saw you leaving momentarily and your assistant Paul read the computer wrong. He took the train on the wrong track."

Annie held her breath then blurted out, "Oh, no! Two trains will collide tomorrow and they'll catch on fire! Everyone on your train will die. You have to pay attention. DO YOU UNDERSTAND?" Annie was shaken.

She had to somehow make Tom understand the severity of the situation. She felt she had to save those 252 souls. At this point in time she knew all she could do was pass the information to Tom and hope he made the right decision. For if he didn't, all would die. All she could do was tell Tom what she saw; the rest was up to him.

She explained to Rob and John that this is where free will comes in. The accident may be fatal. However, if Tom makes the right choices, the train might crash, but all those on it can still be saved. "You see, if you can see the future in time, then sometimes you can change it."

Tom jumped into the discussion. "Annie, I understand what you're seeing. I promise I will not leave my post tomorrow. But will that stop the people from burning to death?" he asked.

"Let me see, Tom." Annie paused. "Tom, the way I see it, you have two possible futures regarding this matter.

"In one future, the train will screech to an abrupt halt. There will be a few minor injuries, people will be all shook up, but you will have saved their lives.

"Sometimes we have more than one future. In the other future you go to the men's room and your assistant handles the train and you know what happens."

Annie paused briefly, then said, "Wait. I have more information coming to me.

"Tom, listen to me. I'm being told you should not take your eyes off the tracks. You will have two minutes to spot the error in the computer while you're traveling at high speed; there will be a light flashing on your board. You need to trace the route at that time, for there will be a malfunction in the computer. You will have less than two minutes to find the malfunction. At that time download the computer and run the train manually. You should be able to save your life and everyone else's, if I'm correct.

"That's all I see for now. I'm sorry, Tom; this is all the information I'm allowed to tell you." Annie broke out in a cold sweat.

Tom said, "Annie, I can't thank you enough for warning me. I'll do everything in my power to change the course of events. I'll call you back on this. Thank you, Annie, from the bottom of my heart."

Rob cut to a commercial.

Meanwhile, all across New York City, people were listening to the radio. The radio station's switchboard was all lit up; it seemed everyone who was listening wanted to speak to Annie. Construction workers had their radios blaring at their work sites. Cab drivers were listening. People in the park with radios were tuning in. A couple pulled their car off the road in New Jersey to listen intently to Annie. She was the talk of New York City.

John shouted, "We're back live in 3, 2, 1." He pointed at Rob.

In a very strange way, Rob felt all of Annie's emotions and more. He felt what she was feeling. He wondered how this could be. "Why do I feel her? Why do I feel what she is going through?" he asked himself.

Rob snapped himself out of it. "Annie, how do you deal with these visions?"

"It's okay, Rob, I'm saving souls. That's my job on Earth. You see, when the listeners call into your station, the lucky ones that make it through the lines are the ones I'm supposed to help," Annie replied with a hint of pride.

Rob noted, "Well, that old clock on the wall is ticking again; it's lunch time. I guess, if we're lucky, we'll find out in a few days how Tom makes out. Until then, we'll wish him well."

"This is Roll-over-with-Rob-in-the-Morning signing off. Have a good lunch, New York City. Coming up next is Dave the Dude. Stay tuned for more of 92.3 FM."

Rob unplugged his ears. "Hey, Annie, Come with me. I have something that just might cheer you up. HURRY. We need to get out of here for a while."

Annie hurried. She followed Rob as fast as her little feet would take her. They took the elevator down four floors. Rob hailed a cab and they were off. "Where are we going, Rob?"

"It's a surprise, Annie. Driver, Times Square, please." Annie was patient. When they arrived at Times Square, Rob asked the driver to circle a little around the block.

"Annie, look up!"

"Oh, my, my! It's a billboard with my name on it!" Annie turned to Rob and smiled.

"Read it, honey. Tell me what it says!" Rob exclaimed. He couldn't wait for Annie's reaction.

"Rob! It's a huge billboard. HUGE." She pointed upward. "Wow!" There was a BIG picture of an angel's wing on it. Annie read the words aloud.

"CALL IN LIVE FOR ANNIE, OUR ANGEL OVER THE AIR-WAVES, ON 92.3 FM EVERY MORNING.

Roll over with Rob in the morning. Listen to our real live angel Annie.

"Whoa! I can't believe this." Annie hugged Rob tightly and kissed him on his cheek. He blushed.

"Driver! Washington Square, please." Rob had a big proud grin on his face as they drove on.

"Here we are. Washington Square," the taxi driver called out.

"Pull over there," Rob ordered.

"Annie, look up!" He pointed to another billboard.

Annie had tears in her eyes. She had dreamt of this moment; she wanted to be known, so she could help all those wonderful people. Rob was making it happen for her. She didn't know how to thank him. Words were not enough. "Rob, what can I say? I owe you so much. I don't know how I can repay you."

"Don't worry, my little angel, you will repay the station as we both watch our ratings soar. Annie, everyone will know who you are and everyone will tune in to our show." Rob smiled broadly.

"This huge investment that we made will make you so famous. Our show will go through the roof, young lady, and no one will be able to touch us. I promise you that." Rob was higher than a kite; he was ecstatic.

He held Annie tightly in his arms as they both stared at her new billboard. "Annie, that's not all. There will be more billboards on buses and taxis and a rotating sign at Times Square. What do you think of that, young lady?"

Annie was speechless. She couldn't believe this was happening to her. Was she dreaming? And if so, her dream had come true right before her very eyes. Annie stared at Rob; she looked into his eyes. She couldn't help but wonder why Rob was really doing this. Was it just for the station and its ratings? Was it for his ego? Or did Rob have deeper feelings for her?

Oh, well, none of that really mattered, she thought. All that mattered was that she would help 1000 souls. Then she could be with Brandon again. She didn't believe Rob really understood how she really felt about Brandon. "Or, for that matter, how it took several lifetimes of our relationship to develop," she told herself.

But one thing was very clear to Annie: Rob was making Annie's dreams come true. At that moment she suddenly realized that Rob was the one who would guide her to Brandon.

Annie bashfully kissed Rob again. "I don't know how to thank you, Rob. Thank you so much. I am truly grateful."

Rob snapped out of his high as reality set in. "Well, I've got to get back to the station, little angel. Can I drop you at your apartment?"

Annie shook her head. "Rob, I need to walk and think. I would love to have some alone time in my life right now. Can you drop me at the zoo?"

"The zoo?"

"Yes, Rob, when I'm with the animals, I can rejuvenate. I'll take a long walk, then I'll go back to my apartment."

"Driver, the zoo, please," said Rob.

When they arrived at the zoo, Annie got out of the cab and waved goodbye. She shouted, "See you Monday, Rob!" She paused for a moment and took a long breath. Leaning slightly into the open window, she said, "Thank you so much. There aren't enough words to describe how happy you've made me. It was a great day."

Rob smiled.

The zoo was such a memorable place for her. She loved animals, and this was where Annie and Brandon met every Sunday. He bought the bananas and she fed the monkeys. Brandon had a soft side that very few people knew about.

She looked around, feverishly hoping to catch a small glimpse of memories of Brandon passing by. Annie was happy when she watched the monkeys in their cage. She wondered, if she thought about Brandon, he would hear her. Would he make his way to the zoo? Her thoughts of Brandon clouded her thinking.

While Annie was at the zoo, Brandon was at the Helen Hayes Theater right next to Sardi's, taping his show and doing his monologue.

"Well, folks, a funny thing happened to me on the way to the studio today. I turned on the radio and heard my friend, Rob—you know the one, Roll-over-with-Rob-in-the-Morning show. Well! Did you hear? He had an angel on his airwaves this morning. How many of my studio audience believe in angels?" There was loud applause and some giggles. "That's what I thought. Well, I'll tell you—I think we need to bring that lovely lady on our show real soon. Wouldn't you all want to meet a real live angel?"

The audience erupted into louder applause. Someone shouted, "Yeah, Brandon!"

"That's what I thought. Well, let's see what my assistant Rose can do."

Turning to a figure standing in the wings, he said, "Hey, Rose, do whatever it takes, but get that angel on our show."

"Yes, boss." Rose knew that Brandon was serious.

Brandon turned back to face the camera and began talking to Annie from television land. "Not to be disrespectful, Annie--I believe that's your name—but if you are listening out there, I really do want you on my show."

Brandon chuckled. The audience laughed and applauded. Everyone was in agreement.

Rose knew her job was on the line. She would have to scramble every which way to get Annie on the show.

Rose was about 40. She had long red hair with highlights of brown and blonde, green eyes, and a slender figure. Ever since Rose met Brandon, she found she didn't have a life of her own. But Rose had been Brandon's personal confidant for about three years now. She adored him; she wasn't going to let him down.

Rose was very well aware of the conversation Brandon had had with Rob, and that her boss wasn't happy about the snub. She had to find her own way to appease him. And she would.

After the show Brandon asked Rose to come to his dressing room. She did.

"Rose, I want this mystery angel on my show! Do you get it?" Brandon yelled. He seemed ready to throw a tantrum. This was very out of character for him.

In a calmer tone he pleaded, "Please, Rose, get down to Rob's show and find her. Try to sneak a peek as to what she looks like. Sweetie, I don't care how much money it takes. Offer her anything and everything. I want that angel on my show. Get her."

"Brandon, I'll do my best," Rose promised and grabbed her purse. "Okay, Brandon, I'm leaving. See? I'm going. But Brandon, I think you're being just a little bit **obsessive** about this." She paused in the doorway and turned to Brandon. "Breathe, Brandon, breathe. Never fear; Rose is here." And with a little laugh she left to take a cab to Rob's station.

Once there, Rose jumped out of the cab, practically tossed her tip to the driver, and raced to the elevator where she pounded the eighth floor button until it lit up. She raced out of the elevator—it seemed to have crawled upward—and approached the receptionist.

"Hi, my name is Rose. I'm Brandon Turner's assistant. Is Rob available?"

"Wait a moment; I'll see if I can get him. He's creating some new commercials, but I'll see what I can do." The receptionist reached for the phone. "Hey, Rob, sorry to disturb you. I have a lady here that says she's from The Brandon Turner Show. She wants to talk to you," she said.

"Don't worry, honey, I'll be right out."

When Rob came out of the control room, he hailed Rose like an old friend. "Hey, Rosie, how the hell are you? Long time no see. What brings you to my neck of the woods? Are you slumming?" Rob held papers in his hand; it was very clear he was busy.

Rose pleaded, hands clasped as if in prayer, "Rob, you have got to save me. Please, Brandon has turned into a raving lunatic. My job is on the line over your angel. He has to have her on his show. All I know is Brandon ordered me to come down here and plead with you about Annie. I have to book her for his show."

Rob did not hesitate with his answer. "Rosie, **No Can Do**. Annie is mine. I have a huge promotion going on. I have to save her from exploitation. Television is not where she belongs right now. Besides, I talked to Brandon yesterday and he was okay with it. What brought this on?"

Rose sighed. "I don't know. He believes he knows her. He feels something whenever he hears her voice on your radio. He's got it in his head that he has to meet her.

"Rob, he has our whole staff half-crazed about her. He even told his viewers on television that she would be on his show." Rose pleaded once again with Rob. "What am I going to do?"

"Rose, you tell Brandon that when the time is right, I will personally bring Annie down to his show. Believe it or not, the one thing Brandon understands is timing. He's so good at it on his show. Let him know the timing is off. Tell him he has my word that, after I work with her a while and get everything in perspective, I will make sure Annie makes an appearance on his show. I have more work to do with her; I can't let her go now like a loose cannon. It will spoil everything." Rob was agitated.

"I understand. I hope Brandon will." Rose gave Rob a kiss on the cheek and motioned goodbye. "Thanks anyway, Rob."

Rob turned and walked back to the control room to finish up his work for the day.

Rose thanked the receptionist on her way out; then, she did a double-take when she spotted a young man sitting in a chair, reading a book. He was the world famous medium, Pat Edwards. Rose had an inspiration. She approached Pat.

Rose stretched out her hand as she greeted Pat. "Hi, my name is Rose from the Brandon Turner Show. How would you like to be on our show tomorrow?"

Pat was startled. "Are you serious? I mean, I came here looking to get on Rob's show."

"Well, that won't be necessary. Why don't you follow me? I'll make sure you meet Brandon Turner. Then we'll see what he thinks," Rose said seriously. "Come with me, Pat."

Pat was mystified. "Oh, well, I guess this was meant to be. I've been trying to get on Brandon Turner's show for well over a year now."

Rose smiled. At least she wasn't coming up empty.

There was much chit-chat in the cab on their way back to Brandon's show. Rose jotted down notes for a bio on Pat.

When they reached the studio, Rose crooked a finger at Pat. "Come with me, darling. I'll get you a cup of coffee and a bit to nibble while you're waiting to meet Brandon. Now stay here in our Green Room. Don't move, please."

"Okay." Pat was in shock. He thought to himself. "Well, that was weird. First, I was at Roll-over-with-Rob-in-the-Morning in his studio, waiting to meet him, and the next thing I know I'm at the Brandon Turner show waiting to meet him. What a day!" Pat looked up. "Thank you, Universe."

Rose, meanwhile, ran into Brandon's office. "Well, where is she?" Brandon asked. He looked around. "Is she outside?"

"Not exactly."

"What do you mean?"

"Well... I talked to Rob. He said that he is doing a HUGE promotion on Annie. Brandon, your timing is a little off on this. He'll bring her to you when they finish with her promotion." Rose shrugged her shoulders and held up her hands resignedly. "What can I say, Brandon? I tried. Fire me if you have to."

"Rose, I'm not going to fire you. I'm just disappointed."

"But I do have a BIG surprise for you," Rose gushed.

"You do?" Brandon smiled.

"Yes, I stole Pat Edwards, the medium, from Rob's show. He's sitting out there in the Green Room. If anyone can compete with Annie, I do believe it's Pat Edwards. Do you know who he is? He channels people from the other side and reunites them with their relatives right here on Earth. Pat talks a lot about soul mates. Twin souls. Everyone will watch your show if you put him on. Trust me on this. He also sees the future. He's good, you know. He's hot right now. Do you want to give him a try on your show?" Rose shrugged.

"Twin souls? What is that all about?" he asked.

Rose replied, "You know what twin souls are—people that are supposed to be together, each and every lifetime. They promise each other that they will come back. Their souls are intertwined. It's that missing part of you that you have been searching for when you are looking for a mate. It sometimes takes a lifetime after lifetime before they can be together again. They have to get it right. Then they can be together forever." Rose sighed softly.

"OKAY! Book him for tomorrow. Rose, how do you know all this stuff?"

Rose shrugged her shoulders.

"By the way, you're not out of the woods yet, though I must admit that this was a good save. Keep bugging Rob. Understand?"

Rose felt relieved. "Brandon, you won't be disappointed; I promise you."

Brandon started to walk out of the room but stopped abruptly. He turned around slowly and stared at Rose. "I'd better not be."

After Brandon's brusque exit, Rose hurried to speak to Pat Edwards in the Green Room.

"Hey, Pat, good news. I spoke with Brandon; he wants you on his show tomorrow."

Pat was in Heaven; after all these years, he finally made it. "Whoa! What do I wear? I have to get back to my apartment. I have to check out my clothes. This is so sudden, but great."

"Okay, do you have it together?"

"Yes, Rose." Pat jumped up off his chair. He reached for his cell phone to make a call. "Don't worry, Rose, I'll be here tomorrow. What time do you want me?" he asked.

"I need you here about 3:00 P.M.," she said.

"You got it, girl. I'll be here."

Annie was still at the zoo. She looked at her watch; it was about four. She had a long weekend ahead of her. Annie was determined to spend time with Kate this weekend; she wanted to find out more about her. Annie took a long walk, memorizing the area from Central Park to Soho. It was so beautiful. Annie loved the fall of the year. She felt so alive. She could feel the breeze. The leaves were beginning to change color. People in New York were alive and vibrant this time of year. She walked till her little feet hurt; then, she knew it was time for her to hail a cab back to the apartment.

Chapter 6

"AND NOW, LADIES AND GENTLEMEN … BRANDON TURNER…" (Applause, applause.)

The Brandon Turner show was live from New York City. After his monologue and a few jokes, Brandon announced to his audience, "Tonight we have a very special guest. His name I'm sure you're all too familiar with… it's **world-renowned medium Pat Edwards."** The audience cheered and applauded wildly.

"Yes, Pat will be with us shortly." Brandon held up Pat's latest book, *Conversations with the Other Side.* "Come on out, Pat, and say 'Hi' to our viewers."

Brandon's stage set was simple. To the left was a brown wooden desk and to its left were two beige velvet chairs and a semi-circular couch with similar upholstery for his guests.

Pat displayed little nervousness as he emerged from the curtains and greeted Brandon.

Brandon stood up from behind his desk to shake Pat's hand. "Sit down, my friend. I've heard a lot of great things about you. I hope you can live up to my expectations."

"I'll try," Pat said confidently.

Brandon asked, "Pat, how does this work?"

"Well, Brandon, I can't explain how it works. I just know it does. It all started when I was a very young boy. I hit my head while I was playing outside and developed a concussion. My mother was so worried. I remember I was going in and out of consciousness and there were times I was caught between this world and the other side.

"The most amazing thing that happened was that I brought back information from my dead relatives, information that not even my mother knew. I met my grandmother who passed and she gave me a message for my mother. I met my brother who had died at five years old. My mother was astonished. I also had several conversations with my father who had passed suddenly from a heart attack."

Brandon listened with interest.

"In those days Mom didn't know what to do with the information I gave her. She took me to shrinks, doctors, priests; she was understandably perplexed.

"She finally took me to a very famous psychic in New York, who explained what I had been through and explained to Mom that, in fact, I had been to the other side. I also came back with names and dates of relatives and how they would pass, along with who would greet them on the other side. As the years went by, I further developed my ability.

"When I go to sleep and dream, information is given to me at that time. Not only do I see dead people, but they also give me information to pass on to others who are living. Well, Brandon, that's who I am in a nutshell. You might say I'm a human telephone," Pat explained lightheartedly.

"Whoa! You know, Pat. I'm trying so hard to believe this." Brandon stood up with his mike in hand and went into the audience. "Pat, we have some audience members who would like to speak with you. Are you ready?"

"Yes."

"We have Betty in the audience; she has a question for you."

"Hi, Betty, how can I help you?" Pat asked.

Betty was about 40, with straight brown hair that barely brushed the bottom of her earlobes, and wore a coral-pink cotton blouse tucked neatly into a white calf-length skirt. She stated she had just lost her husband and she wanted to know if there were any messages for her.

Pat paused for a moment to center himself. "Yes, Betty, I am getting that your husband died before his time. He told me he was at a 24-hour convenience store in New Jersey and had just talked on the cell phone with you to find out if you needed anything and you said 'No.' But then someone came in to rob the store and held your husband at gunpoint. When he tried to make a run for the door, he was shot dead."

Betty bit her lip to stifle a sob.

"Betty, he never had a chance to say goodbye to you. He's telling me he misses you so. The loss you are feeling, he is feeling as well.

"You understand, Betty, that the love we feel for those who have passed is felt by them as well on the other side. The more we grieve for them, the more they feel the grief. It holds them back from doing their new job in Heaven. Your husband knows you love him, but he wants me to tell you to go on with your life. He will always love you and your family. The most important message that he is giving me is to take care of your son Joey; he needs you now, more than you'll ever know."

Pat seemed to be drained. Brandon was more than amazed. Betty cried. The show cut to a commercial break.

The audience wanted more. Pat spoke to several others in the audience to help guide them and relieve them of their pain.

Brandon was pleased. He invited Pat back on his show, but not before asking him to come to his dressing room backstage. Brandon had his own questions about his Annie. So after the show was over, Pat followed Brandon backstage.

After thanking Pat for coming on his show, Brandon said, "I must admit I was somewhat of a skeptic, but I don't think I feel that in my heart anymore." Brandon took a deep breath before continuing. "Pat, I'm sure you've read about my wife Annie who was killed."

"Yes, Brandon."

"Can you reach her on the other side for me?"

"I will try," Pat said.

Pat made himself comfortable in Brandon's chair; he was totally relaxed. Pat faced Brandon and touched his hands to make a connection. He looked up towards Heaven.

"I see the wedding. She was shot. You held her in your arms, crying. You made a promise to each other. Brandon, you promised that you would find her."

A tear fell on Brandon's cheek. He said nothing.

"Brandon, she was your twin soul. I'm being told you will find her again on Earth. In all my years of channeling the other side, I haven't known of a love greater than the love you hold deep within you for your Annie. I'm being told she is not in Heaven.

"In fact, I see a man—an angel—who is giving me this information. I don't understand why I can't connect with her."

Brandon was confused. So was Pat. He continued.

"Brandon, I'm being told that you and Annie will meet again, but you'll need to change. You'll need to become more understanding of the human condition. You'll need to become more spiritual before the two of you can meet. There is a block.

"Annie has been searching for you. However, she is not allowed to meet you again until you change. I can see through the veil."

Brandon tore his hands from Pat's and erupted from his seat.

"How do I become more spiritual? Pat, how can I meet her again in this life? This sounds crazy. I don't understand," he cried. Dejected, he sat down again.

"Brandon, it doesn't matter if it's this life or the next life. The two of you can be together. I'm sure of it. It could be as simple as another person who has Annie's similarities that you fall in love with and before you know it, part of Annie floats inside of your new love."

Brandon looked up. "Is that possible?"

"Anything is possible if you believe," Pat said quietly.

"Pat, we need to spend more time together. Do you mind?"

"No, sir, I don't."

"That settles it. You'll be my spiritual teacher so I can meet Annie again."

"Okay." Pat was delighted.

"I have to leave now. I'll call you," Brandon said. He had a lot of thinking to do.

Back in his Park Avenue apartment, he was deep in thought as he pulled off his tie, which was already undone—his usual signature—and unbuttoned his shirt. He poured himself a drink and walked over to the answering machine. He pressed "play."

"Hi, Brandon, this is Susan. Call me when you get in. You know the number, darling. I'll be waiting." (Beep…)

"Hi, Brand, this is Jen. I saw the show; you look as gorgeous as ever. Call me. I just got back in town." (Beep…)

"Hi, Brandon, this is Ali. I'm sorry about the other night; maybe I over-reacted. Please call me." (Beep…)

Brandon pressed "erase" on all of his messages. He was drained, to say the least. He sat in the dark room, staring at the New York skyline, and he drank till the sun came up.

Meanwhile, Annie was just about to put the key in her apartment door when Kate opened it from the other side. "Hey, Annie, you're home early today. I was just on my way out to get some coffee. Do you want to come?"

Annie smiled. "That sounds great." Annie hurried and changed, then she followed Kate. Kate had the keys to her car in her hand. "You have a car in New York?" Annie was surprised.

"Yes, I use it about three times a week. I get tired of waiting for cabs. This way if I feel like going out at night, I have a car. Come, get in."

Off they drove. Thirty blocks later, Kate stopped at a coffee house called Serendipity, a very famous place in New York.

"What a neat name—Serendipity. What does that mean?" Annie asked.

"You surprise me, Annie. You don't know what serendipity means?"

Annie shook her head. "No."

"It means a splendid, fortunate accident." They both laughed, for Kate and Annie knew there was no such thing as an accident; everything happened for a reason.

"I just love this place, Annie; it's so unique. They have every kind of coffee in the world here, and look at the atmosphere—everything is so lit up in here." Kate swept her arms above her as she made a 360 degrees turn. "They have white Christmas lights all over, potted tropical plants, and the food is delicious."

When they were seated at their table, Kate leaned over and said, "So, Annie, I really want to get to know you. Tell me about the radio show. Don't you just love it? I love the way Rob introduced you as an angel; that must be great for ratings."

"I do, Kate. But I have a confession to make." Annie looked straight at Kate and said, "I really am an angel." She waited for Kate's surprised reaction, which never came.

Kate sipped her coffee and looked up. "I know."

Annie was taken aback. "What do you mean, you know? Can you see my wings or something? Is it showing?"

Kate smiled. "Annie, I'm an angel, too."

Now it was Annie who was surprised. "No way!"

"Yes way. You honestly can't believe Gabriel would have sent you down to Earth to be by yourself. I have a mission as well. My mission is watching over you."

"Explain, please." Annie was all ears.

Kate leaned in. "Okay, here goes. I was born in Manhattan about thirty-two years ago. I became one of the leading photographers in this town; in fact, some of my works hang in the Museum of Art right here in New York.

"I was on assignment for one of the papers to cover a very controversial story. I uncovered some information I wasn't supposed to know. The next thing I knew, I was running so fast down the street to make my getaway, I was hit by a car and flung into the air.

"While I lay unconscious in the hospital, I floated out of my body. I was given the choice in Heaven to go back to Earth, but I chose not to."

Annie asked, "Why not, Kate?"

"You see, Annie, I had never had a life. I spent all my time photographing everyone else that I never had a chance to mingle. I never met my soul mate. I never had kids. I never lived.

"So, Gabriel taught me all about life. He taught me how to live in Heaven and, in order for me to get my wings, he gave me this assignment to watch over you. He was the one that picked out your apartment, so you and I could meet."

Annie moved self-consciously in her chair. "Well, I'm not surprised, to say the least, Kate. So I guess you know everything about me."

"Yes, I do, Annie. I had to study everything about you in Heaven."

Annie was curious. "Kate, what happens when your mission is over with me? I mean, when I find Brandon and we're together, what will happen to you?"

"Then I'll have the option to stay on Earth and continue my career, find my soul mate, have children and a life—provided you don't mess things up, Annie."

"Who, me mess things up? I don't think so… not this time… I'm too close to my goal." Annie felt flustered.

Kate sipped her coffee slowly. "Well, that's what I'm here for. I'm here to make sure you get things right this time. Annie, whatever you do will affect my life as well. I'll have the choice to go back to Heaven or stay on Earth. I really want to stay on Earth. I really want what you had with Brandon. I want to find the love of my life. So **please** don't mess up.

"You know as well as I do, life is one big circle; whatever we do in this lifetime will affect all our lifetimes. If you mess it up, I will not have that option of staying on Earth and finding **my** Brandon. And Annie, you must tell no one who I really am—not even Rob. If you tell anyone about me, this could cause HUGE karmic repercussions. Do you get it?" Kate squinted at Annie.

"Yes, Kate, I won't mess up. I promise."

"Well, we'd better get going. You have a show to do tomorrow and I have to sort out my photos."

As Annie and Kate drove back to their apartment, they talked non-stop about the Heavenly Rules.

Annie wanted Kate to find Mr. Right; maybe she could help her in some small way. Annie's head throbbed with all the thoughts going through it. Above all, she couldn't believe that I, Gabriel, of all angels, didn't trust her.

The next morning Kate had a Heavenly breakfast waiting for Annie.

"Annie, do you want me to drop you off at the radio station? I happen to be going in that direction."

"I would love that, Kate."

When Kate dropped off Annie, they just happened to see Rob walking up the street. Annie waved and called him to the car.

"Hey, Rob, I want you to meet my roommate Kate."

Rob peeked into the car and opened the door for Annie. "Hi, roommate Kate, I'm Rob; nice to meet you." He extended his hand to shake Kate's. "Are you an angel, too?" he asked, smiling.

Annie and Kate both said "No" at the same time. "Well then, Annie, let me help you out of the car. Nice meeting you, Kate."

"Likewise," Kate responded.

As Kate drove off, Rob remarked, "She's kind of cute, Annie."

"Do you want to meet her? I mean, Rob, I can arrange it so we can all go out together."

"Annie, you're my girl for now. You're my meal ticket. I have to watch over you, so I don't have time in my life for anything else. I have too much on my plate, as it is. By the way, what are you doing here so early?" Rob asked.

"Kate offered me a ride. I figured I'd read until it's time for me to go on air. That's okay, isn't it, Rob?"

"Yes, my little angel." Rob put his arm around Annie's shoulder as they walked into the studio.

"Hey, John, what's happening?" Rob called out.

John noticed how chummy Rob was getting with Annie—Rob's hand on her shoulder; Annie at the station real early. Had she been with Rob all night?

"Hey, Rob, Annie. I'm getting things ready for the show. We have people waiting on line to speak to her. They've been waiting for well over an hour."

"That's great news, John. I have a few things to do; why don't you keep Annie occupied till I get back," Rob said as he walked off.

"How are things going, Annie?" John asked while he shuffled papers around.

"Just great," Annie replied. "I sure hope that engineer from the train calls in. I want to see how it all turned out."

"Annie, Rob is getting very close to you. I think he more than likes you. What do you think?"

Rob returned before Annie could answer John. "I'm back," he announced to all within earshot. "Are we all ready to answer the phone lines? Annie, put your ears on and we're off."

Rob began, "Good morning, New York. **This is Roll-over-with-Rob-in-the-Morning.** "John, who's our first caller?"

"Rob, we have Tom on the line; you know, the train engineer." John handed Rob a news bulletin as it came over the wire.

"Yes, Tom, you're live on the air with Annie."

"Annie, I just wanted to thank you. Your warning…"

Rob interrupted Tom. "Tom, this news bulletin just came over the wire." He read: "**One Dead, Dozens Hurt in Train Derailment.**

A commuter train derailed Saturday on New York's south side, killing at least one person and injuring 83, officials said. The train was traveling from Penn Station to Long Island, New York, when the derailment occurred around 8:36 a.m., authorities said.

"The Metro spokeswoman said all track signals were working when the derailment occurred, but she did not have any other details on a possible cause. She said she didn't know how fast the train was going.

"The engineer had been operating the trains for many years. She said several passengers were badly shaken and were taken to a hospital for routine tests. The New York State medical examiner's office confirmed one fatality but did not have details. Seventeen of the injured were in serious condition.

"The derailment occurred where the tracks were on an embankment next to a street. None of the cars fell onto the street. Firefighters raised ladders to the track.

"One of the passengers said she heard brakes screeching before the train came to a halt. 'I went flying into the safety seat bar and fell onto the ground,' she said.

"The engine ended up on its side and there was a 30-foot gap between two of the cars. Two remaining cars remained upright but went off the tracks."

Rob finished reading the bulletin and asked, "Tom, are you okay?"

"Yeah, I'm fine," Tom replied. "Just a little bit bruised and shaken, but fine. I wanted to tell you how Annie helped me make the best decision at that time."

"Go ahead, Tom; tell us your version," Rob said.

Tom recounted his harrowing experience: "The train was racing down the tracks. I watched the computer until we got near to Long Island. I noticed a light was flashing, just as Annie said. The computer was going crazy for some reason; all lights were lit. I didn't know what to do at first. Then I calmed myself down. I pushed several buttons to deprogram the train. It wouldn't work, but I kept trying. Annie's voice was so imbedded in my head, I knew what would happen next. I had to keep trying. I found a way. I called for help and we pulled the emergency brake upward. The train screeched to a halt. I watched the other train sideswipe us. That was it. I was hurt, but not badly.

"Rob, I know one person died and several were injured. If it had not been for Annie warning me ahead of time, there would have been many more fatalities and I wouldn't be talking on the phone to you now. I just wanted to thank you, Annie. I understand **now** that when you can see the future, sometimes you can change it. And change it I did. Thank you so much. You probably saved several passengers' lives."

Annie responded quickly. "Tom, I'm so glad you are okay. This was a great lesson in humanity for you. You believed with all your heart and soul in what I told you. You reacted accordingly. You chose the path of least resistance; that is why you are here today. My mission on Earth is to guide people to their destiny. I feel good inside. Thank you, Tom."

Rob cut away for a commercial break.

Rob looked at John and then at Annie. He said, "My head is spinning. I don't know what to say."

For the first time, John was impressed with Annie. He didn't understand, but he accepted it. His respect for Annie grew.

Back on the air Rob asked Annie how she felt about all this.

"I feel good, Rob. I always feel great when I can help someone," Annie replied breathlessly.

"Annie, are you okay? I mean, can you take more calls?" Rob asked.

"Yes."

"John, who's our next caller?"

"Annie, we have Abraham on the line."

"Hello, Abraham." Annie tuned in to his voice. "Abe, if I may call you that..."

"Yes."

"I'm picking up that you left your family in North Carolina. Is that correct?"

"Yes, Annie."

"Why?"

"I couldn't afford to feed them so I took this job in New York City. I'm a cab driver. I send money home every week. It's rough, Annie. Am I ever going to get a better job? Why is this happening to me?"

"Abraham, the way I see it, your family really misses you. If you were to drive them to New Jersey and rent a small house, your wife could baby sit and you and your family can be together again.

"Abe, you will make it. You've been so lonely without them. They need you. You've been scared that you wouldn't keep this job, but you will. Make the move.

"Abe, trust in the higher power. This will all work out. I see that someday, in New Jersey, you will have your own limo service; then, you can pick me up." Annie chuckled.

"You got it. Thanks, Annie; I'll let you know how it all turns out," Abe said. His tone was decidedly upbeat.

John had a question. "Annie, the advice you gave that man was on the order of a psychic, not of an Angel. What's the difference?"

"Well, John, there is a difference. I was sent down from Heaven to guide lost souls. I see what I'm allowed to see with the help of Gabriel, my guardian angel. Sometimes he talks to me in my head; at other times it's a direct message that I'm meant to give to others. Angels who are on Earth—such as me—are here mainly to acquire their wings. The more people I help, the closer I am to getting my wings."

"What happens after you get your wings, Annie?" John asked.

"Well, then, I'm free to choose if I want to stay on Earth and become mortal, or I could go back to Heaven and work up there, helping people cross over.

"Now, John, a psychic is a little different from an angel. Psychics are usually born with an ability to see into the future or the past; they may even channel the other side. However, where we differ is, psychics work on a very different level than angels.

"A psychic may pick up information from many spirit guides. Sometimes a psychic is not sure where he is getting his information from; whereas, an angel has but one source—her guardian.

"Many psychics have been fallen angels at one time or another. That means their lives had not been a bowl of cherries, so they were sent here genetically through their parents, to fix the wrong and make it right.

"Psychics who are good, work on a karma-credit basis. The more people that they help, the more credits they get; which, in turn, allow them to elevate their karma. So, when their time is up and they are ready to enter Heaven's Gate, they will be judged on how many lives that they have affected. If all goes well, they will be taught how to become an angel in Heaven. They will be well on their way to getting their wings.

"Got it, John?"

"Whoa! That's a whole lot of information to swallow."

"I hope you understand. Mind you, angels and psychics can be similar. We all work for the same cause—helping to elevate the souls of mankind. It really is a wonderful job. A psychic is an angel in training." Annie smiled.

Rob ended the discussion. "Well, folks, I think we've worked Annie a lot today. Annie, are you tired yet?"

"Just a little, Rob."

"You heard it here first. Tune in tomorrow for our Annie, an angel over the airwaves. It's time to break for commercial. This is 92.3 FM; keep listening. Up next is sports and weather with Todd."

Rob took his earphones off. "Well, Annie, how about a quick bite to eat?"

"Sounds good, Rob."

A voice in the distance shouted, "Where are you guys going?"

"Down the street to grab a quick bite, John."

"Can I come?"

Rob squirmed. "John, I need to talk to Annie alone, you understand."

John's feelings were hurt. Rob was his best friend; now he had a new best friend, Annie. "Yeah, I understand."

Radio, Annie, Rob, Ice Skating and More

Chapter 7

Annie and Rob bolted toward the Second Avenue Deli. Rob wanted a place where he could talk intimately with Annie.

Rob was on a high again; he rattled on non-stop to Annie. "Have a seat, darling. I can't believe how great that show was. I'll be looking for the ratings to see how well we did. It was AWESOME. I can't believe what you told Tom the train conductor and how spot on you were with him. Annie, a few more shows like that and we'll be rolling off the charts. What do you think?"

"I think I'm very pleased with the way things are going. My only wish would be to help people at a faster pace," she said.

"I know, Annie… so you can hurry and meet Brandon, right?" Rob tried to hide his boredom with Annie's going on about Brandon.

"Yup." Annie smiled.

"Annie, can I ask you something?"

"Yes."

Rob stumbled over his words; he didn't know exactly how to put this question to Annie. He held his breath then blurted it out. "Has this love thing ever happened to you before on Earth? I mean, was there ever someone other than Brandon?"

"Yes, Rob, several times; but not to this extent."

"Several times? You mean you keep coming back to Earth and falling in love and that's it? Does it ever get resolved?"

Annie was ashamed to say, "So far it hasn't, Rob. But I keep trying. I know in my heart Brandon is the one."

"How do you know?" Rob asked with some skepticism.

"I just know…when you know, you don't deny it. You know when you know, and you never let it go. It's something you feel deep inside, Rob. I know I will get it right this time; that's why I'm here." Annie was just a little agitated with Rob's question.

Rob was silently analyzing Annie like a shrink. He couldn't understand why Brandon might be different from all the rest. He needed to question her more to find out. "Annie, if you don't mind, can you tell me about another love relationship on Earth that didn't work out the way you wanted it to?" Rob thought maybe if he could understand her past, he could understand her love for Brandon.

Before Annie had a chance to answer, a waiter appeared at the table to take their order. It was Elle.

Quick on his feet, spry as a teenager, Elle quipped, "Hey, girlfriends, where's the rest of the Olson twins? You know, that crazy, wild guy John?"

"Elle, what are you doing at this restaurant? Did you change jobs or something?" Rob asked.

"I have two part-time jobs now. I float around just like a fairy. The clock is ticking; I have to be quick on my feet. What would you be having for lunch, you sweet couple you?" Elle reached over and put his hand on Rob's shoulder and whispered in his ear while staring at Annie. "Honey, if I were you, I would snatch this pretty little thing up as quick as can be. Don't you let her get away now." Rob blushed a little.

"Now for your order... let me see... Rob, you will have corned beef on rye; and Annie, you will have tea, tea and more tea, with a little lox and cream cheese with a bagel. Do I have it right?"

"You got it, Elle," Rob said. "Why don't you whisk away to fairyland and get our orders?"

Elle danced off to the kitchen, chattering to himself like a little motor mouth. "Off I go. See if you can catch me. Don't blink; I'll be back in a wink."

Rob shook his head while Annie giggled. "So where were we?" Rob asked.

"Well, you wanted to know about another love I had on Earth. You see, just before Brandon there was Richard. When Gabriel sent me down, I was supposed to take care of Richard until his passing. I was to guide him to the light. I met Richard in Hawaii through friends."

"My, you do get around. Hawaii?"

"Yes, beautiful Hawaii. Our love was unspoken for many years. I was his caregiver; he was dying of cancer. My mission was to help him, for he had only five more years to live. I was to teach him how not to be frightened of death.

"Every day was a new adventure for us. Richard had quite a bit of money; he lived on a plantation on Maui right next to the ocean. Richard had spent most of his life working and helping others. He helped his workers' families and saw to it that their children got an education.

"My job was to teach him to live every waking moment to the fullest till the end of his time. I taught him what life was all about. We loved; we laughed; we played. As his death drew near, Richard turned his back on me and began pushing me away now and then."

Rob was so totally engrossed in Annie's story, he did not see Elle deliver their lunch and the sounds of the chatter in the restaurant faded out. Rob was glued to Annie's words. "Then what happened?" Rob asked.

Annie looked at Rob with her big blue eyes. "Richard loved me so much he didn't want me to hurt anymore, so he pushed me further and further away. He told me he could see my light. He knew his time was coming. Richard forbade me to hold him in my arms while guiding him to the light.

"Why, Annie? Why did he do that?" Rob asked.

"He didn't feel worthy of me," Annie said sadly. "He looked back at our life together and thought of all the things we could have done, places he could have taken me. We had always talked about going to Paris, but that never happened. Richard was a dreamer; yet, with all the money he had, he never really went anywhere.

"He was so scared that he wouldn't have enough money for his retirement that he saved most of what he made on the plantation— with the exception of helping his workers. Love was unthinkable for him until he met me. Richard felt he had messed up. It was too late for him now and he knew I had to go on with my life."

Rob shook his head in disbelief. "Go on, Annie."

"Rob, I know this is hard for you to believe, but deep inside of me the light of my love and my energy seeped through. My light was so bright and so full of love for him, he ordered me to leave. I fought him, but he won. Richard died seven days later.

"My mission was unfulfilled, according to the angels' rule book. As much as it hurt, I was supposed to keep trying, for if I could help just one soul on Earth, then thousands would follow. I had no choice but to let Richard go and move on with my life. Rob, that hurt more than you'll ever know."

Rob reached across the table and patted her hand. "Annie, you never cease to amaze me. The more I listen to you, the more life makes sense to me," he said.

Rob smiled sympathetically. "Do you need a ride home? You'll have to get up early for the radio show tomorrow. And Annie, if it's any consolation, tomorrow on the radio you'll be helping many people. I'll walk with you outside and get a cab for you."

Rob and Annie got up from the table. They were walking out of the Second Avenue Deli when Elle slid right into them.

"Check!" Elle waved it over his head like a fan. Handing over the check, he added loudly, "Tip, please." Elle was never subtle.

"Oh, Elle, I'm sorry; I forgot about the check." Rob pulled out a few dollars from his wallet and laid them on Elle's outstretched palm.

Elle burst into a rhyme: "Never fear, your fairy is here. Here you go; have a good one, you two." Elle smiled and said aloud to himself, "I just know these two will fall in love. I just know it."

Rob and Annie ignored him.

Rob turned to Annie. "Hey, by the way, this weekend John and I are having a small get together at my house. Do you want to come?"

Annie's face lit up. "Can I bring someone?"

Rob held his breath. "Who?"

"Kate."

"Oh, Kate—yes, you can. By the way, where are you headed to now?"

"To Central Park, Rob."

"Why do you always go to Central Park? What do you do there?"

"I'll tell you later." Annie smiled at Rob.

Rob hailed a cab. "Driver, take the lady to Central Park, please," he said. He held the door for Annie and said, "See you tomorrow."

Annie pleasantly asked the driver, "Sir, please drop me off at the ice skating rink."

"Yes, Ma'am," the driver said as he inched into the New York traffic.

At the rink Annie sat on her favorite bench and watched the skaters go round and round on the thin ice. Annie loved the ice skating rink. She remembered how well she ice-skated when she was a little girl. She wanted to try again, but she was just a little rusty.

She watched a little girl about twelve years old glide around the rink without effort—she skated so perfectly. Annie knew the young lady was in her element when she skated.

Annie was surprised but pleased when the young girl came up and sat beside her on the bench to drink some Gatorade. Annie noted that she was thin, had the biggest brown eyes, and her blonde curls were tied back neatly in a pony tail. She wore the cutest ice skating outfit Annie had seen—her beige tights matched her pretty red dress. She seemed poised with lots of class for a little girl beyond her years.

While wiping the ice off her blades, the girl looked up at Annie. "Hi, my name is Julie. What's yours?" she asked.

"Annie. You know, I come here often and I've watched you skate. I love watching you skate, Julie; you make it look so easy."

"It **is** easy, Annie," Julie responded. "I've been skating since I was five years old. One season I sprained my ankle and I couldn't skate for six whole months. I was scared that I'd forgotten how to skate, but you know what, I'm training for the Junior Olympics now. My mom is over there." Julie pointed to a woman in a beige coat across the way. "She loves to watch me skate." She bent down to tighten the laces on her skates. "Where are your skates?" Julie asked.

Annie threw her hands up in the air. "Don't have them with me."

Julie grabbed Annie's hand and pulled her to the service booth. "Let's get you fitted with ice skates." Before Annie could say a word, Julie said to the gentleman in the booth, "Let's see now. She looks like a size 6; can I have those brown skates up there, Sir?"

"Yes, you can," he said. "That will be five dollars, please." Annie reached into her purse and paid.

As Julie helped Annie lace her skates, Annie flashed back in time and remembered what it was like to ice skate. Annie thought to herself, "I can do this."

Julie helped Annie stand up. Annie held on to the rail with one hand and locked the other hand into the crook of Julie's arm. Taking it one wobbly step at a time, Annie felt klutzy and frustrated. As

Julie and Annie made their way around the rink twice, Annie began feeling much more confident, but she couldn't help giggling.

Just then, Julie let go of Annie's hand, sending Annie into a tail-spin. Annie flew in every direction, her ankles bending every which way. One, two, three skaters just missed Annie as she hurtled through the crowd.

Julie, who was watching the spectacle, raced to Annie and tried to steady her. "Whoa! Annie. I think we'd better sit down for a while," Julie said. She held up Annie as best she could—she was, after all, only a skinny twelve-year-old—as they inched their way to the bench.

Annie was a little shaken, but she giggled and giggled. "See, I told you I haven't skated for a long time." Annie, however, was not one to give up on anything easily. She was willing to go out on the ice again.

Julie admired Annie's resolve but shook her head. "I think you had enough for today, Annie. I'm happy you made it around the rink. How about you watching me for a while? Maybe you'll get the hang of it."

"Okay," Annie agreed.

Julie glided across the ice and skated like a pro; the ice was hers and hers alone. She twirled up in the air, then made several figure eights in the middle of the rink.

Annie watched in amazement. She knew she could do that with just a little more practice.

Like I said, Annie was not one to give up so easily. While Julie was jumping and twirling, Annie got back onto the ice, holding tightly to the rail, and slowly made her way around the ice rink once again.

She waved at Julie and Julie smiled and waved back. Annie was so proud. She knew she had to try her wings at this one.

She looked up toward the sky as if she saw me, Gabriel. She especially wanted me to watch how well she was doing. Annie thought to herself that all work and no play were really not good for her or anyone else. After helping so many people, ice skating was a welcome relief for Annie now.

Time raced by. Annie was hungry; she motioned to Julie to get off the ice and have a hotdog with her. They sat on the bench with their hotdogs and they really got a chance to know each other. Julie was now Annie's new best friend.

Meanwhile, Brandon sat in his penthouse apartment with just nothing to do. He picked up the phone and called Pat Edwards. "Hey Pat, Brandon here. I think I'm ready for my first spiritual lesson. Can you come over? If you can, I'll send a car for you."

"I'll be ready in one-half hour," Pat said. Brandon sent the car. Pat was ecstatic. He thought to himself, "I'll be teaching Brandon Turner how to be spiritual—little old me." Pat chuckled.

When Pat arrived at Brandon's Park Avenue building, Brandon buzzed him in. Brandon stood in the doorway with a drink in one hand and another drink in the other hand for Pat. "Here, this is for you, my friend. Sit down and we can talk," he said, gesturing to a chair.

"Thank you," Pat said, waving away the drink. "Sorry, Brandon, I never drink when I am in a session with someone, but thank you anyway. By the way, how many of those have you had already?"

"I just poured this drink," Brandon answered. "I hardly touched it."

Pat said emphatically, "Brandon, if you want us to work together, you really need to put the drink down."

"Okay, Pal. I usually never listen to anyone, but you have my attention." Brandon set both glasses on the coffee table in front of Pat. "What do you want me to do next?"

"Please, sit down and relax. Oh, by the way," Pat said, pointing to a picture on the mantel, "is that a picture of Annie and you together? If so, can I see it so I can tune myself into her vibrations?"

Brandon jumped up from his chair and gave Pat the picture. "Here."

"Oh, my, my. She certainly was pretty."

"Yes, she was," Brandon said proudly but sadly.

"Just give me a few minutes to adjust to her frequency and let's see what I pick up." But first, Pat made himself comfortable in his big brown leather chair. He propped a few pillows in the back of his neck and wiggled around till he felt everything was comfy.

Pat held Annie and Brandon's photo and stared deeply into Annie's eyes.

Brandon didn't know what to expect. He waited nervously for Pat to say something.

Pat coughed a little to clear his throat, and Brandon leaned forward in his brown leather chair. He didn't want to miss anything that Pat had to say.

Pat spoke. Words were coming out, but Pat seemed to be spacing out. He wasn't looking at Brandon; it was almost as if he were talking into thin air.

He said, "I'm having trouble connecting with Annie; she seems to be all over the place. Wait! There is a man; he's very distinguished looking—almost fatherly—wearing a white suit with a pink tie. He's telling me his name is Gabriel and he's Annie's guardian angel."

Pat now looked at Brandon. "Do you have a question for Gabriel?"

"Who, me?"

"Yes."

Brandon could barely contain his excitement. "Well, let's see… Where is she? Is she okay? Does Annie miss me? Will I ever get to be with her again?"

"Whoa, slow down a little. Just one question at a time, I can't talk that fast," Pat said. "Wait, I will repeat to you what Gabriel is telling me." He cocked his head slightly as if listening to someone whispering in his ear.

Pat repeated whatever I, Gabriel, told him. "Yes, Annie is fine. She is on a very special mission. Yes, Annie spoke of you often; she misses you very much and she wants you to know the love that you had for each other never died. Your question—will you ever be with her again?—I can't answer that. There are certain things between Heaven and Earth that may not be revealed at this time."

Pat was conveying a direct message from me to Brandon at that moment. He continued, "Brandon, you must go on with your life for now. There are many changes and obstacles that you will face in the near future. I have checked in the Book of Life. This book contains everything that you have done and everything that you will do in the future. However, you do have free will choice on minor things and you do have alternate futures. We are waiting to see which path you will take, Brandon. And, might I add, it seems you have picked the perfect person to guide you on this spiritual journey.

"All I can say to you is if there is a will, there is a way; and it will be up to you to find the correct path that will lead you back to Annie. However, if you remain the person that you are now, you will never see Annie again."

Brandon asked quizzically, "What does he mean, Pat?"

"Ask him."

Brandon felt odd talking to someone he couldn't see, but he had to know. "Gabriel, what do you mean? What is wrong with the person I am now? And how can I change to be a better person?"

I, Gabriel, responded through Pat, "We see here that you have spent your life indulging yourself. We see you drink spirits quite often; this must taper down quite a bit. We see the way you treat people—demanding—and such is not the way the world works. You need to develop compassion and understanding for your fellow man. You must learn the world does not revolve around you.

"You were given this mission on Earth to be able to help thousands of people through your television show. We have yet to see you really help anyone in a compassionate way. The way you treat women is deplorable. All this and more must change."

I pulled back my energy. Pat was drained; he returned to his body slowly and shook his arms and hands so he would be connected to Earth.

"What did he say, Brandon? Sometimes I'm a human telephone. I never remember what was said in my channeling."

Brandon bowed his head in shame. "He said a lot, Pat, and all of it was true of me. I have to change. I have to watch my consumption of alcohol. I have to treat women with more respect. I have to find a way on my television show to help people instead of feeding my ego. He told me Annie still loved me very much. He couldn't give me an answer whether we would be together. I get the feeling I'm being tested."

Pat shook his head. "Brandon, this is one of the strangest channelings I have ever had. Usually I can connect with the person who has passed. I'm aware in this case it's not allowed at this time. I don't understand why, but I accept what Gabriel has told you. Looks like we have a lot of work to do. It seems your karma is below par for the people upstairs."

"Pat, is it possible… I mean, if I really change and help people, do you think… I will be able to be with Annie?" Brandon asked.

"Anything is possible. The way I see it, Brandon, you have two ways to be with Annie. One, you will meet someone like her in every way; in fact, her soul may be the same as well. Or two, you may have to pass on to meet Annie. I have no idea what they have planned for you upstairs. If you really want to meet her, you have to abide by their rules. I do know that much."

Pat got up. "Sorry, Brandon, I have to be going. This session has taken every ounce of energy out of me. I hope you don't mind."

Brandon also got up. "I understand, Pat. I just hope I don't have to pass on before I meet her. I'll choose to follow their rules. By the way, how accurate are you when you channel the other side?"

"Oh, about 85 percent. The other 15 percent I usually can figure out what went wrong. Brandon, I really have to go." Pat started for the door.

"I'll get the car for you; and, by the way, to help my karma I want you on my show once a month. Okay?" Brandon said.

"I'll be there for you."

"I'll call you in a week or so for another session. Thank you. You'll never know how much this has meant to me."

As Pat stepped into the limo, he tried to make sense of what had just happened.

Brandon had his first and last drink. He sat in his room trying to figure out how he could make his life better.

Elsewhere, night was beginning to fall on the ice rink; it was time for Annie to go home. She waved goodbye to Julie and promised to see her again. She hailed a cab and went home.

Annie tiptoed into the house so as not to wake Kate and crawled into bed. When the alarm clock blared early in the morning, she felt as though she had only three hours of sleep. After a hasty breakfast of toast and juice, still half-dazed, she made it to the radio station.

"You're live on the air with our angel, Annie!" Rob shouted.

Radio Days and Helping Lost Souls

Chapter 8

"Annie, are you ready to answer the phone lines?" Rob asked. "And Annie, I'm proud of you; you've helped well over three-hundred people and that includes those in the train derailment."

Rob turned to John and pointed to an instrument on the side. "John, see that bell and counter I put on the desk?"

"Yes, what is that for?"

"That's for Annie. Every time she helps a caller, whether it is in groups or just one person, press the counter and hit the bell so we know how many people she has helped."

"Good idea, Rob. Let's see… Annie's up to 325 so far and counting. Shall we carry on?" John asked.

"John, who's our next caller?"

"We have Helen on the line."

Annie said, "Hi, Helen, how can I help you?"

"Hi, Annie, I'm really enjoying your show. I'd like to know about my daughter and how she's doing. Her name is Jamie and she lives in New Jersey."

Annie hesitated before answering; she was uneasy about Helen's question. Something was wrong. She stared off into the distance; a rush of fear, an uneasiness, came over her. The feeling was so overwhelming she forgot that she was live on the radio. Her words poured out as if she had no control.

"Helen, your daughter's in danger. You must go to her now! She's in an extremely dangerous situation. You must stop what you're doing. Get in your car. You must go now!"

Annie caught Helen off guard. Helen replied as if she were in shock, "Annie, I have a few days off in a couple of days. Is it all right if I go then? I don't want to lose my job."

Annie's voice grew even louder. "Tomorrow may be too late! You must get there today, do you understand? Please listen to me; it's a matter of life and death!" Annie shouted.

She regained her composure and said, "I see your daughter is on drugs. Correct?"

"Yes," Helen replied.

"Your daughter has overdosed. I see her lying on a bed unconscious. Now, do you understand?" Annie tried to remain composed.

"Yes, I'll leave now." Helen hung up.

"Whoa!" Rob remarked. "I sure hope Helen gets there in time. Why don't we go to a commercial break while you pause to gather your thoughts?'

During the break Rob asked, "Annie, how do these things come to you?"

"Gabriel shows me visions, or sometimes I get feelings; it's stronger than anything or anyone can describe. Sometimes the knowing feeling takes the form of a very profound vision—you know, like moving pictures. It's something in your gut that's indicating danger. That's the best way I can describe the feeling," Annie said.

Angel over the Airwaves ran one hour overtime due to the overwhelming response. Now Annie was more than a permanent fixture on Rob's show—she was a star. Rob pumped his fists in the air when he checked the ratings. Due to his little angel trying to save souls, his ratings soared.

Two days later, the story of Helen continued on the radio with Annie and Helen.

"We have Helen on the radio," John said.

"Great!" Rob said. "Put her through."

"Annie, this is Helen. I called to thank you," she said.

Rob interrupted. "Helen, why don't you tell the listening audience what happened and bring us up to date."

"Okay," she responded. "Well, you remember two days ago I called in and spoke to Annie about my daughter Jamie?"

"Yes, please go on, Helen," Rob replied.

"You see, I'm a maid at the Hotel Waldorf in New York. I was listening to Annie on your radio show while I made my rounds. I decided to call. I had tried on several other occasions and I was never able to get through; the lines were always jammed. This particular Friday was different. Much to my surprise, the phone rang and immediately I was the next caller. I asked Annie about my daughter Jamie in New Jersey. Your angel Annie frightened me with her tone of voice. It was as if she was giving me a message and I had no choice but to listen. There was something in her voice that made me respond.

"I quickly found my supervisor and told her there was someone ill in my family and that I needed to be let out of work right away." To my surprise she consented without hesitation.

"I jumped into my car and drove to New Jersey. With traffic and all, it took me about two hours. I stopped at my granddaughter's house and asked her to show me where Jamie lived. We arrived at Jamie's house within fifteen minutes.

"I knocked on the door and her husband answered. He was bewildered that I was there. 'What are you doing here?' he asked.

"I said, 'I came to see my daughter, Jamie. Where is she?' I demanded to see her.

"He responded, 'She's in the bedroom upstairs.'

"My granddaughter and I rushed up the stairs to Jamie's room. There she was lying on the bed—she could barely move. There were bruises all over her body. She seemed semiconscious. I was determined to take her back with me to New York. My granddaughter and I carried her to the car.

"Jamie's husband said, 'By the way, your daughter is crazy. Where are you taking her, anyway?'

"My response was 'Don't worry; I agree with you. I'm taking her to a mental institution.' That seemed to appease him. We carried Jamie to the car and I placed her in the back seat with my granddaughter and drove off to New York.

"I remember driving for about an hour. It must have been near midnight when my granddaughter suddenly started to scream. 'Grandma, Grandma! Jamie has stopped breathing!'

"I turned and saw my daughter Jamie lying as if in death. I kicked the car into high gear—speeding, looking for the nearest hospital. We were in luck; the hospital was only a mile away. We rushed Jamie into the emergency room.

"The doctor worked on her until she began to breathe on her own. We found out she had overdosed on drugs, just like Annie said. The doctor told me we got her there just in the nick of time. Her heart had stopped beating and she was dead for about a minute before they revived her.

"I stayed by her side every moment until she recovered. We brought her back with us to New York so she could start her life over again."

Helen stopped to catch her breath before continuing. "If it hadn't been for Annie warning me about my daughter, God only knows what would have happened to her. I want to thank you again, Annie. You gave me back my daughter."

Annie, Rob and John were overwhelmed and lost for words. Annie finally said, "Helen, I'm just doing what I was sent here to do. All that matters is your daughter is alive."

"Thanks to you, Annie," Helen replied.

Rob cleared his throat and said, "That was quite a story, Helen. I wish you the best. Please check in with us once in a while and let us know how Jamie is doing."

"I will. Thank you so much."

"What a perfect end to our show, Annie. This is Roll-over-with-Rob-in-the-Morning. Don't forget to keep that dial tuned to 92.3 FM."

John commented to Annie, "What a great show—beyond great." Then, figuring Annie and Rob would exit for lunch without him, John quickly went about his business. He was used to not being invited and kept himself busy so as not to draw attention to himself.

Rob shouted across the room, "Annie, are you ready to get a bite?"

Annie had a sudden idea. "Rob, why don't we take a walk and go to the park and talk? We can catch a bite of lunch from one of the hot dog vendors."

"Sounds good to me, I'll get my jacket and off we'll go." Rob waved to John. "Later, John."

So Annie and Rob bundled up and walked out of the studio, ready for their new adventure. They walked and walked, past Macy's and several vendors on the street, and they kept walking. They were a contrasting pair—Rob was very tall and Annie was petite.

"Where are we going?" Rob asked.

"I was thinking of Washington Square," Annie said.

"I have an idea." Rob stepped off the curb and waved down a taxi. "Why are we going there?" he asked as he leaned back in his seat, relieved to rest his feet.

"I thought we could grab a hot dog and sit and feed the birds... and look up at my new billboard." Annie smiled.

"Ah, now you're getting it," Rob chuckled loudly. "Look at your billboard? OH, NO! I hope I haven't created a monster."

When they arrived at Washington Square, Annie hurried out of the cab and ran to a round bench where she could sit and watch the pigeons cooing and strutting around to impress—who? Potential mates? Rob noted where Annie was sitting before approaching a hot-dog vendor.

"Three dogs, please—two with kraut, one without. Throw in some fries and two cokes, please." Rob smeared mustard all over the dogs.

Handing Annie the hotdog without sauerkraut, some fries and a coke, he said, "Here you go. Enjoy."

Rob was so hungry he couldn't eat his two hotdogs fast enough. Annie burst into laughter. Rob's mouth was so full that when he tried to talk to Annie his words came out muffled. "What are you laughing at?"

"Rob, you're so funny. Hey! Look at my new billboard. I think I like this one best," she said.

Rob finished up his lunch. "Annie, I don't get it. All the billboards are the same. What is so different about this one?"

Annie looked up at her billboard. "I think it's the positioning of this one; it's just right, Rob." Annie threw out some pieces of her bun to feed the pigeons.

"Okay, whatever you say."

"Rob, I wanted to tell you something that is very important to me. Several weeks ago you asked me about other men that I had fallen in love with in other lifetimes. Well, I didn't tell you everything. Is it okay if I tell you about this one lifetime before Brandon? It would mean a lot to me."

Rob was intrigued. "Okay. I can't wait to hear this." For this story Rob got cozy next to Annie while he observed her closely. "Annie, I really don't know if I believe in other lifetimes. I mean, I'm just getting used to your being an angel, and now you throw other lifetimes at me. Don't mind me; I'm just rambling on," he said as he looked at his watch. "I'll listen. That's what I'm here for."

Annie smiled, grateful for Rob's attention. "Thank you, Rob. It all started when Gabriel sent me down to Earth to help this very lonely young man named Rich. He was about 35 and I was 45. He had blond hair and blue eyes and was tall and thin. His main passion was to surf the world in a spiritual way."

Rob blurted out, "A surfer! You had a relationship with a surfer?"

Annie gave Rob "the look." "Rob, please just listen. Rich was so lonely, but Gabriel loved his spirit. My job was to find out why he was so lonely and to help him through his trying times.

"Gabriel placed me in Hawaii where I met Rich while I was surfing. I fell off my board and lost my bearings and Rich came to my aid. He actually saved me from dying."

"Excuse me," Rob interrupted. "Annie, are you making this up?"

Annie was clearly agitated. "No! Just listen… I need to get this off my chest, Rob."

Rob rolled his eyes upward momentarily. "Okay."

"Rich and I started dating; and after a short period of time, he wanted to take me to a different island to surf with him. I was very intrigued by him; not only was he highly spiritual, he was also very psychic. I was so drawn to his spirit. I would have followed him anywhere."

"That's so nice to hear, Annie," Rob said indifferently.

Annie continued. Whether Rob was listening or not, she needed to talk.

"So Rich bought us plane tickets for the Cook Islands. There was a private island named Tabu that he wanted to show me. 'It's just awesome for surfing,' he said, 'and the waves are so perfect.'

"When we landed at the Cook Islands airport in Rarotonga, we were greeted by six men. The next thing I knew, I was riding with Rich in a big pickup truck with our surfboards on hand. We drove down a dirt road to a tiny beach where there was a boat waiting to take us to the Island of Tabu."

"Annie, this is getting interesting," Rob said.

"So we put all our gear in these canoe-shaped boats and I could see this beautiful island off in the distance. Rob, it was beyond anyone's imagination. The island was shaped like a round sundial.

When we landed on the island, Rich took my hand and said, 'Annie, this is my own private island. Welcome.' We were greeted with flower wreaths by what appeared to be several native islanders."

"Annie, I have a question," Rob interjected. "In every lifetime was your name Annie?"

"Rob, my name is always the same, lifetime after lifetime. Gabriel made it that way, although other angels may have their names changed if they want. I just love my name, so I keep it."

Annie continued her story.

"Rich walked ahead; I followed. We walked on sand and mud for a while till we came to a tree house. I followed him up the steep steps that wound around the trunk of the tree." Annie took a deep breath as though reliving the climb.

"Rob, this island and its people were amazing," she said.

"Rich sat me down and explained how he inherited the island from his family and that only invited guests were allowed to surf here. This was a very spiritual place.

"The native workers served the visitors on the island; that's how Rich made his money to keep up the place. He worked on the island six months out of the year and the other six months he traveled the world in search of the best surf spots."

"Interesting," Rob said.

"I spent several weeks with Rich on Tabu. I learned everything about the native people as well as the visitors who would pay Rich several thousand dollars per week to surf there.

"Rich opened up to me. He told me how unhappy he was. I looked around at what he had and I couldn't understand why he was unhappy. Rob, he had it all... I mean he had it all! Rich explained that, unfortunately, every lady he ever met never loved him for who he was. They only saw what he had and that was the Island of Tabu. Rich wanted to get married, have children, and live a normal life. But that was nearly impossible for him; he had to work the island so he could derive income."

Rob was getting more intrigued by this story. "Go on, Annie, you've got my attention."

"The next day we went surfing, then boating. It was then he told me of his greatest loss in his life...his brother. His brother drowned while surfing at the island in spite of Rich's attempts to save him.

He never got over his brother's death, and staying on his island was a constant reminder."

"Very interesting, Annie," Rob said.

Just then, Annie and Rob were distracted by several birds flying overhead and flapping and squawking right in front of Annie's billboard. Annie wondered if this was a sign. Should she be telling all this to Rob?

Rob was really getting into the story. He did wonder about Annie, though. He knew she was very psychic, and he also felt the warmth of her light. But he didn't know if she was just a great storyteller or if she was, in fact, speaking the truth. It was hard for Rob to believe in other lifetimes. He barely accepted Annie as an angel—and now this. This story seemed contrived.

The shrill ring of Rob's cell phone jolted him out of his thoughts. It was John calling.

"Hey, Rob, are you ever coming back to the studio to work this afternoon?"

Rob answered, "I'm working on it. Annie's captivated me with this new story she's telling me. She won't let me go until she finishes it. John, if you'll pick up some of my slack today, I'll make it up to you. In fact, I could meet you at five at the Second Avenue Deli. We can have a bite to eat and I can fill you in."

John felt good; maybe—just maybe—he could get his old friend back. He really missed Rob. Ever since Annie came along, all Rob saw were dollar signs and how he could generate huge revenues for the radio station. At times it seemed to John that Rob was very determined to make this happen and Annie was his very own Golden Goose.

"Got you covered, Rob, take as much time as you need with Annie. I'll see you at 5:00 at the Deli," John said.

Rob turned back to Annie. "Sorry, Annie. Now, where were you in the story?"

Annie knew she was stealing Rob's time and she felt badly, but she had to get this story off her chest. "That's okay, Rob. I'll continue if you don't mind," she said politely…

Annie continued her story. "The very next morning after breakfast, Rich and I went boating. We took along our surfboards so, whenever the perfect wave appeared, we could go for it. What happened on that outing was even beyond my comprehension.

"I was relaxing in the boat; it must have been 95 degrees under the blazing sun. According to Rich, we were in the same spot where his brother Brad had drowned. As Rich steered the boat, suddenly for no apparent reason, I started to channel his brother Brad. I had no control of what came out of my mouth."

"What did he say, Annie?" Rob asked.

"Well, he said, 'Tell Rich that my accident wasn't his fault. I did something stupid—I misjudged a wave. I thought I could take it, but it was way too big for me. I tried to paddle as hard as I could back to shore, but I lost my breath. My leg cramped up and I went under a huge wave. By the time my body floated to shore, I was a goner. I know Rich tried to save me; I floated out of my body and watched him try to revive me. It wasn't his fault; he needs to stop blaming himself for what happened.'

"Rich looked at me. Tears were running down his cheek.

"He said, 'Annie, ask Brad to tell me something only he and I know. I need to confirm what just came through you.'

"Within a moment, Brad told Rich about the car accident they had in Bali—the one where they went off the road while they were looking at two gorgeous babes.

"Rich cried out, 'That IS my brother! Annie, NO one knows of this.' Rich was blown away."

Rob immediately interjected, "What year did that happen?"

Annie replied, "It was 1971 in the Cook Islands. It made the headline of the *Surf Today Magazine*. The reason I know this is Rich showed me the picture of his brother. The headline was **World Class Surfer Drowns in Freak Accident on Tabu Island.**"

"Annie, wait a minute." Rob picked up his cell phone and called John at the studio. "Hey, John, do me a favor. Go on-line and check *Surf Today Magazine*. Check for a surfer named Brad, World Class Surfer, who drowned in a freak accident in 1971. Check up **Surfer Drowned Cook Islands 1971**. Something should come up. Then call me back. Annie is telling me this story about one of her past lives, and I need to check this out, so please get back to me immediately."

"Okay, boss." John heard the urgency in Rob's voice. He wasted no time.

"Rob, you don't believe me?" Annie felt hurt.

"Annie, it's not that I don't believe you. I have to prove this to myself. Maybe there are pictures on the web of Brad and Rich. I NEED to check this out for myself. I'm not trying to hurt your feelings. I just need to know."

Fifteen minutes later John called back. "Did you find out anything?" Rob asked.

"You're NOT going to believe this!" exclaimed John. "I couldn't find it at first, Rob, so I called the *Surf Today Magazine* and—guess what?—they're still in existence. I spoke to the editor and he gave me an internet link to check out. While I was talking to the editor, I pulled up the link with pictures and all. The editor told me he knew Brad and had personally photographed and covered several stories about him on the Island of Tabu.

"Then I checked a step further. I asked the editor if the Island of Tabu is still operational. He told me that only surfers know of this hidden place. The island is run by a guy named Jeff Clarkson, World Class Surfer. It seems he is the son of Rich, who owned the island. Upon his father's passing he felt he needed to carry on with the Island of Tabu for the sake of his father."

There was silence on the other end of the phone. "Rob, are you there?"

"Yes."

Rob was stunned. He could hardly speak. "John, I'll see you at 5:00; and see if you can print out that story and bring the pictures and whatever else you've got to the Deli. I need to hear the rest of this story. I'll clue you in when I see you. Thanks, buddy." Rob hung up.

"Annie, I don't know what to say. I'm so sorry. My mind is messed up; I just don't understand this whole thing. What you're telling me can REALLY validate past lives."

Annie emphatically tried to make her point. "Look, Rob, all I know is that you don't have to understand; you've just got to believe. What once was meant to be already exists, somewhere in one's past life." She paused and waited for Rob to respond. Rob was silent. So Annie stood up and grabbed her purse. She was ready to leave in a huff.

Rob grabbed her arm. "NO, please don't leave; I need to hear the rest of the story. This is all new to me."

Annie sat back down on the bench. "Okay, but Rob, it's a long story; I could finish it another time."

"No, Annie. NOW, please."

"Okay. Now where was I? I remember... So Rich and I went out on the boat every day and on a daily basis I channeled the information that was given to me by Brad.

"Rich was able to verify a lot of what I channeled by calling his mom. The information came to me so fast and furious that Rich didn't even know what was true.

"All Rich wanted to do was talk to his brother, for he missed him so. A week went by when some very important information came to me. I was very hesitant to repeat what his brother told me, but Rich begged me to tell him."

Rob leaned forward. "What was it?" he asked.

"Hold on to your hat for this one, Rob," Annie warned. "Brad told me that Rich and I knew each other in many previous lifetimes. In each lifetime we were man and wife, but somehow we never got it right."

Rob leaned back and sighed. "There you go again, Annie. I don't know. I'm beginning to wonder if many lifetimes are worth going through—if we never seem to get it right."

"Rob, I don't believe we have a choice on how many lifetimes we go through," Annie answered.

"Then, what is the point?"

"The point is we have to experience many lifetimes in order to grow and serve mankind. When we finally get it right, then—and only then—do we progress to the next level in the game of life? I do believe at that point we have a choice whether we come back to Earth or not. At least that was how Gabriel explained it to me.

"He also told me we are still little children here on Earth. Just like nine-year-old children—when they don't get things right, their parents teach them to do them over and over again until they succeed. It is the same as well, when we experience other lifetimes. In other lifetimes we experience different people, different cultures, different men, different women, different races. In time we get it right. At least I hope so, for my sake."

Annie continued, "Brad, Rich's brother, told me that if I looked deeply into Rich's eyes, the veil would come down and I would be able to see Brad for just a moment in time. I gazed into Rich's eyes and, lo and behold, I saw Brad surfing off in the distance. Brad showed me the surfing accident that he was in.

"Rob, he showed me how he died."

"Whoa!" Rob drew back just a little.

"Then he told me something so profound that it bewilders me to this day."

"I'm scared to ask, Annie," Rob said.

"Brad said that Rich and I would be together in the year 3054. We would marry and have children.

"Rob, I saw it. I saw Rich and myself having a great life; but I was sad, for I also knew we were NOT meant to be together in the life we were leading at that time. I knew it would be a matter of time before we would go our separate ways and Rich would be devastated once again."

"Did you tell him, Annie?" Rob asked.

"Yes, I did."

"How did he respond to what you told him?"

"Not very well; in fact, that was what caused all our problems—the fact that I could see we would not make it.

"Rich argued with me. He wanted to prove me wrong. Rich told me in all his years he had NEVER met anyone like me—that we were perfect for each other in mind, body, and spirit. He could read my mind, my thoughts. If I were away from him for any length of time, he knew what I was thinking. He drove me crazy. Yet a part of me loved him so much. I wanted this relationship to work."

"So what did you do to make it work?" Rob asked.

"Rich had an idea. He thought that if we left the island and traveled to see great seers and mystics, they would hold the answer to our fate. Since I wanted to explore as well as he did, I followed him.

"Rob, the love I had inside for Rich was different," Annie said.

"How?"

"He was like a father, mother, brother and sister all wrapped into one—like the Universe was playing a joke on us. They allowed me to see the future, but I wasn't allowed to play with what I saw. Every which way I turned, I envisioned DO NOT TOUCH IN THIS LIFE-TIME."

"So what did you guys do?" Rob was mystified, yet intrigued, by Annie's story.

"We literally traveled all over. We went to Peru and India and climbed the Himalayas for the answer, but there wasn't a mystic anywhere who could tell us our fate—only Brad.

"We ended up in Hawaii on the beach in Waikiki. We were having a huge discussion on this matter when Rich told me we could make things work, no matter what. I had a very different outlook on this."

"What was it?" Rob asked.

"I explained to Brad that he was 35 and I was 45; we would never have children. I felt way too old for him. It didn't matter to Rich. I explained that I couldn't live with his reading my mind all the time and knowing my every thought. I felt it was an invasion of my privacy."

"How did he respond?"

"He never answered me. Maybe he never heard me. All Rich could think of was that I was his only real, true love and nothing else mattered. He rattled on about our new life together: he would build me a house in the mountains; we would have regular visits to the Island of Tabu; he would build a center for people who could see the future and channel the other side, and I would be a part of that."

Rob was getting it. "Rich seemed a little bit self-righteous."

"A little?" Annie scoffed. "Rob, that was the last straw. He was planning our life together and not even bothering to ask me if that was what I wanted. I could barely put up with his reading my mind, but planning our future—that was it."

"So what did you do, Annie?"

"I suppose I created a scene, Rob. I screamed and yelled; I tore up every picture we had, including the ones that were taken in Peru; I told him I couldn't live like this; I told him I hated him and everything about him. Then I ran as fast as I could away from him. Rob, I ran into the street and was hit by an on-coming car. I died again."

"Oh my God, Annie!"

"You got that right, Rob. Rich was shocked. He cradled me in his arms, laid his head on my chest and cried, 'Why? Annie, why? I loved you…'

"When I got to Heaven, Gabriel was there to greet me. He explained to me that Rich and I would have been together forever, but it just wasn't our time yet. Because I had seen through the veil and peered into other lifetimes with Rich, all was taken away from me. I was never again allowed to peer through the veil. That one single act was my lesson.

"I gazed down from Heaven every now and then and watched Rich as the years went by. I watched as Rich had girlfriend after girlfriend and saw how sad he was. Then one year I watched from above and saw Rich finally meet the right one—the young lady was pretty. They had a son who took on the responsibility of running the Island of Tabu. Rich lived a full life and a happy one without me."

Rob wondered, "Do I detect a bit of sadness in your voice, Annie?"

"Yes," she sighed. "For, you see, I loved Rich, but I couldn't give him what he really wanted—me. In my heart I knew it wasn't in the cards; it was never meant to be." Annie's eyes grew misty and she lowered her head.

"Well, that is my story. I do know I have to get to the Island of Tabu one day while I'm here on Earth. I want to meet Rich's son."

Rob said, "Annie, I think this tops anything and everything you have ever told me. Give me a little time. I'm trying to understand; I really am."

Rob looked at his watch. "Whoa. I've got to meet John at the Deli. Don't be late for work tomorrow, Annie. Where are you going?"

"I need to get home and talk to Kate about your party this weekend."

"Annie, before we leave, I have a question for you."

"Yes?"

He hesitantly asked the burning question. "Have **we** ever been together in another life?"

Annie turned away from Rob momentarily, then she turned back and said, "I'll tell you when the time is right." Rob had to be satisfied with that answer for now.

Annie and Rob shared the same cab. Rob sat in silence. His stop, the Second Avenue Deli, was first. Rob rushed out of the cab, already late for his meeting with John. "See you tomorrow," Rob said.

Annie continued on her way home.

Rob, Annie, John, and Kate

Chapter 9

John arrived at the Second Avenue Deli a great deal earlier than anticipated. He waited in a semi-round booth for Rob, tapping his fingers on the table and constantly checking his watch.

Rob made his grand entrance quite dramatically, calling out to John loud enough to turn heads in the restaurant. "Hey, John, how're you doing?" Rob was well aware of the attention he was attracting. "Do you have those photocopies from the internet I asked for?"

"I sure do. Here, take a look." John spread the pictures on the table; there were four good shots in all.

Rob couldn't wait to see the pictures. Oh...my...God. That's Rich...and there's his brother, Brad. And...and that's Annie. I can't believe this. She looks very similar to the way she looks now, John." Rob looked up in amazement.

"What are you talking about? When I last spoke with you, you told me half a story. Can you fill me in?" John was fit to be tied.

Rob's eyes were wide open. He stammered, "She...she really IS an angel.... That means, there really is more than one lifetime.... This blows my mind."

"Okay, clue me in," John demanded.

"Annie was obsessed with telling me about this other lifetime she had with a surfer—a guy named Rich—who owned an island named Tabu. Her mission was to find out why he was so lonely. To make a long story short, Rich fell in love with Annie and she was able to channel his brother Brad, who had passed away surfing.

"Look, here's the picture of Brad... And there's a picture of Rich and there's Annie...." Rob pointed at the smiling figures then shoved the photos to John. "Anyway, she succeeded in channeling Rich's brother, so Rich and she decided to travel the world and seek out mystics and psychics to find out if what Brad channeled through Annie was true."

"Well, was it?"

"Yes, John, and you have the pictures right in front of your face to prove it." Rob couldn't get his story out fast enough.

"So then what happened?" asked John.

"Well, they found out everything was right on. Rich fell more and more in love with Annie. As time went by, he didn't want anyone around her; Rich wanted Annie all for himself; he felt he had discovered a great prize or something."

"Sort of like you, Rob?" John snickered.

Rob ignored the remark. "Let me finish. So it was then that he started to control Annie's life. She got extremely mad and ran as fast as she could away from him. The sad thing was she ended up dying again because she got hit by a car." Rob threw his hands up in the air. "And that's it in a nutshell." Rob exhaled deeply.

"Okay, buddy, it's time we take you to the funny farm. Do you really buy into this?" John stood up and shook his finger in Rob's face. "How do you know Annie didn't LOOK this information up on the internet as easily as I did?"

Rob mumbled, "I don't know."

John was clearly agitated. "Well, that's my point!"

"John, settle down. Sit down. We can make more progress if you calm down." John sat down reluctantly. "I understand your skepticism towards Annie."

While they were debating the issue, along came their favorite waiter, Elle.

"Hello," he sang. "My men… I love them so, they'll never know, when they take me in their arms…."

John interrupted. "Elle, what are you doing here?"

"Didn't Rob-a-Rio tell you? Guess not. He was so engrossed with Miss Annie the other day he even forgot to pay his check till I slid sideways into his Big Strong Body…Yes. I'm now working two part-time jobs, this deli and the other. I'm so much in demand… SO they tell me. And…where's Mary Poppins, boys?"

Elle glanced toward the entrance. "Uh… OH! I better take your orders. I just saw a sweetie come in. I want to serve this one myself," Elle said. "I need to find out what 24-hour gym he goes to."

Elle snapped his fingers in the air. "Hurry, boys, what will it be?"

Rob ordered coffee and a chicken salad platter. John was surprised at Rob; this order was very out of character for him. "I'll have the meat loaf and mashed potatoes and a Coke," he said.

"I'm off to fairyland," Elle lilted. "I need my magic wand to spread my fairy dust on that guy alone in the booth over there." Elle pointed in that direction. "He must be gay-dar; I just know it." Elle slid across the room to take his order.

John turned his attention again to Rob and spoke calmly. "Okay, Rob, I have an idea. We can manipulate Annie just a little. We can look her up and find out if she's ever been conked in the head."

"John, that's simply duplicitous. I won't have anything to do with it. I believe everything Annie has told me. You want to know why?"

"Yes, I do." John gulped down his Coke.

Rob said, "I've seen her in action; she has a glow like no other. I've watched her answer phone calls and save people's lives. My mind is WIDE open. You know, John, there very well could be other lifetimes. Maybe I knew you once before; maybe you were my brother in my last life."

John spit out his Coke and chuckled. "Okay."

"John, you know what? I asked Annie a question today. I asked her if we had met before in another life and you know what she said?"

"Can't wait for your answer. Well…did you know each other before?"

Rob was unsure. "I don't know exactly. She turned to me and said, 'I'll tell you when it's time.'"

"What kind of answer is that?" John asked, eyebrows raised.

"That's my point, John. I don't know if we met before. But I swear I'm going to find out. I'll try again at our little party Friday night. Speaking of which, what are we going to do for the girls?"

"Girls, such as in… more than one?"

"Yes. I told her to bring Kate, her roommate. You'll like this one; she's cute as a button, single—right up your alley."

Their conversation was interrupted by an excited Elle with their orders. "Guess what? I just got the cutie's phone number. He's taking me to the 24-Hour Fitness down the street right after my shift. I told you guys he was just like me. Will this be all?"

"Yes," they said in unison.

Elle put the check on the table. "I didn't want to lose myself and forget the check. Oh, he's flagging me down; he must want more water. Off I go. See you sweeties next time."

Meanwhile, Annie went home and found Kate sitting in the living room watching television. "Hi, Kate, what are you watching?" she asked.

"Nothing much." Kate hurriedly pressed the power button on the remote control, so Annie wouldn't notice that she was watching the Brandon Turner Show. "So, how was your day, little angel?"

"I'm drained, Kate. Tomorrow night John and Rob are having a bit of a get together and they'd like to make dinner for us. What do you think? Can you go? Are you free?"

Kate ran upstairs to the loft to check her calendar. She called down to Annie, "Yup, I can go. What time is it and what do we bring?"

"Whatever you want, I guess. I don't know the details, but after work tomorrow I'll find out everything," Annie replied.

"Annie, what is John like?" Kate asked as she came back down from the loft.

"He's cute and very intelligent. He has a flaw, though."

"Okay, girl, what kind of flaw?"

"Well, he's somewhat of a skeptic… but, Kate, I know you can turn him around with your charm." Annie grinned mischievously.

Kate wagged her finger at Annie. "I don't get it. He's heard you on the radio; he's heard you help hundreds of people. Why doesn't he believe you?"

"He thinks I'm a psychic, not an angel," Annie said.

"Well, wait till he meets me!" Kate laughed.

"Now remember, Kate, you're not supposed to let him or anyone else know that you are an angel," Annie scolded her.

"Don't worry; I've got the perfect answer for him. I can't wait to meet him, Annie. It's been so long since I've had a little fun. Get the address and details. I've got to take a shower and get up early; I have a shoot at your favorite place tomorrow, the Central Park ice skating rink. I'll talk to you tomorrow. And, oh, Annie, find out what we should wear—casual or dressy."

"You got it, Kate. See you."

Back at the restaurant, John checked his watch. "We'd better be going. I've had a long day. I've got to get ready for work tomorrow; I need to catch up."

Rob nodded. "Yes. Thanks, John, for picking up my slack. Thank God, tomorrow is Friday. Thanks again, buddy; I owe you one."

They left the restaurant, and both made their way home.

Before they knew it, Friday came and everyone was back on the radio.

"Good morning, New York City. This is Roll-over-with-Rob-in-the-Morning on 92.3 FM. We have our lovely angel, Annie, ready to take your phone calls. "Are you ready, Annie?"

"Yes, Rob."

"John, who do we have standing by?"

"We have Steph on the line."

"Good morning, Steph. What can Annie help you with today?"

"Hi, Annie, I have a very special request. My husband, Peter Hurkos, passed away many years ago. I can't seem to get him out of my mind. I miss him so."

Annie glanced upward as if she were accessing information from a different realm. "Steph, I'm so sorry. May I ask you—was that THE Peter Hurkos, The Foremost Psychic of the Century?"

"Yes, Annie."

"What a great loss to all of mankind. Let me see. I will try very hard to pass information on from the other side to you from Peter."

Annie tuned into Peter's vibration… the information flowed.

"Steph, I'm being told that Peter has been around you non-stop. Is that true?"

"Yes."

Annie could see Peter in her mind. He was tall in stature and had a Dutch accent. "He is watching over you all the time; that's why you can feel him. He's telling me it's time to move on with your life. He's telling me next year you will be in for one of the best years in your life financially that you could ever imagine. Deals will come through. Movies will be picked up. He's saying for you to not worry about your health. All will be fine. Peter said that next year there will be a man who walks into your life; he will be a client—salt and pepper hair, around 60. This man will be more than interested in you. It looks like you might find the next love of your life. He also wants to let you know that the love continues on the other side when you die."

Steph couldn't thank Annie enough for the information.

"Commercial break!" Rob shouted.

John went over to the counter and rang up another person that Annie had helped. John called out to Annie and Rob, "She's up to **808** and counting."

Annie clapped her hands and yelled outloud in a most unfeminine way, "Yeah!"

Rob was getting nervous; Annie was getting very close to reaching her goal of 1000 souls. He couldn't help but wonder what would happen once she met it. How would she meet Brandon again? Would all his hard work and billboards that Rob had placed all over New York City be in vain?

John let Annie and Rob know they were back from commercial. "Are you guys ready? I have our next caller."

Rob refocused his attention. "We're back. Annie, John tells me our next caller is Andrea."

Annie couldn't wait to speak to her. "Hi, Andrea." Annie was right in tune with her. "I'm picking up that you left your boyfriend after ten years. You are now making a new life for yourself. You wonder if you will ever go back to him. Am I correct on this?"

"Yes, Annie."

"I am getting direct information on this one," Annie said. "Andrea, I see two different paths that will be open to you. On one path I see your boyfriend is changing; he is trying to mold himself into the way you want him. When you see him again, it will appear to you that he is different. Please understand, he has not changed that much. He really wants you back but is unwilling to marry you. This will be something to consider if you decide to go back to him in the future." Annie paused before continuing.

"The other path shows me there is a new man waiting for you—someone you don't know yet—someone who is more to your liking. He is light-haired, nice, and very spiritual. You will meet him through a friend. You will take it slowly at first, but there will be no denying it. Within six months from today your decision will be made as to… 'Are You Going to Stay with the One Who Loves You? Or Are You Going Back to the One You Love?'… to quote that wonderful country song. This will be up to you."

Andrea seemed a little bewildered. She didn't know what she should do, but thanked Annie anyway.

Rob jumped in. "Well, Annie, that old clock on the wall is ticking away. Looks like we'll have to wait till Monday for you to help all the people out there.

"This is Roll-over-with-Rob-in-the-Morning… on 92.3 FM. Stay tuned for news and weather. Over and out."

Rob took off his earphones. "Great show, Annie," he said.

Annie took off her earphones. "Say, Rob, I spoke to Kate; she wants me to get your address for the get-together."

John looked up at Rob.

"Oh, it's 300 Fifth Avenue. Do you need a ride?"

"No, Kate will be driving. Do you want us to bring anything? And what time should we be there?" Annie asked.

Rob looked at John. "What time is good for you, John?"

"Oh, I'd say about 7:00. And Annie, just bring yourself and Kate."

"Sounds good," Annie said. Annie got off her stool, picked up her purse, and headed out the door. "Bye, guys, see you tonight."

Annie hailed a taxi. She arrived home with ample time to figure out what she was going to wear that night. She laid out at least ten different outfits and shook her head many times over. This night would be so special. She wanted to make a good personal impression, for this would be really the first time she would get to know all about John.

Annie took a long bubble bath; she sat in the tub and thought about how she could get Kate together with John. She wondered if the two of them would get along. She also wondered if she had to be ready to jump into their conversation and save Kate now and then—John was known for his sharp wit. She hoped it would all work out.

The one thing that was very prominent about Annie—she could help thousands of people, but when it came to herself, she was lost. That was why she had me, Gabriel, to guide her. I knew everything about Annie—at least, almost everything. I mean, she had a little free will—not much, mind you—but just enough to get her into a heap of trouble at times.

Hours later Annie heard the door open downstairs. With camera in hand Kate shouted, "I'm home, Annie! Where are you?"

"I'm up here, Kate, getting ready for tonight."

"What are you wearing?" Kate asked.

"I'll show you." Annie ran down the stairs to show Kate and get her approval. "Look, what do you think?" Annie twirled around.

"You've got to be kidding me," Kate said. Annie was wearing tight black pants, a black and white top which she wore off her shoulders, a red sash, and ballet-type shoes.

"You are not wearing that, are you, Annie?"

"Why, what's wrong?"

"It's so… out of style," Kate said. "Come with me to my room and we'll get you all coordinated." Kate shook her head. "I really don't believe you. Didn't Gabriel teach you how to dress?"

"NO!"

"That's why you're so out of synch. Here, try this on for starters." Kate threw Annie a pair of simple black slacks, a pink blouse with an open collar, and a simple, tailored black jacket. She gave her black open-toed, high-heeled shoes and simple jewelry to wear.

Annie slipped out of her choice of outfit and tried on Kate's. When she looked in the mirror, she realized it made a world of difference. "I like this," she said, admiring her image.

"I thought you would. Now, why don't you soften your make-up while I get ready and change."

"Okay, Kate."

Kate took her time and prettied herself up all in red—she wore red slacks, a peach shirt, red shoes, and light make-up. Her hair flowed down onto her shoulders. She looked classy.

The girls were finally ready to go.

Annie told Kate, "You look great."

Kate returned the compliment. "And so do you, Annie, if I may say so myself."

Kate did the driving and drove down a few blocks before stopping at a bakery. "Annie, I really don't like to visit people empty-handed, so I'll park over here and you run in and get a cake."

"Okay; anything special that you want, Kate?"

"No, just pick out something that looks delicious. Here's twenty-dollars; have a field day." Kate blasted the radio while waiting for Annie.

It wasn't long before they arrived at Rob's apartment. Kate was lucky to find a parking spot right in front of the building. They both shared the car mirror for a quick look one final time. "Ready?" Kate asked. "Oh, don't forget the cake."

Kate saw Rob's name on the apartment directory and buzzed in.

"Hello down there," Rob said through the intercom.

"Hi," Kate responded. "It's Kate and Annie."

"Kate, I'm in Apartment 812. Take the elevator to the eighth floor then turn right; we'll be out in the hall waiting for you." Rob buzzed them in.

Just as Rob promised, he and John were waiting in the hall for them.

"Well, here they are," Rob remarked. "Don't you ladies look nice. Kate, this is John." Rob gestured toward John, who held a beer in his hand as he greeted Kate and Annie with a nod. "Come on in, ladies."

Rob said, "I'm cooking, but I'm sure John will show you around. Won't you, John?"

John did just that. "Follow me," he ordered light-heartedly. They ended up on Rob's patio, which was quite large and lit by twinkling white lights. There were several potted plants, a round table with seating for four, and several lounge chairs on each side of the patio.

"Here's our view, the lights of beautiful New York City." John pointed to the right. "And there's the Empire State Building. Look, isn't it just beautiful?" The girls nodded. All the time that John was talking, he couldn't take his eyes off Kate.

John showed them the rest of the apartment. It was decked out in wall-to-wall stereo. Rob had every electronic device imaginable in his apartment. The furniture was simple; the main focus was his new HDTV system.

Rob called them to the counter in the kitchen. They sat and watched Rob cook. Kate asked Rob, "What are you making? Oh, by the way, we have a cake for you. Here." She handed the cake to John.

Rob responded, "Thank you, darlings. What am I making? Well, you have entered the world of Rob-a-Rio." He put on his best imitation of a maitre d' and intoned, "We have for dinner tonight spaghetti and meatballs, home-made at that, plus a great salad with wine and garlic bread." He smacked his fingers with his lips. The girls clapped and giggled.

Rob smiled appreciatively. He turned to John and said, "Hey, John, turn on some music and pour the girls some red wine."

"You got it."

After pouring the wine for Kate and Annie, John looked at Kate and said, "Why don't we look at the view? Follow me, gorgeous." Kate followed.

Annie was left talking to Rob while he cooked in the kitchen.

"You look all dolled up today," he said. "Looks like Kate and John are getting along well."

"Thanks, Rob. I sure hope so. I really want Kate to get to know John."

And that's exactly what Kate was doing. She asked John to tell her all about himself.

John was very charming and charismatic. Kate thought he could charm a snake.

"Well, let me see... I'll give you the short version. I'm single and very happy being single; I'm not ready to settle. I've had my share of women. I love playing the field. I drink a little, party a little, have fun a lot.

"One of my greatest loves is working with Rob at the station—I get a chance to use my creative side. I love music. When I was younger, I had my own rock-and-roll band; that was the greatest passion of my life."

"What happened?" Kate asked.

"Well, the band broke up. I used to sing and play lead guitar. Times changed and for some reason, I never went back to it. I really miss it, though."

John paused. "Kate, tell me about you." As he listened to Kate, John had to stop himself from being mesmerized by her energy and beauty; he had to contain himself, and that was hard.

Kate said, "I'm single and not looking, as well. I travel the world in my dream job of photography. I'm a free-lancer and my job takes me to exotic locations such as the Serengeti in Africa where I photograph animals. You'll like this, John—I get so many calls from rock groups to photograph them, it's amazing. In fact, next Saturday I'm going to photograph Bon Jovi in Central Park."

That got John's attention. "You've got to be kidding! He's one of my favorites."

"Really? Would you like to go with me to the concert next Saturday? I could use the help with my cameras—I have so many to take. All you have to do is hold my camera bag and watch my cameras and I can get you a pass."

"Would I? What time shall I meet you?"

"I can pick you up at 7:00 P.M. wherever you want," Kate said.

Rob hollered from the kitchen; dinner was being served.

"We'd better go eat. After you, gorgeous." John was just a little bit scared of Kate. There was something very different about her that he had never seen in any other woman. She was single and not looking. She was very independent. She was drop-dead gorgeous. She loved her work and she loved rock stars and rock-and-roll. How unusual, he thought—just what the doctor ordered.

He realized with a start that he might have met his match in Kate. He had been a player in the singles game for so long, but Kate was very unusual and different. He noticed that Kate was always one step ahead of him. She was able to read his mind and answer his questions before he asked them. He could imagine himself with her in the future and somehow that scared the heck out of him. He wondered what a beautiful girl would see in him.

"I see the two of you are getting along well," Rob said, raising his eyebrows a little.

John said, "I'm going with Kate next Saturday to the Bon Jovi concert at Central Park. Kate's a photographer and I'm going to help her with the camera equipment."

"That sounds great—right up your alley." Rob smiled. "Well, here we go—enjoy," Rob said as they all sat down to dinner.

That evening was wonderful for Kate. She was very attracted to John; she felt she had a lot in common with him. She would get to the bottom of his skepticism after a few dates. Kate had a very funny feeling about him; she wondered if he was the one. Could he be the love of her life, the ONE she was waiting for? Only time would tell.

The evening sped by; there was laughter and lots of conversation. They were all getting to know one another, and it felt comfortable and good. The hours ticked away before they knew it, and it was time for Annie and Kate to say good night. Rob gave Annie a peck on her cheek, and John graciously kissed Kate's hand. While on their way out, Kate and Annie raved about the dinner. They both mentioned that next time it would be their treat.

Kate spoke fondly of John all the way home. Annie was amused. She knew this would happen. She couldn't be more pleased. When they arrived home, Annie went immediately to her room; she was tired. She would find herself tossing and turning.

"Hey, Annie," Kate called after her, "Get some sleep; I'll talk to you in the morning."

Conversations with Brandon and Pat

Chapter 10

Annie couldn't help herself as she lay in her bed staring up at the ceiling. Annie's big blue eyes were wide open as she thought of Brandon... while she slowly drifted off to sleep.

Meanwhile, Brandon paced around his apartment thinking of Annie. He picked up the phone and called Pat. "Hey, Pat, how are you doing? Can you come over to my apartment? I'll make us something to eat and maybe if you're up to it, you could channel some information for me."

Pat responded, "Hello, Brandon. It's so good to hear from you. I thought you forgot about me. It's been a while."

Brandon was sitting on his brown leather couch and staring at Annie's picture on his fireplace mantel while he spoke to Pat. "How could I forget about you? Get yourself over here and we'll talk."

Pat stood up and hobbled around, pulling on his jeans, while listening to Brandon on the phone. "I'll get a cab, Brandon. See you within the hour." Pat couldn't get dressed fast enough.

Brandon looked around his kitchen to see what there was to eat for both of them. He opened the fridge; there wasn't anything appealing so he picked up the phone and ordered pizza from down the street. He walked over to his patio and looked out at Central Park. He wondered if he would ever see Annie again.

It wasn't long before the buzzer rang from downstairs. It was Pat. Brandon buzzed him up.

"Hi, come on in, Pat. How're you doing?" he asked.

"Well... I've been fine." Pat took off his jacket and handed it to Brandon. "I sure am hungry," he said.

"I ordered several pizzas; they should be here soon." Brandon motioned for Pat to follow him. They both walked out onto the patio and were mesmerized by the city lights. "Isn't she beautiful? I just love New York City, especially in the evening," Brandon said.

Pat had his hands planted on the patio rail. He turned and looked at Brandon. "How are you feeling since the last time I saw you?" he asked.

"Surprisingly well, I quit smoking. And I brought my drinking down to a near halt; I do take a drink now and then. I really have been working on myself, and as for the women in my life, there just hasn't been anyone special. I found out that giving up drinking and smoking was easy, compared to giving up women—now, that was a tough one. I really have been trying, but you know us men." Brandon raised his eyebrows.

"I'm very proud of you, Brandon." Pat smiled.

"Late at night I disguise myself so that very few people recognize me; then, I jog down to Barnes and Noble and check out all the books about past lives. You know the ones—like *Many Lives, Many Masters*. I have found them to be very interesting. What's your take on past lives?"

Pat was just about to answer when the buzzer sounded in the apartment. "That must be the pizza guy. Yup," Brandon buzzed the delivery guy in, thanked him and handed him a big tip.

Brandon and Pat practically inhaled the pizza; they both were starved. "Thanks, Brandon. I feel better now," Pat said, as he used several napkins to wipe his face before answering Brandon's question.

"To answer your question about other lifetimes, I believe it's very natural to have had many lifetimes. I believe, when one dies, the soul lives on. The soul goes through an educational process on the next level—what some people might call Heaven, or an interim stop along the way. I believe at that time we are shown our past on Earth and we are encouraged to learn from our mistakes. Then, if we are worthy, we get several opportunities to come back to Earth and try again."

"Very interesting, when we come back to Earth, do we recognize people we knew before?" Brandon asked.

"We recognize some people; we travel with a lot of the same souls lifetime after lifetime. We then get the opportunity to fix or right the wrong that we might have done in the past. You do realize we are responsible for all of our actions here on Earth? You see, whatever we put out there in the Universe will come back to us either in this lifetime or in some other lifetime.

"To give you a good analogy… If you, Brandon, treat women without respect and use them, then the next time around you will feel their pain and you will be the one that will be used. Get it?" Pat felt comfortable answering these questions for Brandon.

"I think so. So, you're saying, if I step on people, if I hurt them, if I treat women without the respect they deserve, that all those terrible things I once did will come back to me in another life."

"Yes, most definitely." Pat was emphatic about this point.

"Do we fall in love with the same people we loved before?"

"Many times we do, Brandon; however, they may not look the same. I have noted in my studies there is a familiarity about them—we feel comfortable around them without ever knowing why. Sometimes we can look in their eyes and know we have met them before. It's hard to prove; but they say when you know, you know."

Brandon questioned Pat on a deeper level. "Pat, let's say I meet Annie again in this lifetime. How would I recognize her? How would I know it's her?"

"Brandon, there is a very thin veil. If we have the gift—such as many psychics do—we can pierce that veil for just a moment in time; which means that just for a fragmented second, time stops. At that moment in time we can see who the person really is. Not only would you know it was Annie, you would feel it in every part of your soul. This is sometimes known as *déjà vu*…meaning 'haven't we met somewhere before?'"

Brandon started to pace while trying to fathom the depth of the conversation that at times baffled him. He was sucked in. He had to have answers, for in the deepest part of his soul he knew he would meet Annie again. Brandon wanted to be prepared for what might happen at that time. He didn't want to mess things up. He wanted it to work so that Annie and he could be together again.

"Brandon, I totally understand where you are coming from. If you just take it at your own pace, things would fall into place a lot better for you. Don't rush things. If it is meant to happen, you'll be together again with Annie—but only if it's meant to be. Remember, Brandon, the Annie you meet now might be very different from the Annie you once knew."

"Say that again, Pat."

"Well, when you come back to Earth after passing away, several things can happen. She might be younger and growing up in a different place, and when somehow you bump into her—say at the local bookstore—you sort of recognize her. Your mission would be to test the situation—feel it out. There would be several traits that only you would recognize. Somewhere along the way you would know it is Annie.

"You see, when the soul enters the body of another person, sometimes there is bewilderment, shock. It takes time for the soul to get used to the new body. Then, let's say a series of events may occur that causes that person to be physical, where they are usually not. For example, say you drive to work the same way every day for a year, then something inside of you says, 'I think I'll drive to work another way.' You do, and you come upon an accident on the street and someone needs your help, so you jump out of your car and you tend to that person. You help her. Not only do you help her, but you also look into her eyes and in some small way you recognize her. This is what we call 'meant to be.' You never know how the Universe is going to play things out for you. Life can be one big adventure and one big surprise."

Brandon shook his head. "Whoa! This is mind boggling, Pat. How do you know all this? And how do you know this is not just contrived?" he asked.

"I have witnessed too many situations like your Annie in my lifetime. I myself could recognize her if given the opportunity to do so. I also have been privileged to witness several past-life regressions and future-life progressions to know this is based on what we call 'fact'—at least, what we call 'metaphysical fact.'"

"What is a past-life regression?" Brandon asked.

"Brandon, a past-life regression is, when I hypnotize you and take you back in time. You will recognize several past-life situations and partners that you have been with along the way. You might even experience situations like, say, an incident of you drowning before. That might contribute to your fear now of drowning. Once we find out why you are afraid of something in your past life, most of the time we can correct it in this life."

Pat paused and peered at Brandon. "Do you understand what I'm teaching you, Brandon? I mean, I'm not getting in over your head, am I?"

"No, I totally understand what you are saying," Brandon assured him. "But how do I know my mind is not making up any of this?"

"You don't know," Pat replied. "What we do know is this...there have been many documented studies done of past-life regressions and several have panned out. For example, five-year-old children who never knew how to play the piano are given a few lessons and suddenly, without any effort, are concert pianists.

"Brandon, there are so many stories involving past lives; it's endless—the books alone could fill your living room. The best advice I can give you is to go to the bookstore and look up 'past lives.' There are times in our life we JUST have to believe, and have faith. We have to trust that there is more to life than we could ever imagine." Pat was very convincing.

Brandon needed to express himself further. "I'm sorry I have so many questions, but this is all new to me. It's like a light bulb lit up in my head, and for some reason there is no turning it off. I wish you could understand. I feel Annie every minute, every second of the day. I feel she is thinking about me. I feel she is talking to me in my head. I know it sounds crazy, but it's just what I feel. Pat, I just want to know why this is happening to me."

Pat placed a hand on Brandon's shoulder. "Exactly my point Brandon. With all my experience in life so far on this subject, I know the information will be revealed to you somewhere in the future. You just have to be patient, my friend."

"I know."

Brandon stood up to stretch his legs. Pat gulped down his soda and ate what was left of his pizza.

Brandon walked around, thinking about what he would ask Pat next. He had so many questions. This conversation with Pat was helping him to understand life in a new way. He wondered if all of this was true. Then maybe he would meet his Annie in this life and maybe, just maybe, he would finally get it right in this life.

"Pat, why do we keep making the same mistakes over and over again?"

"It's really very simple, Brandon. Usually, when you make a mistake, you learn from it—sometimes, that is. However, when emotions are involved, especially LOVE, they cloud our vision. When we think we love someone SO much, nothing matters."

Brandon was all ears. He latched on to every word that Pat was saying.

Pat continued. "Sometimes our vision is so clouded we never think of the consequences. So we end up making the same mistake over and over again until we learn our lesson. Love is so powerful; sometimes we don't want to learn our lesson. Sometimes we think we can handle any situation when it comes to love.

"For example, let's say you have this tendency to fall in love only with powerful, beautiful women who are unavailable. You've been through this situation so many times in this life, but this new love that you may be seeing now—you believe she's different from all the rest of the ladies you have dated. This love is clouding your vision.

"As time goes by, your rose-colored glasses come off and you realize that she's the same lady in a different dress, one you cannot love. So you walk away and get out of the situation three years later. Did you know you wasted three years of your life trying to fix her and mold her and make her yours?"

Pat lectured, "Brandon, life is so precious; every moment counts. Those three years could have been spent on finding Miss Right, not Miss Wrong. When we repeat our mistakes enough times, we sometimes get it and we supposedly learn; on the other hand, other people may go lifetime after lifetime trying to figure it out. It's that simple. It's so sad but true. I wish we could all learn the first time—including myself. Brandon, do you understand what I'm telling you?"

Brandon bent his head down. "Yes, I get it."

He thought about all the loves of his life and how he always picked the same type of girl—over and over again—just like Pat said. What Pat was explaining to him finally made sense.

Brandon realized that the one exception was Annie. When he found her, she was so different from everyone else that he never wanted to let her go. He also realized that when he finally was able to make a commitment, she was taken away from him. He now knew there would be more lessons to learn. He felt that Pat was sent to him to help guide him to his destiny…that destiny would be a repeat of Annie in some way, shape, or form; he was positive of that now.

"Pat, you know how strongly I feel about Annie. Was she my true soul-mate? Is that why I feel the loss of her so deeply?"

Pat spoke very softly and candidly. "Brandon, we have many soul-mates—friends can be soul-mates; our bosses can be soul-mates—we have many. What you had with Annie goes well beyond all that. Annie is the missing part of you that you have longed for lifetime after lifetime."

Pat continued. "She was taken away from you for one of two reasons. One…you probably had to learn a lesson. Or two…she herself had to learn some sort of lesson that had nothing to do with you. To say the least, that was her karma, her learning lesson."

Pat asked abruptly, "You say she told you that she was an angel?"

Brandon jumped up. "Now we're getting somewhere! Yes, that's what she told me."

"I have never heard of an angel marrying a mortal." Pat shook his head. "This can't be, Brandon."

"Pat, that's why I didn't believe her. I just let her rattle on about her being an angel, figuring she meant she was pure of heart."

Pat seemed excited; he had a strong vision at that moment. "I think I'm getting it. I think I understand."

Brandon demanded that Pat share his vision with him. "What?"

Pat jumped up. "I get it now," he whispered. Pat sat right next to Brandon on the couch and looked straight into his eyes. "Don't you get it?"

"No, explain it to me—what you're seeing." Brandon was squirming.

Pat explained, "If, in fact, Annie was a real angel, she must have broken a rule up there. I mean, angels aren't supposed to marry mortals…everyone knows that. And, if she broke a rule, then her Guardian had to intervene. So if I'm right—and I think that I am— he plucked her right back to Heaven."

At that very moment a mirror over Brandon's fireplace came crashing down and shattered into pieces.

The crash of the mirror startled Pat and Brandon. "Why did that happen?" Brandon shouted.

Pat cried out, "Oh, my God! That happened because I'm RIGHT. I guess they're a little angry up there because I figured it out. You know what, Brandon?... I think I'll have a drink now if you don't mind, pal. I'm spooked."

"You're spooked? I'm sitting here with a broken mirror that came crashing down from nowhere and you're telling me that Annie really is an angel? I don't know who is more insane—me or you."

Pat got down on the floor with Brandon and helped him pick up the pieces of the mirror. "I got it—this was a sign. Not only did the mirror fall to the ground but it's also telling us if we put the pieces back together we might be able to understand the rest of this puzzle."

Brandon stared at Pat in a very strange way. "Pat, do you really believe that Annie was an angel?"

"YES."

"So how can I ever be with her on Earth?" Brandon asked.

"Well, according to everything I've read, there is a way. She would have to come back to Earth on some sort of mission to forgive her past. After she's accomplished her mission, somehow in some way the two of you could meet. Then she would have the choice of giving up her wings and staying on Earth with you and living out her life. She would then become a mortal until she died of natural causes, at which time she would return to Heaven and start the process all over again. She would be an angel until her next lifetime."

"How do you know all this?" Brandon looked up at Pat from the floor.

"I just know. And I know I'm right on...or the mirror wouldn't have fallen from your fireplace." Pat kept picking up pieces of the mirror.

"Brandon, I hate to say this, but you have to get spiritually ready for Annie. You have to cleanse yourself of all your past karma. If you really want to be with her, and if you love her as much as you say you do, then you'll have to change.... I mean you'll HAVE TO CHANGE. It may mean you will have to give up everything in order to spend the rest of your life with her. Are you willing to give up your fame? Are you willing to give up your money? Are you willing to give up everything in your life as you know it today?"

Brandon answered without hesitation, "YES."

"Then we have a lot of work to do. I'll have to teach you everything and then some. Brandon, promise me you'll tell no one about what we're doing."

At that very moment a picture of Annie and Brandon flew off the mantle and landed on the floor right at Brandon's feet.

"Oh, my God!" Brandon shouted. "I hope I'm ready for this."

Pat said calmly, "The way I see it, Brandon, you're more than ready. We've had every sign right here in your apartment today. Sit down. I have more to tell you."

Brandon's voice quavered. "More?"

Pat started to pace around Brandon's apartment as if he were on to something. "You see, I have never experienced something like this before—I mean, an angel and a mortal. I find this very interesting, to say the least. You're like a test case for me. Brandon, have you had any dreams or signs about Annie since she passed away?"

"Dreams, no. Signs—let me think—yes." Brandon looked up at Pat. "You know that angel that's on Roll-over-with-Rob-in-the-Morning? Well, I've been listening to his show and her name is Annie. I feel like I might have known her before. In fact, I've been asking my assistant Rose to book her on my show, but it seems we can never get hold of her. I don't get it myself."

Pat said quickly, "Brandon, I know about that angel. From what I heard, Rob won't let anyone see her. He's using her as a HUGE marketing ploy. Rob feels it will drive people mad if they don't know what she looks like. I'm really not so sure that she is an angel…she could be a very good psychic. Whatever Rob is doing, it's working; the whole town is dying to meet this one."

"Including me, Pat," Brandon said. "While I have your attention, I have a few more questions that are plaguing me."

"Shoot."

"What goes on in Heaven? Is it predestined whom we will be with on Earth?" Brandon sounded serious.

"Brandon, I don't know exactly what goes on in Heaven. I only know what I've read and what people feel and what people think.

"I do know Heaven is where the future is born and everything in Heaven somehow makes its way to Earth eventually. I believe that in each lifetime we are predestined to be with someone. However, we are not always with the same person."

"What does that mean?"

"Well, take Annie and you. It seems to me that you haven't finished your karma together in this life. So you are bound to repeat it again somewhere, sometime on Earth.

"When the two of you get it RIGHT… then each of you will come back in a different lifetime and maybe you will be with other people. You see, Brandon, you have left-over karma with other people as well."

Brandon was getting more inquisitive. "What happens when we die? Where do we go?"

"Ah. When we die, we have a physical body and a spiritual body. Our soul, or our spiritual body, leaves the physical body. It travels upwards through time and space. We travel through a tunnel where we are met by people who have passed on before us—relatives, friends, et cetera. We are debriefed about our life; in other words, we are given a life's review—a retrospect.

"You will experience your life in a mere flash of time. You will feel everything that you have done, people you have hurt, people you have loved, people you have helped through life. The best part of this review of your life is that you are the one who will be judging yourself.

"Example: Let's say you are a hunter of deer. Just imagine that, after you shot the deer, you go over to its lifeless body and touch it. Suddenly you can feel all the pain, all the horror, all the fear that the deer experienced. At that moment, after that life-altering experience, it's you who will decide if you will ever kill a deer again. You see Brandon, that is how we learn our lessons in life. That is how we learn whether we will repeat our mistakes or not."

Brandon was stunned. "Pat, I don't know what to say. This evening has been very emotional for me; it's been an eye opener. I need time to process this. You see, I've never believed in anything that wasn't in front of my face. Now I'm finding out there is a whole new world out there and we are players on Earth. I'm not so sure I like my role."

"I understand, Brandon. The same thing happened to me." Pat stood up and headed for the door. "I'll get my coat and leave you alone to think about what I've said. If you have any questions, call me." He left Brandon to process all that he taught him.

Radio, Kate, Rob and John and Brandon

Chapter 11

The alarm went off in Annie's room. It was 6 A.M.; she had had a good night's sleep for once. Annie smelled the coffee downstairs, so she made her way to the kitchen.

"Good morning, Annie. Coffee?" Kate asked.

"My, you're up early," Annie observed.

"Yes, I have to get things ready for the Bon Jovi shoot; I have pre-production tonight all the way into Friday night. It's a really big weekend for me. I can drop you off at the studio if you want."

"I'd like that very much."

"What are you going to do this weekend?" Kate asked.

"I really don't have any plans; I have to see what will turn up."

Kate quickly turned to the subject on her mind. "Annie, I really feel a connection with John. We had a great time last night. I wonder if he could be the one." Kate stared at Annie as if she had the answer to her question.

Annie shrugged. "Kate, I know very little about him. I spend most of my time with Rob; we talk a lot. I can find out, though."

Kate blurted out jokingly, "Annie, I thought you're supposed to know everything."

Annie responded with a giggle, "Kate, I'm an angel—not a bloody psychic."

Kate laughed. "Well, hurry, if I'm going to get you down to the radio station on time; we're running a little late. Have you noticed the weather is changing? I feel winter coming on."

Annie hurried through her breakfast and she and Kate were soon on their way. Kate drove as fast as she could—without getting cited—and let Annie off at the radio station.

"Bye, have a good one. Oh, Annie, see if you can pump Rob and find out just a little about John." Kate smiled.

111

Annie said, "I'll see what I can do," and dashed up the stairs to the entrance.

Noticing the light flashing ON AIR over the doors to the studio, Annie tiptoed in and waited for Rob to cut to a commercial.

"Good morning, sweet angel," Rob greeted her. "Did you sleep well?"

"Yes, I did," Annie replied truthfully. She saw John in the corner and gave him a little wave with her fingers. "Hi, John."

"Back to you," he said. "Hey, your friend is really cute. I can't wait to go to the concert with her on Friday. Will you be going?"

"Yes, she is cute, and she thinks you're very attractive. No, John, I won't be going to the concert Friday. It's not my kind of music."

Rob asked, "Annie, what will you be doing Friday night?"

"I really haven't thought about it," she said.

"Well, why don't we go out to dinner together? You pick the place and I'll pick you up."

"Sounds good to me." Annie thought to herself, "Well, now I won't be all alone this weekend."

John called out, "Hey, Rob, hand her the ears; we're about to go live." He started the countdown—"3, 2, 1"—and pointed at Rob.

"Good morning, New York City. We're live on the air with our Angel Annie. John, who's our first caller?"

"Rob, we have David. He's ready to talk to Annie."

"Good morning, David. How can I help you?" Annie said.

"Hi, Annie. I had something very strange happen to me this weekend; I wonder if you can help me figure it out."

"I would love to, David. Please explain what happened."

"Well, my cousin was visiting me from Hawaii; it had been a long time since we'd seen each other. She insisted on visiting my mom—her aunt—in the nursing home where she's been for years. Now, my cousin is a very famous psychic and that worried me; I thought she might be getting some information about my mom's passing and I wasn't ready for that kind of news." David choked up just a little.

"Go on; I'm listening," Annie said.

"I told my cousin that my mom had not been speaking to any-one in the last few weeks. I didn't want her to be disappointed if my mom said nothing to her. But what I saw that morning I can't explain.

"My cousin sat beside my mom's bed and held her hand and started to talk to her. My mom's name is Esther, by the way.

"She said, 'Hello, Aunt Esther, how are you?' My mom opened her eyes for the first time in days and recognized my cousin. My mom spoke. 'Hello, so nice to see you,' she said. 'Have you come all the way from Hawaii to see me?' My cousin responded with 'Yes.'"

David sputtered, "Annie, I couldn't believe it. My mom had not been speaking to anyone for quite some time, and now she was talking a mile a minute and she recognized my cousin. She was speaking in full sentences."

Annie said, "Catch your breath, David. I'm getting the picture loud and clear. And David, sometimes people who may be passing get a second wind."

"Well, my mom got a second wind, all right. So my cousin continued to talk to her. This is what I heard: 'Aunt Esther, I came to tell you about the other side. You know, it's so beautiful over there and you will be free of pain. First, there will be a tunnel, then a bright beautiful light, and there will be relatives waiting to see you if you decide to go.'

"I then asked my cousin what she meant by saying if my mom decides to go.

"She explained it this way: 'Our time of death is written in stone, but sometimes up there they will give people a second chance to say their goodbyes on Earth. Maybe it's one hour; maybe it's several years—they decide.' My cousin pointed upward to the heavens."

Annie nodded. "I got it."

David went on. "Their conversation continued. My mom started to channel information for my cousin from the other side. She said, 'When you go back to Hawaii, there will be a German lady you will have to help.' My mom was very insistent. 'She needs your help. You must help her; you must guide her.' My cousin nodded and said she would. She gave my mom a long goodbye kiss, knowing she might not see her again.

"We left the care home and walked the few blocks back to my house. My cousin was a bit baffled. She turned to me and said, 'I don't know any German ladies. I don't understand why your mother said that.'

"I told her not to worry; sometimes Mom was delusional. My cousin got a little upset with me; she said my mom was not delusional. Then she turned to me and said she would wait this one out. She felt that this channeled session was based on truth.

"About three weeks later when my cousin arrived back in Hawaii, she called me with the strangest news. She said she had a friend that needed a place to stay in Hawaii. Her friend was distraught so she offered to help her out. Little did she know then that her friend was leaving her boyfriend after ten years; she felt useless and at times wanted to end her life. It turned out her friend was German."

"Whoa," Rob and John both said in unison.

Annie said, "David, these things happen sometimes. That is why some persons are the lucky ones who are allowed to stay on Earth just a little bit longer; sometimes they have wonderful messages for the people on Earth. It's so important that we pay attention to each and every message. We call those messages 'signs.' You see, sometimes there are secret messages in signs.

"We may hear a song on the radio that reminds us of someone that we haven't heard from in a very long time. The song plays and we hear from our friend.

"You see, David, your cousin went to see your mom to help ease her pain, but what really happened was your cousin was the one who got the direct channeled message from up above. It's a two-way street, my friend."

David said, "Annie, my mom passed away six months after my cousin's visit. Do you feel she is okay?"

Annie tuned in. "Yes, Esther is fine. She says she is with her husband, Sam—he looks so good. She has taken up painting through someone here on Earth. She loved to paint in real life; now she can channel her energies into a famous painter on Earth."

"Annie, I can't thank you enough for listening," David said. "I feel so much better now. I understand now."

Rob went to a commercial break. "That was a long one, Annie; it ate up a lot of our time, but it was a good one as well. Hey, John, are you punching the counter over there?"

"Yes, I am," John responded. "Annie, you're really moving along nicely; looks like you're up to 909 people and counting. Within a few weeks or so you probably will hit your mark of 1000 souls."

Jokingly, Rob said, "Not if I have anything to say about it."

Annie stared at Rob. "You **are** joking, Rob, aren't you?" she asked.

"Yes, Annie, I'm just kidding."

That morning Annie took call after call on the radio. She was really on top of things. Rob pushed every button that had a light lit up and John kept hitting the counter. They made a great team.

Rob finally said, "Well, our show has come to an end for today, folks, but hang in there; we have news and your weather coming up. Looks like a cold one today, so don't turn your dial; we'll be right back with the weather."

Rob pulled off his earphones. "We're out."

Before Rob could say anything else, John said to Annie, "Hey, how about a cup of coffee downstairs? I want to ask you something."

"Okay, but that's about all I have time for today," Annie replied. "I have lots of errands to run and I want to go shopping before the Christmas rush starts."

Rob gave John a strange look. He knew he wasn't invited.

John and Annie went to a small coffee shop right next door to the radio station. They both ordered coffee and a pastry.

"Annie," John began, "I asked you to join me because I need to know about Kate. You see, Annie, to be truthful, after my last marriage many moons ago, I became a player. There wasn't any woman who walked who I didn't want to take to bed."

Annie blushed.

John cleared his throat. "I hate to brag, but I love my women. But when I met Kate, there was some energy about her that was familiar. I mean, she's the marrying kind—not the playing kind—and, Annie, that scares the living heck out of me."

"John, you're right. Kate is attractive, very self-sufficient, and very loving. She was with someone before, I believe. She has devoted her life now to photography and travel—but you know what?"

"What?"

"I believe she's doing all of this to keep herself busy. I believe she wants to find someone to love her."

John was lost for words for a moment. Then he said softly, "I never thought I'd ever say this, but I think I could be that person."

"John, Friday isn't far off; I'm sure the two of you will have a great time together. Let things unfold the way they are meant to be. Don't push anything. Take it slow."

"I will. I'll go at a snail's pace for Kate," he said.

"John, I have a question for you."

"What's that?"

"It's about Rob."

"Yes, I knew this would pop up eventually."

"Does he date?" Annie asked.

"Only you lately." John smiled.

"I've only had lunch with him a few times."

"Annie, I think Rob is still waiting for his wife to come back to him. He has never expressed any interest in anyone else, but when he's with you, he lights up. He loves building up your career. Annie, how do you feel about him?"

"John, to be honest, I find Rob mildly attractive. He's a bit quirky, but very nice. He's been very good to me. That's it in a nutshell." Annie hoped she had made her point.

John studied Annie as she spoke to see if she was hiding some of her feelings about Rob. "Would you ever allow Rob to be more than a friend?" he asked.

"I really can't answer that; I don't know. But what I do know is my heart belongs very deeply to another. I totally understand why Rob is waiting for his wife, John; I'm waiting for my love, Brandon, to come back into my life."

Annie looked at her watch and stood up. "John, it was so nice talking to you. I really have to go now. I need to go shopping; they're having a huge sale at Macy's."

"I got it, sweet one. Well, I'll see you soon. By the way, I'm real proud of you; you're almost hitting your mark of 1000 souls to help."

Annie waved, "Bye, John."

John went back to the station. Rob was still working. "Well, did you have a nice coffee break with Annie?" he asked condescendingly.

"Yes, I did. And you don't have to be so huffy about it. All I did was ask her a few questions about Kate."

"John, that's not what's bothering me."

"Well, what is?"

"Annie will hit her 1000 mark real soon; I hope she won't leave us. I mean, I put a lot of energy into promoting her. Look at our station now; we are number one. I can't afford to have her leave."

"What makes you think she'll leave?"

"I don't know. That's why on Friday I'm going to take her to a really nice, elegant-dining restaurant and have a long talk with her about her future plans.

"By the way, we'd better get our act together. I want to put together one HUGE promotion about Annie hitting her first mark on the radio. Something like, 1000 souls and counting. Annie makes her mark just as she approaches 999 souls… we have balloons and lots of noise as if it were New Year's Eve. **Come join us for one big party bash at 92.3 FM.** Then shortly thereafter I'll schedule a television spot for Annie, so the world can see her. John, I want this to be big…HUGE."

"I hear you, pal. It will be done," John assured him.

Meanwhile, while Annie shopped for something cute to wear for Friday night and Kate was checking out the Bon Jovi concert, Brandon was at the television station getting ready for his show. Scripts were flying at him. He had to memorize everything that would be going on that night. He smiled when he saw Pat Edwards' name on the guest line-up for that evening.

"Rose!" he shouted. "Where are you?"

Rose came running with her little puppy, Bo, following on her heels.

"There you are, Rose." The puppy began barking and chewing on Brandon's left shoe. "Rose, I love dogs, but do you think you can do something about him?"

Rose picked up Bo and cuddled him in her arms. "What can I do for you, Brandon?" she asked.

"Is Pat here yet? If he is, I want to talk to him."

"You got it. I'll check; if he's here, I'll send him to your dressing room."

Pat was sitting cozily in his dressing room when Rose peeked in. "Hey, Brandon wants to see you."

"Okay," he said, and hurried down the hallway.

"Hi, Brandon. What's up?"

"I see you're on the show tonight; I can only give you about fifteen minutes with the audience. Is that okay? I have so many guests to fit in tonight I don't know where to put them."

Pat replied, "Brandon, that's more than okay. I can't thank you enough for all you've done for me. My business is booming; I barely have time to breathe."

Brandon dropped his talk-show-host persona and pleaded, "Pat, help me out here—I've been dreaming of Annie a lot."

"What have you dreamt?" Pat asked.

"I dream the same dream night after night. It's always the same. In the dream it's snowing outside. It's cold. I hear music and I see people—like they're dancing. I can't make it out. Then the next thing I know, Annie is in my arms; I'm holding her. Same dream, night after night."

"Well, you could be dreaming of her in the future, of some event where the two of you meet." Pat paused. Without looking at Brandon, he said, "I feel Annie coming closer to you. The stars might just be in alignment. It could be just a matter of time before the two of you meet."

Brandon turned and looked at Pat. "Do you really think so?"

Pat nodded.

A voice in the distance shouted, "Brandon, get ready! You have 10 minutes to AIR." Brandon scrambled; he wasn't quite finished dressing. Pat left to get ready for his part of the show.

The announcer shouted: "AND NOW, LADIES AND GENTLE-MEN, BRANDON TURNER!"

Brandon made his entrance to wild applause and, after acknowledging the screaming fans in the front rows, took his seat. "Good evening. We have a really great show for you tonight; and we've brought back, by popular demand, Pat Edwards. You know what a great hit he has been, helping our audience members." The audience went wild; they loved Pat. "Well, I guess we'd better bring him out. Come on out, Pat."

There was a chair waiting at the center of the stage. Pat sat in it and waited for Brandon to take the mike to the audience.

"Any questions for Pat?" Every hand went up in the audience. Brandon picked a cute girl who said her name was Cathy.

"Hi, Cathy. How can I help you?" Pat asked.

"I know this sounds strange, but do all dogs go to Heaven?" she asked. "You see, Pat, I have been having dreams about my dog Sasha. She was thirteen years old and the love of my life. When that dog passed, I never got over it. I even purchased another dog, but it was never the same. Recently, I've been having dreams of Sasha, and when I wake up in the morning, there is a tuft of dog hair on my bed. I can't explain it."

The audience responded with "Whoa...."

"Cathy, to answer your question... Yes, all dogs go to Heaven, but it's a little different from the Heaven we know; it's what you might call a separate dog heaven. They are allowed to wander freely to our side of Heaven. They are indoctrinated as well, and they are debriefed.

"You see, they feel the separation anxiety as well as we do. Sometimes they are so lost and miss us so much that on occasion they can find their way back to Earth to visit us for a short period of time. And, Cathy, that's what I think happened with your Sasha—you had a real visitation from your dog. She's trying to tell you she misses you as much as you miss her.

"But, Cathy, I'm getting that there will be another dog in the future that will be as meaningful to you. It looks like you'll name her Sasha as well. Look for the little white spot on her tail as a sign," Pat said.

"Thank you so much, Pat." Cathy was crying, but she was happy.

Brandon cut to a commercial break. After that Pat answered several other questions from the audience. The show continued.

Meanwhile, Annie made her way back to the apartment with several shopping bags. Kate was in her loft, sorting out her photos. "Hi, Annie, I guess you went shopping today. What did you get? Let me see," she said.

Annie took out all her things to show Kate. "By the way, Kate, I had coffee with John," she said and twirled around.

"What, you had coffee with John? What did he say?" Kate was going through Annie's new clothes and she didn't know what to do first—look at the clothes or talk about John. John won out. "What did he say, Annie?"

"Well, let's see…" Annie said teasingly. "He thought you were cute; he asked me a little about your past; he felt as if he had known you before."

Kate stopped Annie right there. "What? He felt as if he knew me before?"

"Yes."

"You know, Annie, I never thought of that. I wonder. Could it be we had met before?"

"It's possible, you know."

"How will I know? I only remember you because Gabriel allowed me to. But John—I guess Gabriel gave me my memory shot on that one."

Annie was puzzled. "Memory shot… What's that?"

"That's a shot that we all get in Heaven so we don't remember our past lives, although I've heard of the shot wearing off now and then. I even heard of angels piercing through the veil to see their past-life partners. But you, Annie—I wonder if Gabriel forgot to give you your shot. You remember almost everything. Why is that?"

"I didn't even know there was such a thing as a shot, Kate, but what I do know is I'm allowed to speak with Gabriel any time I want. I can even travel back to Heaven, if need be."

"Annie, you must be a lot more special than I thought. Or you are more evolved than me," Kate said. "Anyway, what else did John say?"

"He said he couldn't wait to see you tomorrow night. He also explained that he was a ladies' man."

"A ladies' man—what does that mean?" Kate asked.

"It means he's a player; he loves his women, but only for play." Seeing Kate frown, Annie quickly added, "Except for one thing… when he met you…there was something very different about you, he said. You scared him because you were marriage material."

Kate was taken aback by this revelation. "Marriage material! I'm not ready for that one yet."

"Oh, Kate, you know you are," Annie huffed. "Well, enough about all this. Help me to decide what to wear tomorrow night when Rob picks me up for dinner."

"Okay."

So Kate went through all of Annie's new clothes. "How darling can it get? Try this on, Annie; I love this."

Annie modeled her cute, simple black dress for Kate. It had white lace on the sleeves and all along the v-shaped neckline. A very petite white flower enhanced the left bodice of the dress. Annie had black tights to match the outfit. Her shoes were black shiny heels with bowties. According to Kate, she looked darling.

"That is great. I love that outfit," Kate said. "Do you know where you are going for dinner?"

"Rob said he would take me anywhere I want. Where do you think I should go?"

"There's this cute new restaurant on Fifth Avenue; everyone's talking about it, and it's very posh. It's called The Looking Glass. I hear you have to make reservations way ahead of time," Kate said.

"Kate, the one thing I learned about Rob is that he is a very simple man. He loves great food at affordable prices, so where do you think we should go?"

"Let me think." Kate paused for a long time. "I have an idea—get me the yellow pages." Annie did. "Open it to restaurants." Annie did. "Let's see what we have here. Ah, this looks good. It's on the Upper East Side. In fact, I've been there before. It's called the Blue Moon. It's a theme restaurant; they have several rooms you can choose to dine in—the 60's room, 80's room, 90's room, et cetera. Each room features different food and the prices are moderate."

"That sounds great. I'll let Rob know; I think he will enjoy that."

The phone rang while they were discussing the restaurant. Kate picked it up. "Hello."

"Hi, Kate, it's John here. I'm still at the radio station with Rob; we're working on a big promotion for Annie. What time do you want to pick me up?" he asked.

"I can pick you up at 7:00, if that's okay," Kate said. "You can wear jeans—something simple. Will you be at the radio station?"

"Yes, and seven-ish is fine," John said.

"Oh, by the way, can Annie talk to Rob for a moment?"

"Sure. I'll go get him."

Kate turned to Annie. "It's John; he's still at the station. He's getting Rob for you. Tell him about the new restaurant and see if he's interested."

When Rob came on line, Annie grabbed the phone and said, "Hi, Rob. I found a new restaurant that Kate recommends…"

"Say no more," Rob interrupted. "I'll pick you up at 7:00 P.M. at your place. Make the reservations and when I pick you up you can tell me where it is."

"That sounds good. See you then," Annie said. Turning to Kate, she said, "I think I'd better change; this restaurant sounds like I might be just a little overdressed."

"I agree. Grab those cute jeans and wear your white blouse— you know the one—it has the lace all over it. Here's some jewelry to finish you off. High heels would be cute and I have a great Prada purse for you to carry."

"Thanks."

The next night, while Annie was getting dressed, Kate assembled all of her camera equipment for the shoot and lugged them to the door. She shouted up to the loft, "Annie, I'm leaving! I'll be home real late tonight. We'll talk tomorrow."

"Okay."

Kate made her way out the door and down the stairs and ran smack into Rob who was just starting up. "Hey, do you need some help with that, Kate?" he asked.

"No, I have it under control. But thanks. Annie's waiting for you. See ya."

Rob walked quickly up the stairs, skipping several till he reached the apartment. He knocked.

Annie opened her door; she was all ready to go. "I made reservations at the Blue Moon," she said.

"I heard of that place. I hear the food is great," he said.

Annie handed Rob the directions to the restaurant and they were off.

When Kate arrived at the radio station, she parked the car in a loading zone and called John on her cell. "Hi, John, I'm downstairs," she said.

"I'll be right down." John stopped momentarily to look in a mirror and brush his hair before dashing down the stairs to greet Kate. "Hi."

Kate reached over and opened the car door for John. "John, I'm running late, and with this traffic—well, you know." John barely made it into the car when Kate screeched off into the night. They arrived at the concert hall at 7:00 P.M., right on the dot.

John helped Kate with all her equipment. The band was gearing up. People were just being let in for the concert. The energy of the place was exhilarating. John looked around in awe. The hustle and bustle of the people—all the lights, cameras, and music—he was in his element. It had been a very long time since John had been a part of something like this.

John flashed back in time. He remembered how he loved playing his guitar when he was in his teens growing up in New York. His parents helped him form a band, for he was quite good. He always dreamt of being a rock star. John tried for several years to make this happen. He and his band, The ZZZZ'S, played every gig they could. John played not only the guitar but also the drums; he knew some day he would make it.

His first wife, Lisa, was a singer in his band. They were well on their way to success. John played at the Treat Night Club when he was discovered by a talent scout for the Carson show. He was given his opportunity to make it big; he couldn't contain himself. That night he and his band were on the way to the Tonight Show in his van. Although The Tonight Show had offered them transportation, John and his band turned down the offer; they were very particular about their instruments and his van was big enough to transport all his equipment and musicians. John never forgot that; he knew he should have taken that ride—after the fact.

That night it was raining very hard; the roads were slick; the windshield wipers were going full blast—John's dad could barely see out the van's window. Suddenly, it was all over. A car out of control smashed into their van. Within minutes there were ambulances all over the place. John was transported to the hospital for major cuts and bruises, none of which were earth-shaking at the time. But it was the first and last time that they were asked to be on the Carson show.

Shortly thereafter, John gave up his band. The pain of almost making it was too much to bear. He and Lisa soon divorced. It was then he found himself working with Rob at the radio station; at least he could still be a part of the music scene.

And now here he was—looking all around at the concert, wondering what might have been—this time a little wiser and a little older. John was having a good time while forgetting about his past.

The audience was loud—screams could be heard all the way down the street. The music of Bon Jovi was happening. Kate took all the great shots she could with the help of John. When she was finished with her shoot, she took John backstage with her to wait for the group. The highlight of John's evening was Kate's introducing him to Bon Jovi and his band.

Kate then grabbed John's hand and they were off.

Kate, John, Rob, Annie, Brandon and Gabriel

Chapter 12

"John, did you have a good time?" Kate asked.

"Are you kidding? I didn't know you were THAT connected. KUDOS to you, Kate."

Kate smiled as she drove. She couldn't wait to be alone with John and have a nice conversation with him at the restaurant. They reached the Second Avenue Deli around midnight. Both were starved; both could not wait to eat. After ordering, Kate watched John—he was so animated and so alive. He explained to Kate about his budding rock star career and how wonderful it was of her to introduce him to Bon Jovi.

"Kate, tell me about you," he said.

"John, I love my work. I have so much fun traveling the world and photographing anything and everything. The best part about it is that I get paid for doing it. What more can I really ask for?" Kate smiled.

John fiddled with his fork and knife when he asked, "Kate, do you want to get married some day and have kids?"

"Oh, I suppose so. I'm young; I still have time for that."

John was extremely interested in Kate's line of work and her personal life as well. "I'm sorry if I sound like I'm prying, but what about relationships? I mean, with your schedule, don't you find it hard having a relationship? One minute you're in New York and the next you're in Japan.... How does that work?"

"John, I've had my share of relationships and all the hurt and pain that goes with it. I guess that's why I've thrown myself into working so hard. There just hasn't been anyone out there. It's not like I don't want to get involved—I need to be very careful this time. I really don't have the luxury or time to get hurt. Besides, I made a promise to someone to help Annie, as well. I need to help her fulfill her dream."

"Kate, what happens when you help Annie reach her goal?"

Kate reached over to John and rubbed his cheek with her soft hand. "I guess I'll be free to love whomever I want." She winked at him.

John smiled shyly. He stared at Kate as if she were the biggest challenge of his life. John thought that Kate was surprisingly refreshing. She was highly intelligent, creative, into his music, and very independent—although being too independent did bother him a little. He thought the woman with whom he wanted to spend the rest of his life should share a lot of things with him. He wanted to travel and go places with his lady. His attraction to her was overwhelming.

John did everything to calm himself down, for he wanted to be lying in bed with Kate that very moment. He knew he had to move slowly. So he put on his mental brakes, mixed up a little charm and wooed her with his charisma.

"John, do you still want to have your own band?" she asked. "I have connections."

"I think about it now and then, but I feel I'm getting too old for it. But I do practice on my drums a lot," he said.

"You do? I would give anything to watch you do that," she said.

John looked at his watch; he didn't want the evening to end, but he said, "It's getting real late; I have to be at the radio station around six in the morning." John stood up. "Do you mind?"

"No, John. Time just flew by—I really had no idea. I don't mind; let's go."

John helped Kate with her coat and paid the check, and they walked arm in arm out to the car.

"Kate, I would really like to see you again. Is that okay with you?"

"Yes, John, as long as you invite me over to watch you jam on the drums," she answered with a grin.

"It's a date; I'll call you in a day or so. You can come up to my apartment and I'll show you around. I promise…I'll let you watch while I jam on the drums. Okay?" John smiled.

"Okay." That was just what she wanted to hear.

When they got to John's apartment building, he thanked her for a great and unforgettable time. He reached over and kissed Kate on her cheek, then let himself out of the car. He waved goodbye and didn't look back.

Meanwhile, Annie and Rob arrived at the Blue Moon Restaurant. The place was so cool—with a capital C. When they walked in, they were greeted by waiters and waitresses dressed up in costumes of the 60's, 70's, and 80's. Rob, tall as he was, bent down to Annie and said, "You remember Elle, our favorite waiter? He should work here; I can't wait to tell him about this place."

Annie laughed.

The headwaiter came over to Annie and Rob; he was dressed like Captain Hook. "And which room would you like to dine in this evening?" he snarled.

Annie pretended to flinch and shrugged her shoulders. Rob made the decision. "How about the 80's room? That looks like a fun room."

"Thank you, sir; follow me." Rob and Annie didn't know what to expect. The waiter sat them down right under a picture of President Ronald Reagan—the music, all the décor, and even the menu was right out of the eighties.

Rob looked at Annie. "Isn't this place something?" He chuckled.

"It sure is," she agreed.

A waiter dressed as Ronald Reagan himself, with a mask to boot, came by to take their order. "Let me introduce myself. I am Ronald Reagan, the President of the whole United States, and I will be pleased to take your order," he said.

Rob and Annie laughed, then ordered very simply steak and lobster. Rob made sure he also ordered a nice bottle of wine, for he had a lot to say to Annie.

"Annie I have a lot on my mind tonight. Do you mind?"

"No, Rob, what seems to be bothering you?" she asked.

"Well, I know we're coming very close to helping 1000 people on the radio." Rob squirmed. "I'm concerned, Annie."

"Why?"

"Well, when you reach your goal, will you be leaving the radio station?" Rob looked down. There was silence.

Annie paused, then, answered slowly but deliberately, "No... I don't... think... so. Where did you ever get an idea like that?" Annie was baffled.

"Well, you told me your guardian angel Gabriel will allow you to hook up with Brandon, once you have helped 1000 souls, so I figured you would leave me and the station at that point."

Rob's voice cracked as he continued. "Annie, I've poured so much money into this station over you. I even made a fool of myself at times. The owner thought I went out on a limb, but I proved him wrong. If you leave the radio station **now**, my world will crumble." Rob was dead serious; he stared straight into Annie's eyes. "Annie, you know how I feel about you."

Annie turned toward Rob and frowned. "I...leave my show? Are you kidding? I have so many people to help...why would I leave? And Rob, all those billboards that you put up all over New York City...how can I leave all that? Leave our audience and everything that we built together for almost a year now? Rob, I don't think so." Annie shook her head in disbelief.

"But Annie, what about Brandon?"

"Rob, when I reach 1000 people, all I really want to do is take a vacation—I think I deserve that. As far as Brandon is concerned, I have no idea when I will meet him. I have no option but to let Gabriel decide when and whom I meet.

"I never planned on leaving you. I know when I get the chance to be with Brandon again, that will be wonderful—I will be ecstatic— but he has a television show to run and I have a successful radio show." Annie rolled her eyes and shook her head as if she couldn't believe what Rob was saying.

Rob said nothing for a few seconds; then he said quietly, "I get it. I feel better now."

Rob composed himself enough to start talking about their radio show again. "By the way, Annie, John and I are planning your party for the show. We want to make it big—HUGE. We want all of New York City to listen to your show. Now I can add that you'll be taking a vacation for a few weeks. Where will you be going?"

"I really thought I'd take a trip to Hawaii. I want to explore the islands.... I need to feel the ocean, see the waves...re-energize, as you might call it."

"That sounds great. Wish I were going with you." Rob moved closer toward Annie.

Annie and Rob spent the rest of the evening catching up; Rob talked non-stop about the radio show while Annie listened. It was getting late, and Rob had to be at the radio station early in the morning. Shortly thereafter they left the restaurant and Rob drove Annie back to her apartment.

"I guess I'll see you tomorrow at the studio, Annie. I know it's Saturday, but we're having a special show for you. I hope you don't mind coming in." Rob parked the car in front of Annie's apartment building.

"No, I don't mind, Rob, and thank you so much for dinner." Annie reached down for her purse on the car floor; Rob reached for the door handle on her side at the same time. Their eyes locked. Rob could not hold back his emotions any longer; he kissed Annie passionately on her lips…she kissed him back. He was surprised that Annie didn't pull away. Rob breathed heavily… "MMMM."

Annie shyly said, "See you tomorrow." She closed the car door and waved goodbye.

Rob took off in his car, grinning from ear to ear. He wondered if that was the right thing to do. But it didn't really matter—the damage was done, and it felt so good.

That was the very first time in a long while that Rob had kissed a lady other than his wife.

Annie went up to the apartment. She really needed to think, but there was Kate waiting to tell her all about her adventures with John.

"Hey, girlfriend, how did it go?"

"I'll tell you later. What happened with you and John?" Annie asked.

Kate gave an animated resume of her night. "It was amazing. We had a ball. I took John down to the Bon Jovi concert—he had the time of his life. I found out he once had a rock band and it fell apart. We had the most amazing dinner and we talked for hours. Annie, he wants to see me again. I played it cool, though; I didn't want to let on that I would drop my life and spend every waking moment with him. But I did ask him if I could watch him jam on his drums. He said 'yes' and he would call me in a few days."

Annie laughed. "Would you?"

Kate answered coyly, "I don't know…maybe. So what happened with you and Rob?"

Annie undressed and folded her clothes while she spoke to Kate. "Well, we had a great dinner at the Blue Moon; it was everything you said it would be…and more. Rob was very worried about my leaving the show after I hit my mark of 1000 people. I assured him that I really wasn't going anywhere. I did tell him I wanted to take a vacation in Hawaii for a few weeks. Kate, he was so relieved."

"You're going to Hawaii?" Kate was surprised.

"Yes, I really want to—I need to rest. Then, Kate, the most amazing thing happened. He kissed me."

"What…?" Kate leaped out of her chair.

"He kissed me so passionately; I actually felt something."

"Annie, what are you saying? Did you kiss him back?"

"Yes," she replied softly.

"Oh, boy! What about Brandon?"

"Kate, nothing's changed. I love Brandon with all my heart and soul. We will be together forever."

Kate started to pace. "Annie, you kissed Rob back and you say you felt something. You crossed the line, don't you think? Remember, Gabriel sent me down here to watch over you." Kate shook a finger at Annie. "If you pull this Love-Addiction Co-Dependency thing with Rob, both of our gooses are cooked. What are you going to do?"

"Nothing, Kate. It was just a kiss."

"What did you feel exactly?"

Annie turned dreamy-eyed. "I felt little balls of energy ignited when he kissed me. It was as if he were familiar to me in some way. Kissing Rob was so different…I really can't explain it. I'll know more tomorrow when I see him."

"Tomorrow is Saturday," Kate reminded her.

"Yes, I know. We have a special radio show tomorrow... Oh, my, is that clock correct?"

"Yes, it's about two in the morning."

"I'd better get ready for bed. I have to get up early for the show." Annie headed for her room to set her alarm clock.

Kate followed her and leaned against the door jamb as she tried to talk some sense into Annie. "Annie, you've got me worried. If you mess up again, I may never end up with John—and, for that matter, ever find the love of my life. Please think this through. Push him away, girl. **It's not meant to be.**"

"Don't worry, Kate, I am in control. Get some sleep now."

"That's exactly why I'm worried."

"Why?"

"Because you're in control."

Annie was up at the crack of dawn, got dressed and made a cup of coffee. With coffee in hand she raced out the door and down the steps, and hailed a cab. Since it was the weekend, the streets were practically empty and she arrived at the radio station right at 6:30 A.M., ready to go on air.

"Hey, Rob; hi, John. I'm ready." John handed her the earphones.

Rob shouted, "We're live on the air with Annie, our very special angel! We've asked Annie to come on this weekend especially for you folks out there who have been sending an overwhelming number of e-mails to our station."

The aura this morning was different. Rob couldn't take his eyes off Annie, and Annie avoided looking directly at Rob.

The phone lines all lit up. "John, who's our first caller?" Rob asked.

"We have Susan on the line for Annie."

"Hi, Susan, how can I help you this morning?" Annie sipped her coffee.

"Hi, Annie. I had a very strange experience, you might say. I just started dating a guy named Bill. We get along so well; we share everything in common. Last night he took me out to dinner—it was wonderful and romantic. When Bill walked me to my apartment building—such a nice gentleman, I thought—he kissed me so very gently. But something happened that had never happened to me before."

"What was it?" Annie and Rob asked in unison.

"When Bill kissed me, I saw our future, but it wasn't in this life."

Rob interrupted abruptly. "Come again...? What do you mean it wasn't in this lifetime?"

"Well, it's as though I saw us together in our next life. It was a flash forward in time. It looked about eighty years in the future. I saw space travel. I saw space stations. I saw that Bill and I were getting married at a space station chapel. Annie, this was so real to me. Did I imagine this, or was it real?" she asked.

Rob remarked, "Are you sure you weren't on something?"

Annie gave Rob a reproving look. "No, Rob, she wasn't on anything. Susan, what you saw was very real and very rare. Sometimes, if we have a gift like yours, we can pierce the veil of time and see far into the future—and honey, that's what you did."

Rob listened with great interest as Susan whimpered, "Annie, does that mean I won't have a chance to be with Bill in this life?"

"Very good question. Usually, when we pierce the veil of the next life, our chances of being with that person in this life is really rare. But then again, who knows? I would say enjoy the time you have together for now and let nature take its course—you will find out soon enough. I've had incidences of this happening to me as well."

Rob stared at Annie, trying to figure out what she was really saying.

Annie continued. "So please call me back and tell me how it ends up in this life with you and Bill."

"I will, Annie. Thank you so much for not deeming me crazy." Susan hung up.

As the day moved on, Annie answered call after call while John kept hitting the counter button. "980 souls and counting!" he shouted. All of radio land must have heard John calling out 980 souls. John felt just like Santa Claus. Then he said, "Rob, we're just in time for a commercial break."

Rob told his listeners, "Thank you, New York, for listening and making us Number One in the ratings. We've plumb run out of time for today. This has been a special edition of an Angel over the Airwaves."

John counted down to one and pointed. "We're over and out." Annie and Rob handed their earphones to John.

Rob turned to Annie; he really wanted to speak with her.

He cleared his throat and said, "Annie, next weekend is Christmas and then New Year's Eve. We'll be giving you some time off for the holidays; we usually just play pre-programmed music until New Year's Eve and on New Year's Day.

"Why don't we plan to have your Big Radio Bash on New Year's Eve? That way we can all celebrate the New Year and go out with a bang. And when I announce to the listeners that you'll be taking a few weeks off, it will sound very natural," Rob said excitedly.

John looked at Rob. "Buddy, that sounds great. We can even celebrate at your apartment on New Year's Eve."

Rob raised his eyebrows in delight.

John continued, "I wonder if Kate will be busy shooting, or if she'd like to join us. I think I'll call her tonight and invite her. What do you think, Annie?"

"Yes, John, call her and invite her." Annie giggled.

Rob asked Annie, "Are you busy for the New Year, my darling angel?"

"No…" She paused. "I don't have any plans. Rob, the New Year's Eve Bash sounds great. What a wonderful idea. We can all celebrate together." Annie smiled.

Annie looked at her watch; there was still plenty of time left for her to go Christmas shopping. Annie said her goodbyes; she peeled herself off the chair, waved to Rob and John, and quickly left the building.

She loved to walk down Fifth Avenue and look in the shop windows at the displays of wintry villages, animated North Pole toy makers, mannequins dressed in their holiday best, and Christmas trees glittering with tinsel and ornaments. She watched several Santa Clauses ringing their bells for the Salvation Army. Christmas carols filled the air.

This was her favorite time of the year. Snowflakes brushed her rosy cheeks. She tossed her red scarf across her neck and bundled up tightly. Annie felt vibrant.

Back at the station, John and Rob were discussing an upcoming show. When they were finished, Rob said, "John, have lunch with me. I really need your advice on something."

"I'll be ready in a few minutes. I want to call Kate first and ask her out for New Year's Eve."

"Oh, that's right. You had a date last night. How did that go?"

"I'll tell you all about it at lunch. You go on; I'll meet you at the Stage Deli," John said.

As Rob went off, John dialed Kate's phone number. He was a little nervous, and that was out of character for him. He paced while the phone rang three times.

"Hello."

"Hi, Kate, this is John. How're you doing?"

"Just fine."

"Did I catch you at a bad time?"

"No, John, not at all. What's up?"

"Kate, Rob is throwing a huge party on New Year's Eve for Annie on the radio and we'll continue the party at his place well into the night. Would you like to join us?"

"Wait… Let me check my schedule." John began pacing again while Kate checked her date book. "John, I can go. I'm free New Year's Eve and Day. I'm so excited—this is the first year I have it off. By the way, John, want to have a bite to eat tonight?"

"Sure, where do you want to go?" he asked.

"Let's do Italian. I know this place right close to your neighborhood; it's called Stefano's. I hear the food is great there. Then, if I'm lucky, maybe I can watch you jam on your drums," she said.

"Kate, that place is just a short hop from my apartment. I eat there all the time and, you're right, the food is great. Can you get off early—say, five o'clock? We can spend more time together and I'll show you my drums and my apartment."

Kate didn't miss a beat. This would be her night. "See you, John; got to go." She hung up the phone without saying goodbye.

John rushed out of the studio and ran all the way to the Stage Deli. He didn't want to keep Rob waiting; he knew Rob was a stickler for being on time. He pushed open the big glass doors and slid into the booth as fast as he could. "Hi, Rob," he panted.

Rob asked, "What did she say? And, by the way, I ordered for us."

John had a huge grin on his face.

Rob said, "I gather she said yes."

"I'm seeing her tonight."

"Okay..."

"So what did you want to talk to me about?" John asked.

Rob hesitated before answering. "Well, this is hard for me... I mean, it's been a long time and I don't exactly know how to put this."

John was concerned. "Spit it out."

"Okay, here goes. Annie and I went to dinner last night at the Blue Moon restaurant."

"How was that? I've heard a lot about that."

"Surprisingly good," Rob said with a smile. "Anyway, I drove Annie home, and when we reached her apartment I opened her car door from the inside."

John let out an audible gasp. "You didn't, Rob! You didn't...! Tell me you didn't."

"John, I couldn't help myself...I kissed her. Not only did I kiss her, I kissed her passionately. I can't stop thinking about her. John, I want her. What am I going to do?" Rob sank his head onto the table.

John was at once surprised, yet not. "Rob, I'm stunned. I thought she was just a MEAL ticket!"

Rob straightened up. "I don't know what happened. I don't even know **why** it happened. All I know is it **did** happen."

"Did she...kiss you back?"

Rob nodded vigorously. "Yes."

"I think we have a bit of a problem here," John said candidly. "The way I see it, someone's going to get hurt, and I'm guessing it won't be Annie." John slapped the table and glared at Rob.

"Rob, are you crazy? All she talks about is Brandon. Did you NOT... hear her? She loves him. Soon she'll be with him. What is it about this picture you don't understand?"

Rob slumped in his seat. "You're right...I'll get a grip. But why did she kiss me back if she loves Brandon?"

John responded, "I don't know." He looked around at the other deli patrons and lowered his voice. "I don't understand this whole thing... an angel, in love with a mortal from her last life, chasing him in this life, when she probably met Mr. Right—YOU—and doesn't know it. This could be a book. Rob, pull it together."

They both had a good laugh.

Rob needed to change the subject. "How was your evening with Kate?"

"Now we're talking! She's a BABE! Talk about attraction—I nearly went through the roof. I wanted her so badly I couldn't help myself. But I was good. Rob, she's smart and intelligent. This could be a keeper—I feel it." John checked his watch. We'd better get back; I have to finish my work. Kate and I are going out to dinner tonight. And then...I will show her my apartment."

"Sounds good. Let's go," Rob said. They walked back to the radio station to finish their work.

Annie, meanwhile, was tired of shopping and decided to walk up the street and get a cup of coffee. Feeling a little winded, she sat down to rest for a short while on a bench nearby.

She looked up towards Heaven. The snow had stopped, and a feeling of loneliness swept over her. She really missed her guardian angel and soon it would be Christmas Day. "Gabriel, where are you?" She called to me.

I immediately appeared sitting next to her. "I'm here, my little angel. What's wrong?" I asked. Only Annie could see me.

Annie turned and smiled. "Gabriel, you're really here."

"Have I ever let you down? You called... I appeared."

"Gabriel, I have a bit of a dilemma. You see, the other night when Rob drove me home, he kissed me."

"I observed that; and you, Annie, kissed him back. So what's the dilemma?" I asked innocently.

"Well, Gabriel, I'm supposed to be with Brandon...I love him. But now when Rob kissed me, I felt something. If I really loved Brandon, why would I feel anything at all for Rob?'

"Good question, Annie," I said. I held her hands in mine and peered into her lovely face. "I knew this day would come and it's time I explain, my dear. Please understand this. **You are not meant to be with Rob in this life.** But you will be with Rob in ONE of your next lives. That's why you had those strong feelings for him. Your soul remembered and longed for him."

My explanation simply confused Annie. "How can my soul long for something or someone I don't recognize? You're telling me I have to wait until one of my next lives to find out the answer? What happens to Brandon? What will happen to Rob? Will Rob just sit around and wait for me till his number gets picked?"

Her voice took on a higher pitch. "I don't understand, Gabriel. I've done everything that you've asked of me. And I still haven't met Brandon. I just don't get it." Annie shook her head; tears were running down her face.

I put my arms around Annie and gave her a hug. "Have patience, my dear, all will work out...I promise. All I can say is you did know Rob one lifetime before. And that is why your soul remembers him. Each of you has something to finish in this life before you can meet again in one of your next lives."

I pointed my finger at Annie and firmly cautioned her, "Ask No More.... That's all I'm allowed to tell you about this situation."

Annie cried, "But, Gabriel, I need to know what happened to Rob in our last life so I can fix it now, before I meet Brandon."

I was moved by her distress, but I had no recourse but to say no more. "Annie, I have to go. I'm being paged, my dear. Don't worry; it will work itself out." With those words of consolation I disappeared.

Annie looked at her watch; it was time to go home. She hailed a cab and went home with loads of Christmas packages. When she got there, the apartment was empty; Kate had already left to meet John for dinner. Annie kept herself busy the rest of the evening until she fell fast asleep.

Kate, John, and the Whole Family

Chapter 13

When Kate arrived at the restaurant, John was waiting with a dozen roses. They chatted and laughed for several hours while they drank a bottle of wine.

After dinner John and Kate went up to his apartment. He showed her around and Kate was impressed. The apartment was very neat and clean and it was very spacious. His drums occupied one corner and pictures of days gone by of John and his group sat on tabletops and hung from walls.

The furniture was ultra-modern and the bedroom was spectacular. She figured he spent a lot of time in there. John had a waterbed—a relic from the sixties—but she was game.... Why, she had never slept in a waterbed before.

She heard music in the background and when she turned around John began jamming on his drums. She stood in the middle of the living room and watched as John jammed away. He was quite good—actually, he was great. She enjoyed his performance for a while; and when he stopped she didn't know what to say, so she APPLAUDED.

John reached for a bottle of wine; they drank and drank. One thing led to another and the next thing she knew, John had carried her into the bedroom—right to that great big wonderful waterbed.

He carefully undressed her and kissed every part of her body. His sweet lips tasted like wine. They made mad, passionate love till the sun came up.

On the other side of town, Rob was fast asleep and Annie had been in her bed for hours. As for Brandon, he was wide awake, chatting with Pat in his Park Avenue apartment.

The phone rang.

"Excuse me, Pat," Brandon said as he looked at his watch. "I wonder who would be calling me at this hour." He checked his watch again.

"Hello..."

"Hi, Brandon, this is Ali."

"Hi, Ali." Remembering what Pat had taught him, he vowed to be nice to her.

"I just called to find out what you're doing New Year's Eve. They're having a HUGE party at Elen's house and everybody who is somebody is going to be there. Would you like to go?" Ali couldn't wait for him to answer. This was the tenth time she had called Brandon. She wasn't going to give up. She forgave him so many times because she believed they were meant to be together. She felt Brandon was still grieving over Annie. Ali was patient.

"Hang on, let me check." Brandon muffled the phone with his hand, looked over in Pat's direction and motioned for him to come closer. He spoke softly.

"Pat, Ali wants me to be with her New Year's Eve. They're having a party at Elen's house... Should we go?"

"No," Pat said firmly. "We have too much work to do. My guides have told me you will be reunited with Annie soon; I have to prepare you so you don't mess up."

"Okay, I'll tell her," Brandon agreed quickly.

"Ali, I checked my calendar. I'm so sorry... I have a previous engagement that I can't get out of. I'll see you in a few weeks." Brandon had to say something to appease her.

"Sorry, Brandon. I'll call you in a few days. 'Bye, darling."

"Oh, Ali, say 'hi' to Elen for me. Make my apologies."

"I will. Love you... kiss, kiss..." she said.

Brandon and Pat resumed talking the night away.

"Pat, I've been thinking... This will be the first New Year's Eve that I'll be home—I think I need this." Brandon paced around his apartment. Brandon flashed on ingenious. "I know... New Year's Day I'll do something different."

"What will you do, Brandon?"

"I don't know yet, but I'll think of something."

Pat smiled. "Now you're getting it. Go with the flow. Well, I have to go; I have to write my lecture tonight for tomorrow." Pat reached for his hat and coat. "Brandon, what are you doing for Christmas? I really don't want you to be alone."

"I have some very good friends who've invited me to their house for dinner. Don't worry, I'll be fine. Just knowing I'll be seeing Annie again makes my heart all fuzzy inside."

Pat felt relieved. "See ya New Year's Eve."

It was early morning when Kate made her way home. She tried to sneak into the apartment, but Annie was up and getting ready for her radio show.

"My, my... look what the cat brought in," Annie teased. "And you're still dressed in last night's clothes. What have you been up to?" As if Annie didn't know.

"Annie, I can't talk now. I have to go to sleep; I'm exhausted." Kate turned around and did a double take. "Annie, where are you going at this ungodly hour?" She asked.

"Well, unlike some people, I have to go to work and do my radio show. And I have all these presents for Rob and John for Christmas. I figured I'd put your name on them along with mine and drop them off."

"Sounds good. I have to get some sleep. I hope John is okay. We really had an amazing time." Kate chuckled. "I'll tell you all about it later. Oh, Annie, on your way home see if you can pick up a small Christmas tree; we'll decorate it tonight. And Annie, please understand. I'm so... so... tired. See you later."

Annie made her way to the radio station. John was late. Rob couldn't understand why John hadn't arrived yet; he was concerned.

Annie felt Rob's concern. "Rob, don't worry. I just left Kate—I think they had a good time last night. From what I understand, he'll be here shortly."

Just then in walked John, dragging himself. "Morning... where's the coffee?"

Rob looked at Annie and shook his head. "Where it usually is!" he shouted.

The morning show went by really fast since John was hung over. Annie was quickly approaching her 1000th caller. She needed to save a few callers for the radio show on New Year's Eve.

"Rob, what will you be doing for Christmas?" Annie asked.

"I'm going to spend Christmas with my boys. I have tons of presents for them. And Uncle John will be right with me. Won't you be there with me, John?"

"UH… Yes…"

Annie said, "Thank you, guys, for everything. I'll see you for the New Year's Eve show bright and early. I have to muster up a small Christmas tree. Kate and I will celebrate together. Oh, I almost forgot…here, just a little something from Kate and me for you guys to show our appreciation."

"Thank you. In fact, John and I got you and Kate something for Christmas as well. Here."

John stared. He didn't know what to say—obviously, Rob did this on his own.

"Merry Christmas!" Annie blew her goodbye kisses to all and left. She decided to go shopping and let Kate sleep. She was in search of a small Christmas tree. After several hours, Annie went home with a little tree.

"Good afternoon, Kate. I see you're up and at 'em."

"Coffee…" Kate croaked. She was hung over.

"We need to talk, Kate," Annie said as she fixed a cup of coffee for her bleary-eyed roommate.

"Okay, put the tree over there, sit next to me and we'll talk this one out."

Annie and Kate talked for hours as they decorated the tree. Annie heard all about John and how wonderful he was. Kate felt that he could be the ONE, especially since she made love to him. She knew they would be seeing more of each other.

Kate and Annie spent a wonderful Christmas Eve and Day together. Kate made a turkey with stuffing and cranberry sauce, chestnuts were roasting on the fire, and the eggnog was delicious. They exchanged presents and chatted up a storm as the evening drew to a close.

The rest of the week sped by. Annie did a lot of catching up on things around the apartment. She was into organizing her room and sorting her clothes for Hawaii. Kate stayed busy working while lining up her new photo shoots for next year. The days hurried by. The evenings were hectic with the New Year holiday approaching fast.

From Christmas to New Year's Eve Kate and John were on the phone non-stop. Annie and Rob spoke but once.

After a long day Annie went to bed early.

Now the big crescendo was about to emerge. When Annie awoke that morning, she was getting ready for her New Year's Eve show. She got dressed and waved goodbye to Kate and said, "Well, this is it. This will be my big day. I'll finally reach my 1000th caller," Annie smiled.

"I'll be listening, Annie. Give it everything you got, girl. I'll see you tonight. I can't wait, Annie; this party that Rob and John are throwing is going to be awesome. So hurry home after the show. We can lay out our clothes and decide what to wear." Kate was bubbling over with excitement.

When Annie arrived at the radio station, both boys greeted her with kisses on her cheek. Balloons and streamers were hanging from the wall; there were *Happy New Year* banners congratulating Annie.

Rob was all animated. "Well, this is it, Kid. Are you ready? Are you ready to hit your 1000th caller?"

John jumped into the conversation. "Annie, this is it, girl… this is the BIG ONE… the one you have been waiting for."

Of course, as Annie's guardian angel, I, Gabriel, attended the party—peering down from Heaven, that is. I wouldn't have missed this great event...not for a moment. I observed Annie while she took her…**Last…Calls…**that morning. I noticed how overwhelmed with callers they were. Ah, this was a good thing. There were Tom, Joyce, and Sarah…standing by on the phone.

John pressed the LAST lit button of the phone line.

"Hi, this is John. You will be our last caller. Please hold."

"John… My name is Lenny." He was stuttering and spoke very slowly. "I really need to speak to Annie. It's really important," he said.

"Okay, Lenny, just hold."

Everything was moving so fast, John could barely keep up. The next thing he knew, Rob shouted, "Well, that's a WRAP!"

Rob announced, "It's over. Our Annie will return next year. Oh, by the way, folks, Annie will be in the Hawaiian Islands for a few weeks, taking a long overdue vacation. And thank you folks out there in radio land, for making this all possible. And for making our station Number ONE in the morning." Rob spoke proudly.

John tapped Rob on his left shoulder and whispered in his ear, "Hey, Rob, I have one more caller on the line that needs to talk to Annie."

Rob waved him off and continued with his speech. "**This is Rollover with-Rob-in-the-Morning signing off on 92.3 FM… Happy New Year!**" Rob blew his horn. The music was loud. Streamers were all over the place. Rob handed his earphones to John; he was off the air—for this year, anyway.

John quickly went back to the phone line. "Sorry Lenny; are you still there?"

"Yes."

"Rob ended the show. Annie can't speak to you now; we have utter chaos in this studio. I'm sorry. She'll be back in a few weeks—call her then," John explained apologetically.

"You don't understand, John; this means so much to me," Lenny said, desperation in his voice. Talking to Annie could change everything in my life; I'm now at a fork in the road."

"Sorry, Lenny, Rob is off doing something else now—I can't break away. Please understand…I'm sorry." John hung up the phone. That's all he could do, for Rob was motioning to him to come over.

What Rob didn't know was that Lenny was on his last legs. He was calling from a phone booth near Central Park and was in dire need of help. But how could Rob know? It was just another phone call for Annie.

I, Gabriel, watched and observed and recorded everything that went on that day. Suddenly, my pager went off in Heaven. I had to leave Annie's grand finale; but rest assured, I really didn't think anyone would have missed me. I watched a little longer as they partied on. Then I—PUFF—disappeared.

Annie smiled and said, "Guys, I'm so happy and so sad." She had tears in her eyes. "I can't thank you enough."

Annie turned toward Rob and smiled. "Finally… it's over."

Rob yelled out loud, "1000 souls… saved!"

Rob and John were jumping up and down in the studio. Their joy was unbelievable.

"Annie, are you okay?" they asked.

"Yes, I need just a few minutes. Is that okay, guys?"

"Annie, we more than understand. We'll leave you alone for a little while." Rob patted Annie on her back and said, "You relax a little, darling." Both boys left Annie to herself.

Annie gazed out of her window; she was mesmerized by the falling snow. She watched the snowflakes as they fell ever so gently and covered the ground. She thought about all the good times she had had at the radio station and all the souls that she had helped. Time was speeding up; soon the New Year would begin. This year she had worked incredibly hard to reach her goal of helping so many lost souls on the radio—yet, a part of her soul felt lost. She glanced down at her watch, checking the time—Heaven time, Earth time. As if she were waiting for a miracle—hoping the miracle might be Brandon. No such luck.

It was then John motioned vigorously for Rob to come over to his side of the room, while the party was going on. "Rob, I think we have a slight problem here," he said.

"What is it, John?"

"Well I re-checked the counter of how many people—souls—Annie had helped. The counter is at 999 souls. Rob, that means she hasn't hit her 1000 mark. She NEEDS to help just one more person."

Rob was annoyed, and he explained to John how he felt. "The show is over. We made a big hoopla to our listeners about how Annie helped 1000 souls. Are you trying to make an idiot out of me? And besides, John, what's the difference of ONE… little… tiny soul? Must I remind you that Annie has more than contributed to the world? I don't think it really makes a difference upstairs—999 or 1000, it's all the same, pal. Give the kid a break."

"But Rob, what if you're wrong?" John raised his voice.

"I'm not wrong!" Rob huffed, and turned away abruptly from John; he was fit to be tied. "John, you'd better check that counter one more time, PAL…because Annie HAS hit her 1000 mark."

Rob went back to the party, put his arm around Annie, kissed her on her cheek and congratulated her again. "Aren't you excited?"

"Yes, I am." She smiled. "I can't wait for the real New Year's Eve party tonight," she said.

Annie smiled and thanked Rob and John once again. Unbeknownst to her, she had helped only **999 souls.** John was right.

Rob asked Annie if she needed a ride home. "I just happen to have my car today."

"No, I'm fine," she said.

Annie waved goodbye, and off she went to catch a cab home. During the cab ride, Annie was deep in thought.

Rob also left the station but without saying goodbye to John. He muttered to John, "Later… See you tonight." Rob huffed off.

It was the first time in well over five months that Rob drove to work in his car. He was proud of his old T-Bird. Rob got into his grand car, admiring every inch of it. This car was special; he kept it locked up in his apartment's basement garage most of the time; it was only on rare occasions that he drove.

Rob was on the road for a short while when suddenly he heard and felt an explosion. His car swerved to the left, then to the right. He gripped the wheel of his car to steady it, but nearly hit three people crossing the street. The car came to an abrupt halt.

Rob got out of the car to find out what had happened. "Holy Mother of Mary!" he shouted. His tire was blown to shreds; there was nothing left. Rob was shocked. He looked at his tire again, then looked up at the sky and shouted out loud, "KARMA…!"

Rob couldn't believe what happened. Rob shook his head in disbelief then picked up his cell phone and called Triple A. Rob was in a hurry to make it home; he had to prepare for his party.

When Annie arrived at her apartment, Kate was laying out all of her clothes. Annie and Kate were getting all dolled up for the party. They both were excited. Annie checked her watch constantly; she could hardly wait for the New Year's Eve bash to begin. Soon the year would commence; in her heart she knew this would bring her closer to Brandon.

"Annie, are you ready to go?" Kate called out.

"I'm ready. Let me grab my purse and we're off."

"Annie, I planned to take a taxi this evening—the party could end very late—so do you mind if I don't drive?"

"Not at all, Kate; I agree. I can always take a cab home, anyway." Annie checked her watch one more time. It was 8:45 P.M. "Kate, we'd better hurry; we don't want to be late."

They arrived at Rob's apartment around 9:15 and Rob buzzed them in. John was all decked out. He grabbed Kate and planted a huge kiss on her.

Annie heard a huge POP. "What was that?" she exclaimed.

"That's just me opening some champagne." Rob reached out and handed Annie and Kate each a huge glass of champagne. "Happy New Year, girls!"

Annie looked up at Rob; she noticed how handsome he looked tonight. There was something very special about him—he seemed to have a very special charismatic energy. Maybe it was his cologne...she couldn't put her finger on it.

The apartment was decked out with streamers overhead, balloons in one corner of the room and noisemakers in another, and there were tons of food everywhere—caviar, cheese, crackers. Rob left nothing to chance that evening. Annie was most impressed by the twinkling white lights that lined the patio. She loved Rob's heated patio. The table was set for four and each place setting had noisemakers and glasses for wine. To the left of the patio was a very small Christmas tree glowing under the dim yellow lights. Off in the distance Annie could see all of New York, especially the Empire State Building—SHE was all lit up for the New Year.

Rob motioned to Kate and John to join Annie and him on the patio.

Rob spoke so proudly. "This young lady certainly has made my life wonderful this past year. I think we all have a lot to be grateful for." Rob smiled at Annie.

"Well, John, Kate, Annie, thank you for coming and making the end of my year so perfect." Rob raised his glass and toasted them. Rob moved closer to Annie and put his arm around her.

Annie reached up and kissed Rob on the cheek to thank him.

"John, did you tell Kate how great the radio show was this morning?" Rob asked.

"No, I didn't, Rob, but I will now." John grabbed Kate's hand and took her into the living room. She sat on the couch as John mesmerized her with his story.

When Rob peeked in, they were making out on his couch. Rob didn't want to disturb them; he continued to talk to Annie out on the patio while he checked his watch.

"Annie, it's getting close to that time." Rob was drinking quite heavily; Annie barely touched her drink. He leaned over the patio, checking out all of New York. "Isn't it beautiful out there? I love this town." The time had run away from them. "You know, Annie, I've been thinking…when you come back to the radio in a few weeks, I thought we would have another great promotion for you."

"Rob, that sounds great. I miss the radio already."

John interrupted them. "Rob, I'm turning on the television. Look, you guys, there's Time Square and Dick Clark there getting ready for the countdown. Come on into the living room; let's all watch. Look at all those people—there must be thousands of them. I'm sure glad we're here instead of at Times Square."

Everyone laughed and agreed. John shouted, "There's the ball… it's getting ready to drop! Everyone, pick up your champagne glass. I'll pour…and don't forget your noisemakers." They all gathered around the HDTV. "Here we go; the ball is dropping at Times Square."

Rob, John, Kate, and Annie started their own count-down, shouting in unison, "10, 9, 8, 7, 6, 5, 4, 3, 2, and One…!" As the music played on, "**Happy New Year!**" they shouted.

John reached for Kate and kissed her overpoweringly. He then kissed Annie gently on her lips. Rob reached for Kate and planted a quick kiss on her lips.

He then grabbed Annie's hand and pulled her gently with him to the patio. "Come here, you," he said. Rob put down his drink then touched Annie gently. He bent down slowly. He pulled Annie so close to him their bodies were one. Rob kissed her passionately… then paused for a moment and pulled away. He looked deeply into Annie's eyes and whispered, "Happy New Year, babe."

Annie's whole body felt alive. She felt tingly inside and out. She wanted him. Annie was the one who wanted Rob now, more than ever. Annie reached up toward Rob and, with her hand behind his neck, gently pulled his head toward her lips. She passionately kissed him back and loved every minute of it. In that brief, loving moment they were one.

Suddenly, Annie felt a tug on her blouse. She turned around. "Oh, my!" she exclaimed. Annie abruptly pulled away from Rob, taking several steps backward.

"Gabriel," she whispered, like a child being caught with her hand in the cookie jar.

My voice resonated in her ear. **"NO, NO, NO, ANNIE! THIS... WILL... NOT... HAPPEN!**

"Annie, what are you doing? Annie, this is so wrong!" I scolded her.

Rob couldn't believe what was happening. He saw Annie talking to someone, but it was into thin air. He stepped back to listen to her conversation that he thought she was having with herself.

At one point Rob thought he had had a little too much to drink; but on the other hand, he had never really kissed an angel before. "Time to observe," he thought.

Annie let Rob know that I, Gabriel, was by her side and that I had some issues with her.

"Fine—clue me in," he said sarcastically. "What is he saying, Annie?" Rob waited for Annie to respond.

Annie continued her conversation with me. I had to be harsh. **"Annie, it's not meant to be in this life.** You are supposed to be with Brandon, remember?" Annie nodded sheepishly. "Annie, you are supposed to be with Rob in one of your NEXT lives. And besides, didn't Rob tell you?"

"Tell me what?"

I softened my tone as I explained. "Well, My Dear, while you were doing your radio show this morning, John checked the counter. It turns out that you haven't helped 1000 souls yet.... You only helped 999 souls. Rob was supposed to tell you, and he didn't. Now, go and repeat this to him and see what he has to say for himself."

Rob asked Annie, "What is he saying, Annie?'

Annie was very agitated. She started walking in circles. "Rob, apparently you forgot to tell me something very important today."

"I did?"

"Yes, it seems you forgot a tiny detail, like... I only helped **999** souls instead of 1000. Is this true?"

Rob shrugged. "Well, I didn't think it would matter. Annie, you help someone every day—what's one soul got to do with this?" he asked.

"Rob, every soul in the whole Universe counts; every person affects everyone else. Don't you get it?" Annie was fit to be tied.

"No, not really," Rob said.

I jumped into their conversation and asked Annie to repeat exactly what I was telling her.

Annie did just that. "Gabriel says you really messed up. We were at a fork in the road. I could have ended up with you in this life instead of Brandon, but you really messed up here. It's called KARMA…"

Rob jumped back, remembering the flat tire he had earlier. "Oh, my God, I remember. Annie, is there anything I can do to make this up to you? I didn't mean to hurt you or Gabriel."

I said to Annie, "Repeat this, Annie."

Annie listened obediently and told Rob, "He told me to tell you it's just not meant to be in this life. My God, Rob, the repercussions! We have to remain friends. Because I never got that chance to help that ONE special soul, we can't be together now. That's all there is to it. My mission was to help 1000 souls—not **999**."

John heard some yelling going on and he rushed to the patio. "What's going on here?" Kate was by his side and for the very first time she was able to see me, Gabriel.

"Oh, my God, Annie… it's Gabriel. I see him!" she cried.

John reacted by looking around quickly. "You see WHO, Kate…?"

Rob jumped in and stood by John. "It's Gabriel, the head angel. Apparently, I messed up."

"How?" John asked.

"I never got a chance to tell Annie that she only helped **999** souls."

John became agitated as well. "You never told her?"

"No."

John left the room and dragged Kate with him. He didn't want any part of this.

"Annie, tell Gabriel I'm in love with you. I will do anything, anything just to be with you."

Annie shook her head. Gabriel wants me to tell you that the feelings that you and I feel for each other are from a different life—a past life."

I re-energized and disappeared; I knew Annie would do the right thing.

Rob sat down. "Annie, we have to talk about this. I never understood how important ONE soul is in the whole spectrum of things.

But I do understand now. There must be a way I can make this up to you and Gabriel."

"Rob, please understand, I have very deep feelings for you. More than you will ever know. I also realize I love Brandon—that's why I begged Gabriel to send me back to Earth to begin with."

Annie shook her head from side to side. "I didn't count on falling for you. Now if I don't follow the right path this time, I may never get the chance to come back to Earth and be with you again. Please understand. The love we have continues from past life, to the present life, to our future life. We have to do the right thing in this life, in order for us to be together again."

Rob shook his head. "Annie, tell me **my** future. What will happen to me after you meet Brandon?"

"Rob, you'll be fine. I promise you—I will still work with you on the radio; I'm still going to be there for you. You will meet someone to love you in this life—I promise. Just be my friend; that's all I ask," Annie pleaded.

Rob looked up. This was hard for him. He pretended that everything was all right and smiled just a little.

"I guess you're right, Annie. As John would say, 'get a grip.' Annie, I don't want to lose your friendship; that means more to me than life itself. I love watching you help people. I'll try to understand."

Rob stood up and chuckled a little. "At least I know you'll find me next time around." He bent down and kissed Annie on her cheek and vowed to be her friend forever. "Happy New Year, Annie," he said.

Rob looked at Annie with so much love in his heart. "Annie, you'd better go."

Rob walked into the living room and announced that Annie was catching a cab; he would walk her downstairs.

Kate appeared. "Annie, do you want me to go with you?" she asked.

"No, Kate. I need to be alone. You have fun. See you tomorrow," Annie said.

Annie half-waved as Rob walked her downstairs to catch a cab.

"Annie, I have a lot to think about. Call me tomorrow?" Rob pleaded.

"I will," she promised.

"Annie, I have something to say before you go. I'll wait for you; I don't care how long it takes. I know what love really is now. But more than that, if I lost your friendship and you... I just don't know." He shook his head sadly.

She turned to Rob and placed two fingers over his lips. "Rob, I will always be there for you." She then kissed him lightly.

The cab arrived; she got in and closed the door and waved goodbye.

Rob was determined to make it all up to Annie and fix his karma. On his way back to his apartment, Rob thought to himself that he... MUST... he... WILL... find... A WAY... to be with her.

New Year's Eve was not a total loss for Rob; John and Kate were there to console him. They explained that his friendship with Annie was more important to have, at least for now.

There was a knock on the door. Rob jumped up. "Maybe Annie changed her mind," he exclaimed hopefully. He opened his door. There was a beautiful blue-eyed blonde lingering at his door step. "Excuse me," she purred. "Is this Shelly's apartment?"

"No, I'm sorry. Shelly's apartment is two doors down on the left." Rob pointed, while Kate and John leaned half-way out the door to see who was there.

"Sorry. Happy New Year," she said as she walked down the hall.

"Happy New Year to you." Rob closed the door.

John said loudly, "You see, Rob... you never know... she could be the one."

Rob shrugged off John's comment. "Oh, please, give me a break! It's been a long night; I'm going to hit the sack."

Kate and John stayed the rest of the evening. They ended up in Rob's second bedroom, rocking and rolling the night away.

As Annie made her way home, she felt she could sleep for a hundred years. She thought back over the events of the day and night. First, the party at the radio station; then, the HUGE New Year's Eve party at Rob's apartment. She was all partied out. All she wanted to do was sleep until noon. Soon it would be New Year's Day.

When Annie awoke, Kate was nowhere to be found. Annie got dressed, ate, and went down to the rink at Central Park. She also wanted to see if she could catch Julie at the ice skating rink. When Annie arrived at the rink, she noticed that the ice was crisp and special—within months to come, all would change as the seasons changed. She watched the ice skaters going around the rink while she anxiously looked for Julie.

Annie decided to take a brisk walk for a few minutes. She heard music off in the distance, so she walked in that direction. She spotted a merry-go-round and watched as the children went round and round on bouncing horses. She noticed children eating hot dogs and other children with very sticky hands eating their cotton candy. Annie kept walking until she came upon a small amphitheater—twenty bleachers in a semi-round configuration—where a flutist and violinist played to the delight of passersby. Annie paused to listen—the music was heavenly. After a while, she decided to head back to the ice rink.

As she sat down on a bench, she noticed Julie right beside her, lacing up her skates nice and tight.

Julie looked up in surprise. "Hi, Annie," she said excitedly.

"Hi, Julie; I was hoping I would see you here."

"Did you want to skate with me?" Julie asked.

"Yes, I do," Annie replied and went to get her ice skates.

As they made their way onto the ice, Annie held onto the rail and Julie's hand, taking one cautious step at a time. Annie was still quite clumsy, but she was beginning to get the hang of it. After several times around the rink, she started gliding on the ice. There was a new rhythm to her skating.

Annie's ankles started to buckle a little, but Julie held her hand tightly. Annie was determined to skate well. One, two, three skaters passed Annie, just missing her as she skated through the crowd. The ice was slick and smooth; music played in the background. Annie felt confident. She let go of Julie's hand and glided around the rink several more times.

Finally, Annie felt that sense of freedom she once had as a child. Flashes of her past filled her thoughts with every breath that she could muster as she skated. The world seemed to fade away while she glided on the ice, carefree and not paying attention. She could feel the wind brush up against her rose-colored cheeks. When she looked up, a little snowflake touched her soft skin so gently.

Suddenly, out of nowhere, a gentlemen skating on the same path as Annie collided with her.

Everything happened so fast that they both wobbled rather comically together in a circle. Gravity took over; they fell down together on the ice. Trying to pull herself up, Annie literally fell on top of him.

Annie grabbed onto the left sleeve of his black wool coat while she tried to steady herself. When she finally stood up, she reached out her hand to help him up.

Annie giggled, "I'm sorry."

The gentleman clutched her hand. Upon rising, he couldn't help himself—he stared into her eyes. He brushed the ice lightly off his jacket and hers.

Out of sheer fate, this gentleman had found himself at the Central Park ice skating rink. He had no clue with whom he had collided; but when she spoke, her voice was familiar to him.

"I'm so sorry," he said. "I haven't skated for years; I don't know what possessed me to do this. Are you all right?"

"Yes, I think so." Annie was slightly frazzled.

Julie raced across the ice until she reached them. "Are you both okay?" she asked with some concern. Realizing everyone was all right, Julie made her way back to the bleachers. She giggled to herself, "Yes!"

As the gentleman was busy brushing the ice off Annie's coat, he asked, "Pardon me, haven't we met somewhere before?"

Annie looked up. "No, I don't think so."

"I think so..." he said. "Your voice...I know your voice."

Annie peered into his eyes. Annie saw beyond the veil... It was Brandon—THE LOVE OF HER LIFE. She cleared her throat and wiped a tear from her eye. Annie composed herself. She must not let on that she knew it was HER Brandon—at least, not yet. She had to wait for the timing to be just right.

Annie tried to act surprised. She put on a big smile. "Oh my, you're Brandon Turner, aren't you?"

He nodded. "Yes, I am."

"I'm Annie," she said softly.

At that revelation, Brandon stepped back and gripped the rail to steady himself. He took a deep breath…then, for a moment, he gazed into her beautiful blue eyes. He shook his head just a little.

Annie changed the subject rather quickly. "Brandon, I think my voice sounds familiar to you because I'm on the Roll-over-with-Rob-in-the-Morning show. Maybe you've heard of me?"

He snapped his fingers. "Yes… that's where I heard your voice before. Let me think. You really are that angel on the radio, aren't you? Did you bump into me on purpose?" They both giggled.

"I've been trying to find you for my television show. Can I buy you a cup of coffee?" he asked. Annie nodded.

"I know this wonderful patisserie called Serendipity. Why don't we go there?"

"I love that place," Annie said.

Annie and Brandon sat on the bench, chattering away as they unlaced their ice skates. They walked arm in arm to the taxi stand. Brandon helped Annie into the cab and sat beside her. "Driver, take us to the Serendipity Shop, please, 225 East 60th Street."

"Yes, sir," the driver said.

"Annie, don't you just love the dessert menu at the Serendipity Shop?"

She nodded. "Yes."

Brandon elaborated. "I love their sinful, rich, lush, frozen, hot chocolate. Did you know it was made with fourteen different kinds of chocolate from around the world?"

"No, I didn't," Annie said. "I love their Tiffany style lighting; and, of course, their desserts are yummy."

Annie continued to listen to what Brandon was saying; but then, his voice faded out. She gazed out of the cab window while deep in thought. "My God, I can't believe this is happening to me. I've waited so long. What am I going to do?" Annie was mentally flipping out; she could hardly contain herself. "How do I tell him…that it's me?" She was overwhelmed with memories and the same feelings she once had for Brandon. Her floodgates of emotions were open. What Annie felt cannot be described in an earthly manner.

When they arrived at the Serendipity Shop, they decided to sit in the lit outdoor section that was fully enclosed. They watched the snow fall softly to the ground, layering it in white.

Brandon motioned to the waiter to come to their table. "Oh, Mr. Turner, how can I help you?" the waiter asked.

"We'll have that delightful coffee for two—you know, the one in the huge champagne glass—the frozen hot chocolate with iced cocoa and whipped cream. Oh, and please bring two straws." Brandon knew exactly what he wanted.

"Certainly, Mr. Turner." The waiter scrambled to get the frozen hot chocolate with iced cocoa, stopping only to inform everyone in the kitchen that Brandon Turner was there with an absolutely stunning babe. The kitchen staff peeked around the corner to see.

Brandon couldn't help himself; he stared at Annie. "You're beautiful," he said. He was captivated by the luminous light that Annie radiated.

"Thank you," she said shyly.

They talked for several hours, getting to know each other.

Annie and Brandon Together at Last

Chapter 14

"Annie, do you mind if I tell you my story?" He asked.

"No, not at all," she said.

"This is a bit awkward for me, considering we just met, but there's something about you that is very familiar to me. You remind me of someone that I once loved very deeply. When I look at you, time seems to stand still. And when we collided on the ice, I seemed to be experiencing what you might call *déjà vu* … I don't understand." Brandon shook his head. "Annie, I feel the need to tell you about my personal life and I don't know why. This is crazy… we just met." Brandon was looking for the right words to express himself.

"Brandon, please don't make any apologies. I really want to hear your story," she said.

"Well, where do I start?"

"At the beginning," she said.

"Okay." Brandon moved closer to Annie—he didn't want anyone but her to hear him. He didn't realize, however, that all eyes were on him—his being the HUGE television star that he was.

Brandon looked up and formulated his words carefully. "Here goes…. About a year ago, I had a unique experience with love. Her name was Annie as well. It all started in the spring when we both found ourselves at the book store, picking up the same book at the same time. We laughed. I invited her to this exact same place, Serendipity. She was special, like you."

Brandon paused as the waiter brought their frozen cocoa with two straws.

Annie sipped the drink at the same time Brandon did. She looked up and smiled. "Oh, it's so good," she said. "Go on, Brandon, I'm listening." Annie was intrigued. She wanted to hear Brandon's version of their first meeting and how he envisioned it.

Brandon continued. "Please understand and let me try to explain my feelings for MY Annie." Brandon spoke from his heart. "I loved her like no one else; I lost myself in her. There wasn't a day that went by that I didn't long to be with her. We spent EVERY waking moment together as if it were our last. Our love was beyond any memory that I have ever had. We had passion and deep love; we were one. There were times when we made love that I was breathless. I was swept away by her." Brandon paused for a moment to check Annie's reaction. He didn't want to irk her while he spoke of another woman.

Annie was glued to his every word. While Brandon spoke, she was right with him…remembering.

Brandon continued. "Shortly after we met, I knew Annie was the one. I got down on my knees and begged her to marry me. She said yes. It was the happiest moment in my life. I wasted no time. We set the wedding date almost immediately. Then…well, the rest is history—Annie was shot on our wedding day and she died in my arms." Brandon lowered his head and stared at the floor for a moment.

"I'm so sorry," Annie said, her eyes swollen with tears.

Brandon had to release his feelings; he continued to reminisce. "You know, the funny thing about all this is there isn't a day that goes by that I don't think of her."

He paused before saying softly, "And Annie, when I first laid eyes on you—how shall I put this—? You remind me so much of her."

Annie squirmed; she could hardly contain her emotions. She wanted to shout, "I AM your Annie!" Instead, she took out the gum that she had been chewing while listening to Brandon, rolled it into a ball with her fingertips, then stuck the wadded-up gum under the tabletop. It was a quirk of hers.

Brandon observed what she did and gave an inaudible gasp. "What did you just do?" he asked sharply.

"Oh, I'm sorry; it's a weird quirk of mine—this gum thing." She shook her head. "I won't do it again, I promise."

"Please…do it again," he said.

"Why?"

"Because MY Annie had the same quirk."

At that moment Annie was overcome by the reality of the situation that every human being faces when they get what they want. An intense wave of emotion overpowered her with the love she had for Brandon—she was clearly out of control. On the other hand, Annie also felt the lingering love from Rob.

Before Brandon could say another word, Annie reached across the table and grabbed his hand tightly. She looked straight into his eyes with intense longing and said the words he had been waiting to hear. "Brandon, Remember Me?"

At those words, Brandon recognized her. There wasn't the slightest doubt in his mind. He couldn't help himself—he was the one who was clearly out of control now.

He abruptly got up from the table and grabbed Annie's hand. He said, "We have to get out of here now."

Annie nodded and followed him to the door.

The waiter asked Brandon, "Do you want me to put this on your tab?"

Brandon was clearly in a hurry. "Yeah, yeah…that'll be fine."

Brandon rushed out the door with Annie by his side. Noticing that Annie shook from the cold burst of air that hit them, he wrapped his arms around her and squeezed her tightly. He felt her heart pounding.

Brandon's eyes welled up; his voice quivered as he spoke. "It's really you, Annie." Brandon looked up toward Heaven. "Oh, my God...thank you." He embraced her in his arms. "Annie, this time, I will NEVER let you go...I swear." He kissed her gently, then passionately.

As the snow fell quite heavily and the sounds of the city came back into focus, Brandon hailed a cab.

Annie tugged on Brandon's jacket. "Where are we going?" she whispered.

"Home."

When they reached Brandon's apartment on Park Avenue, they were let in by the doorman and took the elevator to his penthouse suite. Brandon unlocked the door, picked up Annie and carried her through the front door; he kicked the door closed and kissed Annie all the way to the bedroom.

The sensuality of their bodies touching each other was almost too much to bear. Brandon swept Annie away with his emotions. He consumed every inch of her. They were instantly addicted to each other's passion. They made mad, mad, feverish love all night long...till they gently fell asleep in each other's arms.

Annie was still fast asleep when Brandon awoke to the beautiful sunrise. He made a wonderful breakfast for Annie and delivered it to her bedside. He sat on the side of the bed with the breakfast tray in hand and watched adoringly as Annie's eyes opened slowly.

"Good morning, sleepy head."

She kissed him softly on his lips. "Morning."

"Hungry? God, I hope so; I've been preparing this magnificent feast all morning. Here's your coffee."

Annie sat up and reached for the cup of coffee and stared deeply into his eyes.

Brandon's demeanor turned serious. "Annie, how did this all happen? I really need to understand what brought us back together."

Annie explained it all to him. "Brandon, when I died, I went to Heaven. I met with my guardian angel, Gabriel; I pleaded and begged to come back to Earth so I could be with you. Gabriel gave me ONE condition—-I had to help 1000 souls on Earth before we could meet. I ended up on the radio station helping masses of people and one year later—well, here I am."

"Oh, well, that was easy," he chuckled. "I think you left out all the pain and suffering we both went through. You're here to stay this time, aren't you?"

"YES...I AM!" Annie said emphatically.

Brandon explained his willingness to believe her. "You know, about six months ago I wouldn't have bought into any of this, but I met a very gifted young man by the name of Pat Edwards—he's a psychic channel. We became very close and he taught me about spirituality and the other side. Annie, now I believe anything, and everything—and you are my living proof."

"Oh, I've heard of him; he's gifted, I hear," she said.

"Boy, is he!" Brandon exclaimed.

"Annie, I can't let you go. Listen, starting this Monday, my show will be in re-runs for a month. This would be a good time for us to spend every waking moment together. What do you think?"

"Funny thing—I'm off the radio for a few weeks, and my bags are all but packed for Hawaii." Annie smiled coyly. "Would you like to go with me?"

"Hawaii, huh?" He frowned as he gave her suggestion some heavy thought. "I have an idea," he said. Brandon picked up the phone on the nightstand and made a call.

"Hello, Paul, I'll be flying into Hawaii with a lovely lady on Monday. Get the house ready for me, will you? Thanks, Paul."

Annie was perplexed. "House…what house?"

Brandon smiled. "I have a house right on the beach on the North Shore of Oahu. It will be ready for us on Monday.… Okay? I can't think of a more romantic place for us to rekindle our fires, my little angel."

Annie threw her arms around Brandon and hugged him tightly. Just as Brandon was about to succumb to her passion once more, he glanced at his watch. "Holy smokes! It's 3 o'clock; I've got to get ready for my show. Do you want to come with me? I could show you off."

Annie jumped up and got dressed as fast as she could find her clothes. "Brandon, I just realized I've been missing in action for a day; my roommate, Kate, is probably flipping out. I have to get home and straighten out some things. I have to pack and change my airline reservations. My goodness, I have so much to do."

"That's my Annie, my little scatter-brained one that I remember. I tell you what…I'll call downstairs to Howard, my limo driver; I'll have him take you home. You get your things together while I do my show and call me when everything's ironed out. I need a little time to wrap things up as well."

Brandon picked up the phone. "Howard, please take my lady wherever she wants to go. Her name is Annie. She'll be downstairs in a few minutes."

Brandon kissed Annie goodbye. He made sure he had her phone number; then he scrambled to get ready for his show.

Annie collected all her clothes that were scattered around—on the bed, on the chairs, even on the floor. She paused to look at the picture of her that Brandon had on the mantle. She looked very different—yet familiar—in that picture. On her way out, she turned and smiled.

He shouted after her, "I love you!"

"I love you, too," she answered.

Howard, the driver, was waiting for Annie with the stretch limousine at the curb. He gave a slight nod as he opened the door for her. She asked him to take her to Soho; when they arrived, Annie thanked him graciously.

She walked quickly to her apartment. When Annie opened the door, there was Kate waiting for her.

"Oh God, Annie, you're alive...you're okay. Where have you been? Annie, you've been gone a whole day and night. I almost called 911." Kate rambled on. "I have tried every means to get in touch with you. Do you not answer your cell or what? I have so much to tell you."

Annie never had a chance to respond. Kate was furious. "Rob has been calling you all day, asking where you were. Apparently, you told him you would call him. Annie, I can't deal with all this. You left the party in a huff and you disappeared right before our eyes. Please, girl, where have you been?" Kate took a breath and plopped down.

Annie said calmly, "Kate, I found him."

"Him—who?"

Annie paused. "Brandon."

"Oh God... You did? Not now...This is not a good time. How did you find him?" Kate asked.

"I collided with him at the ice skating rink. We went for a cup of coffee and ended up at your favorite place, Serendipity. He talked to me for hours and told me his whole life story, which just happened to include the other Annie, ME."

"Oh boy, what are you going to do now?"

Annie blurted out, "Kate, we have to talk." Annie plopped down in her chair. Kate handed her a small glass of wine.

"Well, let's start with...how did you feel when you were with him?"

"I felt as though time had stood still and we were together again. I looked at Brandon and I studied him. He's so handsome; his salt and pepper hair dips down just a little over his forehead. Kate, I told him who I was—the angel on the radio—then I asked him gently, 'Do You Remember Me?' and he did.

"We rushed out of the restaurant. He held me and loved me all the way to his apartment."

Kate collapsed. "You went to his apartment? You didn't do what I think you did—did you?"

"Kate, we made love all night long. He held me so tight—as if he were scared I might leave him again. He never wanted to let me go, and all those feelings I once had for Brandon came flooding back to me. I loved him once…and I love him still. We found each other. Kate, it's meant to be this time—I know it. Brandon made me breakfast early this morning and we discussed everything. He's going to Hawaii with me. It turns out his show is in reruns for a month and he has a beautiful house on the beach on the North Shore of Hawaii."

Annie stood up; for the first time she took a stand. "Kate, I'm going with him. Gabriel was right."

"Annie, what are you going to do about Rob?" Kate asked.

They were interrupted when the phone rang. Kate grabbed the phone.

"Hello."

A frantic Rob was on the line. "Kate, did you find Annie?"

"Yes, Rob, she's right here." Kate handed the phone to Annie.

"Hi, Rob," Annie said brightly.

"Annie, are you all right? We've been worried sick about you."

"I just got in. I'm sorry I worried everyone. I didn't mean to."

Rob desperately pleaded, "Annie, I really need to see you—just for one hour. I need to talk with you. Please meet me tonight."

Annie had no choice; she needed to talk to Rob as well. "Why don't you come over and we can talk while I pack?"

While hanging up the phone he shouted, "I'm on my way!"

Kate asked, "Annie, what are you going to do about Rob?"

"Tell him."

Kate was uneasy. "I can't stay here while this is going on. I don't want to see a grown man fall apart. You know what, I'll go to John's apartment, and when it's all over, you call me and I'll come home."

Kate grabbed her purse and was out the door in a flash, shaking her head and mumbling to herself.

Annie didn't know where to start packing for Hawaii—her room was in shambles. While she was getting organized, the buzzer rang from downstairs and she buzzed Rob in.

When she opened her door, there was Rob standing in the hall with a dozen red roses. He handed her the roses and said shyly, "Here, these are for you."

Annie smiled at Rob. "Thank you," she said. "I'll put them in water." Annie walked around the house looking for a vase to put the beautiful roses in.

Rob followed her to the bedroom. "I don't mean to be nosy—but where were you?"

"I'll tell you in a little bit. Come sit next to me while I finish organizing my clothes." She patted the bed, motioning for Rob to sit by her.

"Annie, that's tempting—sitting next to you," he said. Rob wanted to hold Annie in his arms and never let her go, but he refrained from doing so.

While Annie was folding and sorting her clothes, she listened as Rob tried to explain himself. "Annie, I'm so sorry for making an IDIOT of myself at the party. The feelings I have for you now are so real. I have a hard time with this future life/past life thing. All I know is what I feel for you now. When I kissed you, I felt something I had NEVER felt before…it was like a memory."

Annie stopped her folding and looked up at him with interest. "Then you and Gabriel told me that that memory was real. If a memory from the past is so real in the present, how do I go on with my life, knowing you ARE the love of my life and knowing I have to wait an eon to be with you?" Rob's eyes pleaded for an answer.

Annie gave him one. "Rob, I understand how you felt, for I felt your love right along with you. You see, that's why people on Earth are not allowed to remember past lives or future lives; for if they did, they would all be really messed up. That's why, when they get to Heaven, they are given a memory shot—so I was told. The memory shot sometimes fades a little, and everyone concerned can see the reality of the situation. One can feel the love inside like no other memory.

Annie looked at Rob and waited for him to respond. She wondered if he understood her words.

Rob reacted cynically. "So what do I do now with all this knowledge? Annie, I hurt inside knowing I can be near you, I can touch you, I can work with you… but I'm not allowed to love you. Knowing you will be with Brandon soon, knowing I CAN'T touch you till another lifetime." Rob raised his voice in frustration. "What do I do?" he shouted.

Annie replied calmly. "Whatever you have felt, I have felt as well. It's sort of a dual memory; you're picking up on my energy, which is causing you to have those deep feelings for me now. In time you won't feel this extreme desire to be with me, but that won't stop you from wanting me. The only difference between you and the next person in love is YOU have all the answers; you were privileged to have a glimpse of who we were. And the poor guy down the street who is madly in love wanders the Earth for eternity knowing he loves someone and never will understand why he can't be with that person. Please believe me, it's a good time for me to go to Hawaii now, for I will be out of sight, and you know what they say—'out of sight, out of mind.'"

Rob retorted, "Annie, I will wait for you. As they say—'absence makes the heart grow fonder.'"

Annie turned around abruptly. "Rob, it's not meant to be right now. I can't go against everything I've been taught by Gabriel and I'm not trying to hurt you. You have to continue on with your life, as I do."

Rob composed himself rather quickly. "How long will you be in Hawaii?"

"Just a few weeks."

Rob said, "By the way, I've been there several times; you'll have a great time. I have an idea; I can work on our new promotion for the show while you're gone."

"Yes, that's an excellent idea."

"Does that please you?" he asked.

"Yes, very much."

Rob felt bubbly. "Okay, Annie, I'll get back to work."

Annie felt more at ease. "Rob, you make the biggest promotion that you can, and when I get back, we'll celebrate. I promise."

That was good enough for Rob right now. He had at least two weeks to think of a way to get her back, he thought. He looked at his watch and said, "Annie, it's getting late; I have to go."

He kissed Annie on her forehead and left the apartment. As Rob left, he mumbled to himself, "I have to get her back—I'll find a way."

He chuckled to himself, thinking out loud, "Unless the memory shot kicks in, then I won't remember this God-awful pain I'm having over her. Oh well." At least he had a big challenge ahead of him, so he thought.

When Rob left, Annie called Kate on her cell.

An anxious Kate asked, "What happened? Is Rob okay? How did you tell him?"

"I didn't tell him about Brandon."

"What—why?"

"Kate, I couldn't; I didn't have the heart— I would have devastated him. I need to wait a while," Annie said.

Kate paused. "Annie, how will you pull this off?" She asked.

"Well, I told him I'd be in Hawaii for a few weeks. I got him going on the new promotion for the radio show—he seemed jazzed. He left my apartment feeling good, knowing he would see me in two weeks. Kate, that's the best I can do for now. I can't HURT him… and besides, he'll never know I'm in Hawaii with Brandon. I'll tell Rob when I get back; it will lessen the blow. He knows I'm coming back to him and the radio. He'll keep himself busy while I'm gone. Get it?"

Kate responded, "I get it, but I don't agree with it. You have to do what you have to do. Annie, I don't understand…an angel like yourself should not mislead anyone, especially Rob—he's been so good to you. I don't want Rob devastated while you're gone. God only knows what he will do!"

Annie replied firmly, "Kate, I'm doing what I have to do. It hurts me to do this to Rob; I feel what he feels." Annie abruptly changed the subject. "By the way, are you coming back to the apartment tonight?"

"No, I want to spend the night with John; I'll see you in the morning before you leave for Hawaii. Love you." Kate hung up. She was slightly disturbed with Annie.

Meanwhile, Brandon had finished his show and the first person he called to meet him at his apartment was Pat Edwards. "Hey, Pat, you were so right—I met my Annie."

Pat raced over to Brandon's apartment as fast as he could. He couldn't wait to hear what Brandon had to say.

While waiting for Pat, Brandon kept busy on the phone getting everything in order; soon he would be leaving for the Islands. He wanted this trip to be special for Annie; he had several surprises up his sleeve for her.

Pat soon arrived. "Hey buddy, come on in and have a seat while I pack," Brandon said.

Pat was perplexed. "Where are you going?"

Brandon grinned shyly. "Hawaii."

"Hawaii? What happened, Brandon? I leave you alone for a day and now you're going to Hawaii."

Brandon explained while he packed. "When you left me here all alone New Year's Day, for some reason I felt a compulsion to go to the ice skating rink in Central Park. I learned to follow my hunches from you. I'll tell you… it wasn't easy, pal… I haven't been skating in years. The next thing I know, I'm skating around the rink and I collide with a beautiful young lady. I pick her up off the ice and offer to buy her a cup of coffee…and to make a long story short, we ended up at Serendipity Shop talking for hours."

Pat listened with rapt interest as Brandon continued his account of the meeting.

"Pat, she was so familiar to me—she was Annie, the angel on Rob's show. I was so happy to finally meet her I couldn't contain myself. In fact, *déjà vu* was a regular occurrence at that point. When we got down to some serious discussions, she said the words I had longed to hear."

Pat interrupted. "What did she say, Brandon?"

"She looked into my eyes and said, 'Do you remember me?' The words resonated in my mind; it was then and only then that I knew she was my Annie…the love of my life."

Brandon implored Pat to explain the situation to him. "Is this really happening? Why is this happening? And what do I do now?"

Pat made himself at home in Brandon's leather chair. He gazed off into the distance; within moments he started to channel information to Brandon.

Brandon sat down as well and focused intently on what Pat had to say.

Pat intoned, "Brandon, the time is drawing near. Yes, we see you have met your Annie…but not without obstacles to come. Gabriel promised Annie that she would reunite with you and he has made good on his promise. We see there is a slight problem in the offing. However, the love that Annie has for you might overcome such obstacles in the future. The love that the two of you have together has overpowered the Universal truths; we find if we separate the two of you now, it could upset karmically all mankind has known. It would create a ripple effect. We have decided as a council to let the two of you play out this love affair without interfering in your lives at this time—which means we will leave you alone for now and let Free Will take its natural course." Pat ended his channeling.

Brandon asked, "Pat, what do they mean?"

Pat responded, "Brandon, I do believe there are several obstacles to come where Annie is concerned. I have no idea what they are and how you will be able to fix them. However, if I understand the spirit world, you'll be tested on how you handle every obstacle that you will encounter."

"This is mind boggling," Brandon said. "Look, Pat, all I know is the love I have for Annie is beyond anything —anyone—can imagine. I swear, she is mine and nobody will take her away from me now...nobody." Brandon was shaking as he resumed packing.

Pat got up, ready to leave. "I understand, buddy. I really feel for you. Well, I'd better be going; I know you'll have a long day tomorrow. Have a great time for me in Hawaii; and if you need me for anything, call. Aloha."

"I will," Brandon said with a wave of his hand as Pat went out the door.

Brandon phoned Annie, and when she answered he asked brightly, "Hello... Did I tell you that I loved you today?"

Annie giggled. "You just did."

"Baby, are you all right? Did you get everything done the way you wanted it? Is my girl packed?"

"Yes, Brandon, I'm all ready to go," she said and giggled again.

"Great! Howard and I will pick you up tomorrow at 10 A.M. I have so many surprises for you; I can't wait to see you. I'm packing now, and I'd better continue or we may never get to Hawaii."

Brandon paused, he then said, "Annie...."

"Yes?"

Brandon felt insecure. "Please tell me this is all real; tell me you will never leave me again—promise."

"Brandon, I promise," she said.

"I love you." He hung up his phone.

Annie held her phone to her chest for just a moment. All the past memories she had with Brandon came flooding back to her now. She sighed and continued to pack until she heard Kate's key in the front door.

She looked at Kate with some surprise. "Hi, Kate, what are you doing home? I thought you were coming back tomorrow."

"I was so tired Annie, all this drama…I had to sleep in my own bed. And besides, I didn't want you leaving without my saying goodbye." Kate grabbed Annie and hugged her tightly. "I'll miss you. I know you are happy. I just wanted to say I'm there for you; whatever you need or want, I will always be there for you, Annie."

Kate held Annie at arms' length and said, "I think we both need to get some sleep; tomorrow is a big day for you."

Early the next day, Kate and Annie busied themselves with last minute chores and details till they heard the buzzer in their living room. "Annie," Kate called, "Brandon is downstairs waiting for you in the limo. Come on, girl, get a move on. I'll help you with your luggage."

When they got down to the street, Kate was mesmerized by what she saw. A huge white stretch limo was parked at the curb, its sun roof open. Brandon held two dozen roses in his hands as he leaned out of the sun roof.

Brandon said proudly, "There's my girl." Howard, the limo driver, opened the door for Annie and took her luggage.

Brandon kissed Annie endearingly. He looked over her shoulder and said, "You must be Kate." Kate nodded in awe.

Annie waved to Kate and said her goodbyes. She and Brandon were off to Hawaii.

Brandon and Annie in Hawaii

Chapter 15

When Annie and Brandon arrived in Honolulu, Hawaii, their senses were titillated by the blue sky and burst of sunshine that peeked through the clouds. The scent of tropical flowers carried on a warm, gentle breeze filled the air and intoxicated her.

They stopped for a moment to absorb the ambience of the island. They watched two Hawaiians sitting under a coconut tree, strumming on their ukuleles, just like the pictures in the travel brochures.

Brandon and Annie were interrupted briefly when a few tourists recognized Brandon. They rushed over to him and said, "Brandon Turner, WOW! Sorry to bother you. Can we have your autograph?"

Brandon smiled and put his arm around Annie. "I'm on vacation," he said, "but I'll be glad to give you an autograph; that's what I do best."

Once his fans were gone, Brandon made sure Annie received an exotic-flower-lei greeting, accompanied by an aloha kiss on her cheek. There wasn't anything he wouldn't do for her.

Their limo was waiting to whisk them off to Brandon's private home on the North Shore of Oahu.

He held Annie close to him in the limo. He asked the driver to take Annie and him on a scenic drive of Oahu, till they reached their destination. Rounding Diamond Head, Annie found the view breathtaking: the ocean was bluer than blue, the waves were pounding the shore, and sailboats skimmed over the waters fringed with whitecaps.

Brandon popped a bottle of champagne as they drove past bronzed surfboarders and bodysurfers challenging the waves. Handing Annie a glass of bubbly, he gazed into her blue eyes and kissed her sweetly on her soft lips. He said tenderly, "Baby, we made it. We're in Hawaii." Their laughter was filled with joy.

Brandon had so many things he wanted to show her on the island. He knew Annie could only be away for two weeks before she had to return to the radio; he was determined to make this trip memorable.

When the limo approached the entrance to Brandon's North Shore home, a security guard nodded and let them into the gated community. Annie couldn't believe her eyes; each home they passed was more beautiful than the ones before. Brandon directed the driver to slow down and the driver turned slowly and carefully into a circular driveway which led to an enormous, beautiful white mansion.

"Here we are, babe; what do you think?"

Annie was overwhelmed. "Brandon, is this it? Is this your home?"

"Yes," he said proudly.

"Oh, my!" Annie couldn't believe her eyes. She stared, spellbound, at the profusion of windows on the building.

As they entered the house, they were greeted by two servants. "Hello, Mr. Turner; so nice to see you again."

Brandon nodded. "Hi, Paul and Nancy. This is Annie; she'll be staying with us. Please take care of her and make sure she gets anything she wants."

Annie smiled and said, "So nice to meet you, Paul and Nancy."

They smiled cordially. Paul said, "Anything you want, Miss Annie, you just let us know. We're at your beck and call."

Paul turned and addressed Brandon. "Mr. Turner, will you be dining in this evening?"

"Yes, we will, Paul. Why don't you fix us some of your magnificent filet of mahi-mahi tonight, and we'll have our dinner on the patio overlooking the ocean while the sun sets."

Paul nodded and he and Nancy left to tend to their chores.

Brandon said cheerily, "Come on, babe, I'll show you the rest of the house."

Annie was astonished; she knew Brandon was wealthy, but she hadn't realized how wealthy he was till now.

She followed him through the house as he described each and every room to her in detail. The house exuded warmth and beauty;

each room was unique and furnished in Hawaiian style, down to the beautiful silk Hawaiian prints. The house was designed solely to bring in the ocean; almost every room had a view. The number of windows was incredible; and Annie wondered who cleaned them, for the servants were well into their fifties and she knew it would be an impossible task for them.

They finally reached the master bedroom. Pink and blue pastels dominated its motif and décor. The room was the size of a house, about 1200 square feet with panoramic ocean views from every corner. The bed was on a built-in pedestal of deep blue marble, reflecting the colors of the ocean.

In the center of the room was a sunken Jacuzzi tub with a massive, spectacular fireplace of rock and koa wood standing right next to it. There was a full kitchen with wet bar; you could cook in the bedroom if you wanted to.

Annie noticed there were mirrors everywhere, including on the ceiling. To the left of the Jacuzzi was a weight room and sauna, with his and her robes hanging on the door. When they opened the sliding glass doors to the lanai, they could hear the waves crashing onto the shore.

Annie and Brandon stepped outside and watched the sky turn from blue to orange as the sun began to set. Annie's eyes widened.

"Oh my goodness, Brandon," she said, "I can't believe what I'm seeing."

"You like?" he asked with a smile.

Annie nodded and said, "Yes, I like. Brandon, this room is warm and beautiful; I never want to leave."

"That's the general idea." Brandon's smile grew broader.

"Brandon, all this—I'm not used to this kind of treatment. This is so overwhelming. I'm used to a one-bedroom apartment without the frills," she said.

Brandon sat next to Annie. "Annie, it's only money; I have millions. This is just one of my homes, but this home is special. I love the ocean, and when I retire I want to spend the rest of my life here loving you. Annie, when I lost you, I had nothing." Brandon reached over and kissed Annie on her lips softly. "Now you're back and I have everything. I have you, Annie."

At that moment Nancy and Paul interrupted. "Excuse us, sir. Dinner is ready to be served."

"Thank you, Paul and Nancy. Why don't you set up everything on the patio for our dinner? What perfect timing; the sun is beginning to set. Babe, have a seat. It's so beautiful this time of year; I love the winters in Hawaii."

As Nancy and Paul poured the wine and served them dinner, Brandon and Annie talked endlessly while watching the sunset. Brandon called it "Magic Time in Hawaii."

He commented to Annie how fragile she seemed to him; he compared her to a glass of fine wine. He said that from the very first time he met her he had always wanted to nurture her.

The hours passed quickly and much wine was absorbed. Brandon seemed to stare right through Annie, his eyes wild with desire. Finally, he spoke. "Annie, do you want to try out the Jacuzzi?" he asked.

Annie was a light drinker, as all angels are—they only drink on special occasions. The wine was beginning to affect her senses. "Yes, of course." Annie had a coy smile on her face.

They made their way from the patio, holding onto the wine and giggling all the way. They watched and waited for the tub to fill. Brandon poured some wild Hawaiian fragrance into the spa that bubbled endlessly.

Brandon reached over to Annie and unbuttoned her blouse slowly, button by button. He undressed every part of her tenderly, kissing each part sensually as he bared it; then, he stared hungrily at Annie. Brandon had waited well over a year to be in the islands with Annie; it seemed a lifetime, never knowing if he would ever see her again. Now, the anticipation of what could be was irresistible. He peeled off his clothes, threw them on the floor, and stepped into the Jacuzzi beside Annie.

He sighed. "Ah, this is so warm and refreshing." He laid his head back and relaxed as he watched the lit candles on the Jacuzzi's rim flicker to the beat of the mellow Hawaiian music. All his senses were alive; he could feel, touch and taste for the want and desire of her.

Brandon slowly motioned for Annie to sit next to him in the Jacuzzi. She slid over with a glass of wine in one hand and kissed him passionately.

He said, "I love you. Are you happy, now?"

Annie was lost for words; she nodded and smiled shyly.

Brandon said, "Annie, tomorrow I want to show you a little of Hawaii; then, I want to take you shopping for clothes. How does that sound?"

"I'm not into clothes that much, but I must confess I really don't have the proper attire for the islands." She giggled, and then said with excitement in her voice, "Okay!"

"Annie, you're a representative of me. You have to look good and act like a lady at all times, a lady with class. I want to see you wearing the finest clothes that money can buy. Do you understand? I know of a couple of places; I want to check out one in particular." He reached over and tweaked her nose.

"Yes, I understand," she said happily.

"Annie, we have less than two weeks together; I want to spend every waking moment with you."

Sadness came over her. "Brandon, please, let's not talk about leaving the islands yet."

Brandon stepped out of the tub and mumbled, "Okay." He reached for his royal blue robe and held it wide open, then motioned for her to come to him. He wrapped the robe around Annie and carried her in his arms from the tub to the bed. He slowly opened the robe and kissed her ears, her neck, her breasts—every part of her body—and he fondled her gently but firmly.

She could feel the cold, smooth satin sheets caressing her body as they made love, their bodies intertwining as one. She loved him, and she made love to him.

Making love to Brandon was like making love in no other lifetime that she could remember. Annie looked at Brandon and said, **"Look at me. I never want to leave you again."** They embraced each other and became one again. Finally, exhilarated but exhausted, they drifted off to sleep.

The next morning Brandon ordered breakfast for two, and Annie and he ate on the patio where they watched the ocean pumping with two-to three-foot waves. They were captivated by the sea.

"Annie, when we finish breakfast, I want to take you to a friend's private showing of unique and sensual swim and lounge wear. I swear it's the top of the line for Hawaii. Her name is Iwalani and her clothing line is called Pualani Hawaii; it is classy and first rate. She'll fit you and give you all the attention you will ever need. She gets her fabric from France, and I swear, babe, you can feel the difference."

Annie immediately got up and left the patio, prompting Brandon to call after her, "Where are you going?"

Annie laughed. "I'm getting dressed; I'll be ready in ten minutes."

Brandon picked up the phone. "Paul, please get my car ready; you know the one, my Classic Mercedes 450 SL convertible, and please bring it around to the front; I want to drive Annie somewhere very special."

"Yes, sir."

Off they went. Brandon drove around the island with the top down, and Annie's blonde hair shimmered in the sun and blew wildly in the wind. The funny thing about Brandon was that when he was with Annie he felt magnificent; she made him forget that he was a World Famous Star. Being a famous star was the one thing Annie never had to worry about. Rob always kept her in tight wraps; no one knew what she looked like; her face was never exposed, though her voice was memorable.

Brandon stopped the car at Iwalani's studio at Diamond Head. Brandon knocked on the door once, and while he and Annie waited for Iwalani to answer, he told Annie a little about her. "Iwalani is beautiful. She has long blonde hair; her tan, thin body was toned from surfing. She was also a stunt lady for water sports on the island; that was how I met her. We go back many years together; a few friends and I helped her put her line together. Oh, by the way, Annie, we call her Iwa for short."

Iwalani opened her door with a smile that broadened into a huge grin at the sight of Brandon. She jumped up and down with excitement. "Brandon, it's you! It's you!" She hugged him to pieces. Out of the corner of her eye, she noticed the pretty blonde lady by his side. Iwa thought this was most unusual for Brandon; he had never brought anyone to her studio before; she must be special.

"Iwa, I want you to meet the love of my life, Annie," he said.

Annie extended her hand to shake Iwalani's hand. "Hi, Iwa, Brandon has told me so much about you. I feel like I know you already."

Iwa smiled.

She walked them inside her studio and sized Annie up and down. "Let's see, Brandon, Annie must be a size 6—if that much. I have something special for her. Iwa handed her several suits and pants to try on.

While Annie was trying on everything, Iwa turned to Brandon and said, "She's special, Brandon. How did you meet her?"

"It's a long story, darling; remind me to tell you some day. But she is the one."

"I can see that. Brandon, she reminds me of your other Annie, and this one's name is Annie as well. How weird is that?"

"You got it."

Annie walked out and modeled each of the outfits that Iwa had selected for her. She looked like a million dollars. "We'll take them all," Brandon shouted.

Iwa's phone began ringing incessantly as Brandon and Annie browsed around the studio. Iwa was on the phone and packing the clothes for Annie to take home, all at the same time.

Brandon didn't want to interrupt her; he waved goodbye.

She put the caller on hold. "Brandon, where you going?" She asked.

"We're going to Duke's in Waikiki; I want Annie to experience the world famous restaurant on Kalakaua Avenue. We'll have a bite to eat on the beach; besides, you're busy." Brandon walked over and kissed Iwalani. "I love you, darling. I'll keep in touch with you. Mahalo," he said.

Annie was intrigued by this restaurant. On their way to Waikiki, she said, "Brandon, tell me about Duke's."

"Duke's is named after Duke Kahanamoku, a world-class athlete from Hawaii. He was pure Hawaiian and a simple man who always knew where he came from. He loved the islands. Duke's Restaurant is known for its stunning ocean views. The food is delicious, so that's where I'm taking you."

The parking valet at Duke's opened the door for Annie, and she and Brandon walked hand and hand into the restaurant.

"Good afternoon," the waiter said. Mr. Turner, it's so nice to see you again. How's the show going?"

"Great, Hoku. I'm on vacation with my lady Annie."

Hoku nodded. "I have your regular booth by the ocean; follow me. Hoku seated them and handed them menus.

Brandon ordered two exotic tropical drinks. He reached over the table and squeezed Annie's hand and smiled.

Annie asked Brandon to order whatever he wanted for the both of them. "This is your special place," she said.

Brandon was so immersed in conversation with Annie that he failed to notice the paparazzi sitting at the next table; little did he know what would happen next.

Within moments the press were snapping pictures of Brandon and Annie; they were all over the place. Brandon lost it; he jumped up from the table and put his hands in front of every camera. The owner of the restaurant and his staff ran as fast as they could to help Brandon. Nothing seemed to work. So Brandon grabbed Annie's hand and ran for the door, hiding Annie's face as best he could. His car was waiting for him at the entrance since Hoku had anticipated that Brandon would be leaving in a huff. They jumped into his car and squealed away from the restaurant.

Brandon was livid. "I can't believe this happened; I thought I was safe in Hawaii. Annie, this has never happened here before." He shook his head in disgust.

"Brandon, calm down. It's going to be okay," she said.

"Annie, why did this happen? Why?"

"Brandon, you said it yourself—when you're with me, you forget about the world. Brandon, you are the world; you have so many fans; they love you."

"Annie, you don't understand; these paparazzi are vicious. I can't even imagine on which talk show we'll end up—CNN, Inside Edition, or Entertainment Tonight. Pick one and you'll see your face and mine plastered all over the place, not to mention in *The Enquirer*. I tried to hide you, but…I just don't know. Annie, I value my privacy, and these maniacs are all out for a lousy buck. They love to ruin people's lives, but not this time; I won't allow it."

Brandon headed back to his house; it was safe there. When they arrived, he asked Paul to pour him a stiff drink. Several hours later, Brandon calmed down several notches. Annie cuddled up to him on the couch as he flipped through the television channels.

Sure enough, Brandon was right. He happened upon Entertainment Tonight. He pointed at the television. "Annie, look." He turned up the volume. "Listen," he said.

"This is Entertainment tonight, and what television star is hanging out in Hawaii? And who is that gorgeous blonde in his arms?" Pictures of Brandon flashed all over the screen; every channel had an item. He began to seethe.

Annie grabbed the remote from Brandon and turned off the television. She said, "Brandon, this is Hawaii; we have the sun, the sand, and the sea right here at your home. If we have to, we'll never leave here for two whole weeks. Let's take a walk on the beach." Annie took Brandon's hand and said, "Follow me." Hand in hand they strolled along the waters washing up on the white sand beach.

Meanwhile, several thousand miles away in New York City, Rob was in his apartment, chatting with John; and, as usual, the television was turned on, although neither one paid much attention to it. But then, John noticed Brandon Turner on the screen, then Annie.

"Rob, turn around!" he shouted. "Look at the TV; it's Annie!"

Rob walked over to the television as if he were in a trance. "What is she doing in Hawaii with Brandon? I can't believe this, John," he uttered hoarsely and slammed his fist into a pillow.

"Calm down, Rob. You knew Annie was going to Hawaii, and you also knew Annie was about to meet Brandon, so why are you acting so crazy?"

"John, I was with her when she was leaving for Hawaii. I was in her apartment with her, and she never told me she was going to Hawaii with Brandon. Do me a favor; call Kate and see what she has to say about this."

John speed-dialed Kate's number. He explained what had happened and asked if she knew anything. He switched on the speaker phone so Rob could hear Kate's response.

She said, "I knew something like this was going to happen. I warned Annie, John. I told her what she was doing was wrong; she should have at least explained to Rob about Brandon. I'm sorry, honey; I tried. Tell Rob how sorry I am. She didn't want to hurt him; she felt nobody would find out about her trip."

"Kate, she was wrong."

"I know."

"I'll talk to you later." John hung up and looked at Rob. "Rob, you heard. What can I say?"

Rob was disgusted with Annie. "It's okay, John. I should have known she and Brandon would find each other. It's me who was stupid for believing we could ever be together. I thought I could alter her future. Well, John, it will be back to business as usual with Annie when she comes back. I'll just visualize the dollar signs." They continued their conversation.

Back in Hawaii, Annie and Brandon were enjoying their leisure together. Brandon nuzzled Annie and said, "You know, you're right. Maybe it's time the press gets to know you. I'm not going to stop my life because of the paparazzi. I know...tomorrow I'll hire a plane and we'll go to the island of Kauai. Babe, you will love it. I'll take you to a very special place of mine."

Annie was happy that Brandon had recovered. She would go with him wherever he wanted to take her. Exhausted, they fell asleep in each other's arms. When they awoke, Brandon asked Paul to find a pilot to fly them to Kauai.

Once the arrangements were made, Brandon and Annie made a mad dash for the Honolulu airport where a private plane was waiting to take them to the Lihue airport in Kauai.

"Welcome aboard," the pilot said. "Good morning, Mr. Turner; hello, Miss. Nice day for flying."

Brandon and Annie settled into their seats for their short.trip to Kauai. Annie pressed her nose against the plane's window to better see the disappearing shores of Oahu and the approaching green of the Garden Isle.

Upon landing, Brandon asked the pilot to wait for them, as they would be back in a few hours after their short visit. "I'll see you here about 4 o'clock," Brandon said.

"Yes sir, I'll be waiting," the pilot said. "Would you like to go back to Honolulu? I need to file my flight plan."

Brandon replied, "No, we'll be going to Maui."

"Yes, Sir."

Annie turned to Brandon. "Where are we going?"

"Annie, I have some very special friends I'd like you to meet on this island; this will be right up your alley," he said. Brandon hailed a cab.

"Aloha, where to?" the cab driver asked.

"Kauai's Hindu Monastery."

Annie turned toward Brandon and smiled. "Brandon, I can't believe you're taking me to a monastery. I've never been to one, you know. I've always wanted to do something like this." Annie reached over and kissed Brandon on his lips.

It was only a few short miles till they reached the monastery. As Brandon tipped the driver, a sense of peace came over him; for the first time in a long time he felt safe. Brandon and Annie removed their shoes, which was the custom in the islands, and walked barefoot along the dirt and rock path, taking in the overwhelming beauty around them—a small waterfall, trees shimmering in the sunlight, island wind chimes sounding as if fairies were dancing among them.

At the arched entrance they could hear Hindu prayers being said throughout the temple. Upon entering, Annie noticed a HUGE crystal. She turned to Brandon and whispered, so as not to disturb anyone, "What is the meaning of this crystal?"

When Annie looked up, a rather tall, slender gentleman wearing an orange robe approached her and Brandon. His long whitish-gray hair was tied back in a ponytail, and his eyes were piercingly blue.

He gave a little bow to Annie and explained, "The crystal in our temple collects prayers. When people pray, the crystal will absorb the negativity. We have many customs in our monastery." The gentleman turned toward Brandon and smiled. "Hello, my friend; it's nice to see you again. It's been a while, Brandon," he said.

Brandon introduced Annie to his long time friend Ceyon. "Annie, Ceyon and I go back at least twenty years. I used to come here to get away from the world. Ceyon would protect me and nurture me, and he took away all my pain. They say when you come to visit this monastery you will receive many blessings. And thanks to Ceyon, I have." Brandon turned and bowed to Ceyon. He couldn't thank him enough.

Ceyon asked Annie and Brandon to follow him; he wanted to show them the grounds of the temple and how much progress they had made. Ceyon pointed out to the left a valley with sacred pools and waterfalls which very few individuals are privileged to see. Annie was in awe; she couldn't believe the beauty of the temple and its surroundings. There were no words that needed to be said; Annie absorbed all the nurturing energy and she felt the tears and laughter of the thousands of people who came to visit the temple.

Ceyon pointed to the new temple. "Each stone was brought here from India and blessed." The temple was massive and beautiful; each stone was hand-carved. Ceyon drove them around the grounds by cart for almost an hour, explaining every detail about the monastery.

They heard three bells ring in succession; it was time for lunch. "Would you be kind enough to join us for lunch?" Ceyon asked.

"Yes, we would; mahalo, Ceyon."

As they lingered over lunch for an hour or so, it was Ceyon's turn to observe Annie.

Ceyon stared at Brandon and then quietly spoke. "Brandon, this young lady is special. She shimmers with light. She is not from this world."

Brandon was taken aback. How could he know Annie was not from here? Why could he see what everyone else could not? "Ceyon, how do you know this?"

"My thoughts are clear," Ceyon replied. "I meditate at a very high frequency; I can see the goodness in people, and the evil. Annie is special; she helps many. This is her destiny; this is why she is here in this lifetime. The love she has for you is very deep, Brandon. With this love the both of you can move mountains together—please remember what I have told you." This one sentence was very important to Ceyon.

The hours passed quickly and the visit to the monastery had been enlightening, to say the least.

It was time for Annie and Brandon to leave, for the monks retired early. They both thanked Ceyon for all his knowledge, and Ceyon provided a ride back to the airport for them.

When Annie and Brandon arrived at the airport, it was almost 4 o'clock and the pilot was waiting for them. They were on their way to Maui. Brandon had a wonderful hideaway there; he had access to a friend's small cabin on the slopes of Haleakala Crater. This was a very special place for him; it was his retreat from the world.

Haleakala sits high above the clouds on Maui—over 10,000 feet above sea level. Annie would be as close to Heaven on Earth as she could wish.

When they landed on Maui, there was a driver waiting for them. "Thank God for cell phones," Brandon thought. The driver took them to a small, quiet place to eat before making the long drive to heaven, Haleakala. As they drove high up the mountain, they could see the setting sun dipping into a golden ocean.

Annie sat in awe of this entire day. First Kauai, then Maui—what more could anyone ask for?

They reached the cabin in the sky, which was on ten acres of property with a panoramic view of the island's West Maui Mountains. Brandon reached above the door ledge to get the key. Once inside, Brandon showed Annie around the cabin; then, he lit a fire in the fireplace, laid out several blankets and pillows on the floor next to the fireplace and motioned for her to sit next to him.

"Babe, it's been a long day," he said.

Annie nodded. She was tired. She laid her head on the pillow and was slowly drifting off to sleep when Brandon reached for her under the blanket. Her breathing became heavy. He took off his shirt and slowly unbuttoned her blouse. He lay on his side next to her, feeling every inch of her breasts with his hands. Her lips parted; she could feel the warmth of his tongue. They made love and cuddled in each other's arms for hours, till they fell fast asleep.

Early the next morning after breakfast they went hiking along the Crater; they were like two children exploring the island. When the high altitude began to affect them, they sat down on a large rock overlooking the Crater to catch their breath and take in the beautiful view of cinder cones and rare silversword plants.

They had been in the islands for almost two weeks; soon they would be heading back to New York. They still had a little time left; Brandon would make every moment count.

The flight back to Oahu was smooth and quick and they soon arrived at Brandon's North Shore home. Brandon was happy to be in his own home; he could relax in this place like in no other. Paul greeted them once again and asked Brandon what time they wanted to have dinner.

Brandon replied, "As soon as the sun begins to set."

While dinner was being prepared, Annie and Brandon took a nice, long warm shower together. He held her up against the tiles, loving her like at no other time. He stepped out of the shower first and grabbed a huge, fluffy towel to dry himself off; he then dried her off. He reached for a robe and wrapped it around Annie. He whisked her up and carried her to the bed, just before the sun was beginning to set.

They made love one more time before they heard Paul saying, "Dinner is served." Annie and Brandon chuckled in bed out loud. Brandon put his hand over Annie's mouth. "Don't," he giggled. "Don't let him hear you laughing." Brandon laughed, hoping Paul had not heard them making love.

"Thank you, Paul; we'll be right there," he said. His voice was higher pitched than usual.

Annie and Brandon went to dinner dressed appropriately; they wore matching robes out on the lanai and watched the sun set as they ate. They could hear the crashing of the surf and they could see the ocean shimmer in the glow of the full moon as it rose above them.

"Brandon, after we eat, can we take a walk along the ocean? The moonlight is simply beautiful," Annie said.

And they did just that. After dinner Annie put on her island wear, a bra top and sarong, and Brandon wore an aloha-print shirt. Together they walked hand in hand along the beach, barefoot in the sand.

Annie and Brandon talked and walked for about an hour; they had so much to say to each other. They spoke of their trips, the monks on Kauai, the Crater on Maui, and went into detail about their adventures.

Annie stopped briefly and turned toward the ocean. She stared at the full moon as it reflected across the water. She was wearing the pretty pikaki lei that Brandon had given her earlier that evening.

"Annie," he said.

She turned to face him, "Yes?"

"There is an old custom in the islands." He reached over and took off her lei and tossed it playfully into the ocean. Brandon explained, "If your lei floats back to you, it means the islands are calling you home and you'll return to the islands again."

Brandon and Annie watched excitedly as the lei washed over several waves and it was taken farther out to sea. Suddenly, a huge wave collided with Annie's lei, and the lei slowly made its way back to shore.

Brandon picked up the lei and returned it to Annie; he placed it around her neck and smiled. He couldn't take his eyes off her. She was surrounded by a luminous light that glowed under the moonlight. The light almost blinded him. Brandon reached for Annie's hand and said the words he never thought he would ever say again.

He held her hands together as if in prayer; he looked deeply into her eyes. "Annie, marry me."

Annie threw her arms around Brandon. Tears floated down her cheeks as she whispered, "Yes."

He held her tightly. "I never want to leave you, and I never want you to leave me ever again." Brandon had tears in his eyes now. They embraced each other and kissed. He held her hand and they took a long walk down the beach. No words were said.

They made their way back to the house and Brandon asked Annie to have a seat on the lanai. He returned shortly with a bottle of champagne to toast their upcoming wedding.

As Brandon poured the champagne into her glass, he said, "Annie, I have a favor to ask of you."

"Yes?"

"I would love to get married here in the islands, but we've run out of time. Let's get married in New York next week, where we collided into each other at Central Park."

"Brandon, you are so romantic," she sighed.

"We could have a small wedding, just a few of your friends and mine; that way the press won't be on to us. We could come back here and honeymoon. I'm sure Rob would give you a few weeks off, wouldn't he?"

Annie frowned. "That's a tough one. When I return to New York, he has this big promotion all lined up. I really don't know what he will say or do."

"We'll cross that bridge when we come to it. I'm sure Kate will help you get the wedding together; I mean, a real simple wedding with a preacher and just a few close friends. Get it?"

"Yes I do, Brandon."

Brandon squeezed her hand. "That's my girl. Annie, one more thing. While we're here in the islands, I want to stand under the moonlight with you now; there is something I want to say to you."

"Okay, what could top this?" she said.

Annie followed Brandon down the path that led to the beach. The path was paved with white sandstone tiles that shimmered with the lights from Japanese and Hawaiian lanterns that lined the path to the ocean.

Under the moonlight, Brandon held Annie's hands. *"Annie, you are the love of my life, from here to eternity; I can't imagine a lifetime without you, nor do I ever want to. You are my life, my breath and my love. I thank God that you were returned to me, and with that gift from Heaven I promise to take care of you for the rest of our lives. I love you, Annie."*

Annie responded with *"Brandon, I've searched a lifetime to find you again; without you, my life is empty. I've never been happier spending the time with you in the islands; it's been a dream come true, My Love. I promise to love and cherish you for the rest of our lives. I love you, Brandon, always and forever."*

Tomorrow evening they would be back in New York City where reality would set in. So, Brandon and Annie recited their spiritual wedding vows to each other on the Island of Oahu, at the North Shore. Brandon was moved by the ocean and the moonlight. Hawaii was where they left their imprint in the sand forever.

New York City Bound

Chapter 16

Annie and Brandon just barely made their evening flight from Honolulu to La Guardia Airport in New York City. As the plane took off from the reef runway and climbed high above the ocean, they waved goodbye to the beautiful Honolulu city lights. Tears ran down Annie's face; she held onto Brandon's hand tightly and laid her head on his shoulder. She sobbed, "Brandon, I don't want to leave."

He smiled and wiped away her tears with his handkerchief. "I know, babe, but all good things must come to an end. I promise you, we'll come back real soon; we'll spend our honeymoon in the islands." Annie managed a smile and dabbed at her misty eyes with a tissue.

Exhausted from their whirlwind two weeks in Hawaii, they soon drifted off to sleep. Some ten hours later, they landed at La Guardia; Brandon's limo was waiting for them at the airport.

At 7 A.M., New York City was alive and vibrant. Impatient taxi drivers were honking their horns, impatient ambulances with sirens screaming were streaking past cars too slow to move aside, and impatient people were shouting at anyone within earshot—culture shock, to say the least.

Brandon asked Howard, his limo driver, to take them to Annie's apartment in Soho; he wanted to drop her off first.

"Annie, I have so much to take care of at the studio, and you need to hook up with Kate to help you get the dress you want. I'll pay for everything. I'll have my confidante Rose arrange for a minister and flowers and all the goodies. Now remember, I only want a few of our friends at our wedding; and I don't want the press nosing around, so tell Rob to keep this on the QT. I want our wedding to go off without a hitch."

Annie was still in her Hawaiian mode; Brandon seemed to be talking a mile a minute to her. "Don't worry, honey; we both need a few days to catch up on things," she said.

The limo stopped at Annie's apartment; Brandon kissed her goodbye and said he would call her later that evening.

Annie felt lost without Brandon, but she knew he had business to take care of, and so did she. Sighing, she unlocked the door to her apartment.

Kate jumped up when she heard the door opening, and ran to the door. When she realized it was Annie, she threw her arms around her. "You're back! What a tan you have! I can't believe it," she exclaimed. "Annie, I have some time before I have to do a shoot; tell me everything. I'll help you unpack." Kate grabbed a cup of coffee; she was ready to hear Annie's story.

Annie was overwhelmed with the fast pace of life at the moment; she was still on Hawaiian time and tried to compose herself as she spoke. "Kate, it was awesome; there aren't enough words in the English language to describe the beauty of our trip."

Annie began to unpack. "Brandon was so romantic. We stayed at his house on the beach on the North Shore of Oahu; he bought me clothes; and we went to Kauai and met with monks and visited a monastery. We went to Maui and went to Haleakala Crater; it was amazing. Time went by so quickly."

Kate noticed that Annie was a bit fidgety. "Annie, sit down for a moment; stop unpacking. What are you leaving out?"

Annie ignored her and continued to unpack.

Noticing this, Kate nonchalantly said, "Rob and John saw you on television with Brandon last week."

Annie whirled around and stared at Kate. She plopped down in a chair. "Oh, my God, that wasn't supposed to happen," she cried.

Kate replied, "Well, it did."

Annie was slightly agitated, to say the least. "What did he say?"

"I don't know; all I do know is he was shocked. I think he's probably okay by now. You really need to call him."

Annie finally told Kate what she had been holding back; her words tumbled out in a rush. "Kate, Brandon asked me to marry him on Saturday, and I said yes. I really need you right now to help me pull this off."

Kate wasn't the least bit surprised. "Annie, it finally happened. Gabriel is making good on his promise to you. That means there's hope for me and John. I'm so excited. How can I help you?"

"Brandon wants us to get married Saturday at Central Park by the ice skating rink. He wants a small wedding, just a few friends. Kate, he doesn't want the press to know; he doesn't want anyone to know. We already said our vows to each other in Hawaii, so this is just a formality. Then we plan to go back to Hawaii for our honeymoon. He asked me to ask you if you would help us."

Kate clapped her hands in glee. "Annie, I'm so happy for you. I'm free tomorrow; we'll go shopping. I'll arrange everything with Brandon; you won't have to do anything—I know how frazzled you get."

Annie gave her a great big hug. "Thank you so much, Kate."

Kate checked her watch; she would be late for her shoot if she didn't leave now. "See you later. So great to have you back home, little angel. I love you. I've got to run." Kate bolted out the door.

Annie finished unpacking and checked the time; it was just about 11 A.M. She knew Rob would be off his show soon and she decided to call him.

"Hello," he said, figuring it was Kate calling from her home.

"Hi, Rob; it's me, Annie. I'm back from Hawaii."

There was a long pause on the phone. Rob was hurt; Annie could hear it in his voice. "Hi, Annie, what can I do for you?" He asked.

"Rob, we need to talk. Can I meet you somewhere for lunch?"

"Well, I guess. I have to move some things around first. Meet me at noon at the Second Avenue Deli, our regular booth."

"Okay." Annie didn't know exactly how she was going to handle this situation, but she was going to give it her all. She hailed a cab and arrived at the Deli at 11:30; she needed time to compose herself.

When Rob walked into the Deli just before noon, Annie, who was now totally calm, was surprisingly happy to see him.

"Hello," he said, as if greeting an old friend. Rob pretended to be jolly. "My, what a tan you have; Hawaii agreed with you, I see. So what did you want to talk about?"

Annie reached for his hand. "Rob, Kate told me that you saw Brandon and me on television; I'm so sorry you found out that way. You have to understand I never meant to hurt you. I mean, this all happened so fast I didn't know how to tell you without hurting you."

Rob lowered his head and said quietly, "Annie, you really did hurt me." Before a guilt-stricken Annie could react, he said cheerfully, "But I accept your apology. I had a lot of time to think. I was out of line; I knew you were meant to be with Brandon in this life. What was I thinking?"

Annie giggled and became her old self. "Rob, I'm so happy. Now I have my friend back—you."

"Yes, you do. So, when are you coming back to work?" he asked.

"Now, don't kill me…I'm going to say this real fast, so you won't go crazy on me," she said.

"What are you talking about?"

"Rob, I'm getting married this Saturday to Brandon, and I want you to give me away."

Rob's voice elevated to a new height. "Are you crazy? You're getting married! I have a million-dollar promotion going on, which just happens to include you, and you want me to give you away? Why don't you just kill me now; why wait, Annie?"

Annie grabbed his hands and pleaded, "Rob, please, you know I'll do anything in the world for you; just do this one thing for me. I'll make you millions and make sure you get the ratings you've always wanted. I promise."

Rob perked up. "Millions, huh? Okay, you got me where it hurts; you said the magic words: Ratings and Millions."

Rob turned serious. "Annie, you know I'll do anything and everything for you. You've been my shining light and my special emotional lover. We've been through a lot together this year. I know you're supposed to be with Brandon—I even like the guy, a little—so just let me know where the wedding will take place; I will be honored to give you away." Rob took Annie's hand and kissed it tenderly.

He stood up abruptly. "Annie, I've got to get back to work; I've got to bolt. Give me a call with all the details."

"I will, Rob. Thanks." Annie nursed her cup of hot coffee; it was too cold outside to leave now.

The snow was falling when Rob left the restaurant and he quickened his steps back to the station. The meeting with Annie was hard for him. He hurt badly; he didn't understand why he couldn't be with her now. At best he could only be her friend—he could watch her grow; he could work with her on the radio; he could dream of the life they would have had together. He wasn't used to settling for second best, but he had no choice. He wanted to be with Annie at all costs, so he would pretend that everything was all right; he would give her away at her wedding, no matter how much it hurt him.

In the meantime, Brandon was in his studio, frantically trying to catch up on so many things, he didn't know where to start. "Rose!" he barked. "I need you in my office now!"

She came running. "Brandon, what are you doing here? I thought you were still in Hawaii."

Brandon nervously paced the floor while Rose anxiously watched her boss who seemed to be falling apart. He stopped pacing long enough to say, "Rose, I'm getting married Saturday at Central Park. I need your help."

Rose was shocked. "Getting married? Who are you marrying, Brandon?" Rose answered her own question before Brandon could speak. "Oh, I know—Ali."

Brandon shook his head. "No, I met someone who reminds me of Annie. I'm totally in love with her, and we spent the last two weeks in Hawaii together. Rose, this means so much to me."

"Brandon, who is this girl?"

"Sit down, Rose. She's the angel on Rob's show. We met when we collided on the ice at Central Park. I fell in love with her at first sight."

Rose gave a little gasp. She had always had Brandon's confidence— he always told her everything—and she hated not being kept informed. "You mean the girl you wanted me to book on your show… THAT Annie?"

Amused at her reaction, he said, "Yes, that Annie." Brandon kept checking his watch. "Rose, focus here. I have to catch up with pre-production programming and set up everything before I leave on my trip."

"Trip? Where are you going now?" she asked.

Brandon ignored her question. "Okay, I see I'll have to catch you up on a few things. First of all, I'm getting married to Annie in Central Park this Saturday. I need you to find me a preacher."

Rose was taking notes. "Got it."

Brandon was very detailed and exact about the wedding. "Since it's snowing outside, check the weather report for Saturday. Order a few fur coats and hats for Annie and Kate, her roommate. By the way, here's Kate's number, 212-555-5438; you can collaborate with her on the wedding. There is to be no press; I want one photographer and only ONE. Call Joe from the East Side; he's a great photographer. Get with Rob; I want music playing in the background while we say our vows—you know, like in the movie *Dr. Zhivago*. In fact, I want its theme song, 'Lara's Theme,' playing at the wedding. You know the song or Rob will—'Somewhere my love…' Rob can be in charge of that."

Rose was writing as fast as she could. She didn't have time to think.

"And Rose, I need the help of the New York's finest Police Department; I need a few men on horseback patrolling the area. The wedding will be sweet and short; and when it's over, Annie and I will exit stage left in a horse-drawn carriage. Here's the guest list: Rob, Kate, John, You, Pat… Oh, Rose, get Pat on the line for me."

Rose dialed Pat Edward's number and drummed her pencil on her notepad while waiting for him to answer. She was stressed; she had this list and only three days to get everything done.

After a number of rings, Pat finally picked up his phone. "Hello," he said.

"Pat, this is Rose. I have Brandon on line one; he wants to talk to you."

When Brandon picked up the phone, Rose left the room; she needed to get to work on the arrangements for the wedding.

Brandon put his feet up on his desk. "Hey, Buddy, I'm back from Hawaii. How are you?"

"I'm fine. Did you have a great time?" Pat asked.

"I really need to see you tonight. Can you come over to my place about 5 o'clock? I'll send out for pizza and I'll fill you in. By the way, what are you doing this Saturday?"

"Relaxing," Pat said.

"No, you're not."

"Yeah, I am."

"Pat, you're coming to my wedding."

Pat laughed out loud. "I knew it! How is Annie?"

"She's great. I love her so much. I can't wait till Saturday," Brandon said. "Look, it's a madhouse down here at the studio; I have to catch up. See you tonight at 5 o'clock." Brandon hung up.

While Brandon was chatting with Pat, Rose was in her office making call after call on the phone. She contacted Kate on her cell and they both agreed to handle all the wedding details without involving Annie; they didn't want her to be stressed about anything. Of course, they would include Rob and John. Rose would work well into the night.

In spite of having to catch up on his work, as he had told Pat, Brandon picked up the phone and dialed Annie's cell number. "Hello, I miss you," he purred. "How's my favorite girl? And where are you?"

"Hi," she said sweetly. "I just got through telling Rob about our wedding and having a long heart-to-heart with him. I'm at the Stage Deli, getting ready to go back home."

"Well, don't get too cozy with him. Remember, you're mine. Annie, why don't you come over to my place tonight? I want to hold you and love you a little."

Annie giggled.

"I'll have my driver pick you up at 8 o'clock."

"Sounds good."

"Pack something to wear for tomorrow, will you?"

"Okay."

"Love you, Annie."

"Ditto."

Brandon hung up the phone; he had to hustle all day to catch up on his work. But he couldn't stop thinking about Annie. Shortly before 5 o'clock, he caught a cab from the studio and went home.

The pizza arrived the same time that Pat did. "Hey, Buddy, have a seat. Let's eat right away," Brandon said.

"So what happened in Hawaii?" Pat asked as he grabbed a slice of pizza.

"Everything. I showed Annie my home in Oahu, we went to Maui and Kauai, and we had a wonderful time."

"Brandon, that's not good enough. How did it come about that you asked her to marry you?"

"We were at my home; the moon was full and she was shimmering and beautiful. It was then I decided I wanted to spend the rest of my life with her."

Brandon laid his hand on Pat's shoulder. "Pat, will you be my best man?"

With his mouth full of pizza, Pat could only bob his head up and down before saying, "Yes; give me the details about the wedding."

"This Saturday around noon Annie and I will tie the knot in Central Park by the ice skating rink. It will be a short wedding; we already said our vows in Hawaii. I want this to go off without a hitch."

Pat listened intently to every word Brandon was saying, but he felt a little squeamish.

Brandon noticed. "What's wrong?" He asked.

"I don't know; I feel a little weird about this. I can't put my finger on it. Sometimes the spirits don't show me everything, because they don't want me to intervene in other people's karma."

Brandon became edgy. "Look, Pat, I went through this before; I have a lot of police protection this time. I will not allow anyone to interfere with our wedding." Brandon's temper was rising. He got up and started to pace around his apartment.

Pat wondered, "Can't you get married indoors or something?"

"No, this is where Annie and I met; this is our place. Why…do you see something happening?"

"That's the problem—nothing is being told to me; nothing is being shown to me. I really don't get it. I'm blanking out; maybe I'm tired or something. I really don't know, Brandon. This has never happened to me before; I really don't know what to make of it."

The buzzer rang from downstairs; it was Annie, 8 o'clock on the dot. Brandon buzzed her in, at the same time telling Pat, "You are lucky, my friend; you're going to meet Annie, the love of my life."

Pat stood up and brushed the pizza crumbs off his shirt as Brandon opened the door.

"Annie!" Brandon grabbed her hand and kissed her on her lips. "Come here; I want you to meet someone. Annie, this is Pat, my psychic friend."

"Oh, I've heard so much about you," she said.

Pat was entranced. The light around her overwhelmed him; it was so bright and filled with love. "Annie, it's a pleasure."

"You are coming to our wedding, aren't you?" she asked.

"Yes, I am; in fact, that's why I'm here—Brandon wants me to be his best man."

"Great!" Annie turned to Brandon. "Rob is going to give me away, and tomorrow I'm going shopping with Kate to get a dress and a few things for the wedding. We have so little time."

Pat put on his jacket and said with a chuckle, "Well, I'd better get going. Judging by the look in Brandon's eyes for you right now, I think you guys have some serious business to attend to." He smiled at Annie. "See you at the wedding."

As Brandon walked him to the door, Pat said, "I can't believe it, Brandon; what a lucky man you are. She's gorgeous. If it's any consolation, I can see Annie's future—it's fine. See you Saturday."

Brandon closed the door. He picked Annie up in his arms and, nibbling her neck, headed for the bedroom. He placed Annie on the bed and undressed her. He slid between the satin sheets and their bodies merged into one. In the midst of their love-making, something came over Brandon; he held Annie extremely close to him and looked deeply into her eyes. He said, "Annie, I love you so much. Look at me; look into my eyes. I want you to memorize every part of my soul. Annie, if anything should happen to me, I want you to remember all the wonderful times we had."

Annie held Brandon close to her and said, "Brandon, nothing is going to happen to you or me. We found each other. You know that I told you I would never leave you; I never will. So stop this nonsense right now."

Brandon was clearly shaken. He remembered the first wedding day with Annie; he was so scared of losing her. He didn't know whether he could go on with his life if something happened to her.

He held Annie and loved her with every breath of his soul. They made love till the wee hours of the morning. They drifted off to sleep wrapped in each other's arms.

The next morning was Friday, one day before their wedding.

After breakfast Annie got dressed and kissed Brandon goodbye; she then picked up Kate in the limo for their long day of shopping. They shopped till they were exhausted. Annie looked at Kate and said, "In less than 24 hours, I will be married. I will be Mrs. Brandon Turner."

The Wedding and More

Chapter 17

It was a beautiful day for a wedding. The sun was shining, but the air was crisp and cold; a few snowflakes fluttered to the ground. Within hours, the ice skating rink in Central Park, where Annie and Brandon would marry, would become vibrantly alive.

A red carpet led to a small podium where the wedding would take place. There were red and white rose petals sprinkled among the few snowflakes that had floated onto the carpet. A few chairs were set up on both sides of the carpet.

Brandon had paid for the rink that afternoon; there would be no skaters on his wedding day. Mounted police officers patrolled the area on their horses. The gang would be arriving shortly.

A white van with big letters touting **92.3 FM Roll-over-with-Rob-in-the-Morning,** pulled up to the left of the ice skating rink. Rob and John quickly jumped out of the van to set up the cables and check the electrical outlets for the music.

Two white stretch limos soon arrived. The driver of the lead limo held onto Annie's hand as she stepped out of the car, then helped Kate out. He walked the two ladies, one on each arm, to the podium.

Annie wore a white round mink hat and a full length white mink coat, an outfit that was the exact replica of Lara's in the movie *Dr. Zhivago.* Kate was dressed from head to toe in a light brown mink coat with matching hat.

In the other limo were the preacher and Rose. She was simply dressed in a light brown mink jacket and a brown mink hat.

Off in the distance a horse-drawn carriage approached, the horse's hoofs clattering on the slightly wet pavement and the driver at the reins dressed all in black.

The carriage stopped abruptly by the podium and its door opened slowly. Annie smiled when she saw Brandon emerge from the carriage with a grin on his face and two dozen red and pink roses for her, the love of his life.

He looked dapper in his black tuxedo and an exquisite black wool coat, the same coat he had been wearing when he collided with Annie on the ice.

The last person to arrive was Pat, who was dressed simply in black.

Rose asked everyone to kindly gather around; the wedding would soon begin. They all gathered at the podium.

John made sure the music was cued for the opening of the wedding. He jumped out of the van and took his place beside Kate at the podium.

Rob escorted Annie slowly down the red carpet to the podium where Brandon and the preacher were waiting. As he turned her over to Brandon, Rob whispered, "You are beautiful, Annie." She smiled nervously.

Brandon and Annie stood side by side before the preacher. Behind them were John, Kate, Rose, Rob, and Pat.

The preacher opened the Bible. "Are we ready to begin?" he asked. Brandon nodded.

"We are gathered here to unite Brandon and Annie in holy matrimony." As the preacher continued, Brandon vaguely heard his words; that is, until the preacher closed the Bible and said, "I now pronounce you man and wife. You may now kiss the bride." Brandon turned to Annie and kissed her long and tenderly.

While the ceremony was going on, a lanky man wearing a gray trench coat neared the white van. His salt and pepper hair was straggly and long; his thin face was sunken and marred with acne. He was distraught.

He read the letters on the van out loud: **92.3 FM Roll-over-with-Rob-in-the-Morning**. He snapped with rage. He hid behind the van, out of sight of the wedding party and the police patrols. He reached into his coat pocket and pulled out a gun; steadying his hand, he aimed it straight at Rob. He mumbled under his breath, "You S.O.B, you deserve this; you never let me talk to her." His hand shook. "I have to do this; I have to teach you a lesson. All I wanted in my lousy, stinking life was to talk to an angel."

He fired. At that same moment, Rob bent down to tie his shoelace. The shot ricocheted off the chair next to Rob. Rob hit the ground.

Pandemonium set in. Everyone hit the ground. Brandon held Annie and covered her with his body. Another shot rang out. It missed Rob and hit Brandon in the neck. There was blood everywhere.

John sprang into action; he tackled the shooter to the ground and tore the gun from his hand. The mounted police surrounded them as John grabbed the guy's neck and shouted, "WHO THE HELL ARE YOU?"

In a crusty voice, the shooter managed to say his name. "LENNY." John stepped back as the police pulled the guy up and handcuffed him.

John shook Lenny and yelled in his face, "Why? Why did you do this?"

Lenny smirked and said angrily, "Did I get him? That S.O.B Rob screwed up my life. I was waiting on the phone a few weeks ago to talk to Annie the angel, but that bastard cut me off."

Lenny's voice grew weary and his shoulders drooped. "My life was in shambles; I **needed** to talk to her. I'm not a violent person. I carry a gun for my own protection; everyone is always out to get me. That's why I needed to talk to Annie. I didn't want to carry this gun anymore; I thought she could help me get rid of this habit." Lenny straightened up. "I was walking by the park when I noticed the radio van. I looked up and saw Rob; I was pissed off."

A light bulb lit up in John's head. "My God, you were the **1000th** caller! **You're the one Annie never got to read.**" John took a long breath before he spoke; he shook his head and muttered, "I can't believe this." Then he was overcome with anger; it pulsated in him. He kicked Lenny hard in the shins several times, till the police bodily pulled him away. He screamed at Lenny, "You shot the wrong man, you degenerate maggot!"

John was sick at the sight of Lenny. "Get him outta here," he said as he took off at full speed to reach Kate.

"Is everyone okay?" he asked, huffing and puffing to catch his breath.

A shaken Kate pointed toward Brandon and Annie. "Look," she said. Rob was pulling Brandon off Annie, who was in shock. Her white mink coat was now stained with Brandon's blood. Rob loosened Brandon's shirt collar and tried to stem the flow of blood as best he could.

Pat assisted in every way that he could, shaking his head. "Why didn't I see this coming?"

The police call had gone out only moments before, but there already were photographers snapping away.

Brandon was still alive when the ambulance arrived. Kate and Rose rushed to Annie's side as the emergency medical team put Brandon onto a gurney and wheeled him into the ambulance.

Annie got up from the ground, brushed herself off, and ran to catch the ambulance; she had to be with Brandon.

With the red and white lights spinning and sirens blaring, they sped through the city to a trauma center. Inside the ambulance, the medics worked feverishly to stabilize Brandon. "We have a pulse." His blood pressure was dropping to a dangerously low level; they managed to apply pressure to his neck.

Annie held Brandon's hand. "Brandon, please don't leave me," she pleaded, "**please**. I love you." Annie couldn't control her tears. Sobbing, she laid her head on his chest.

Brandon could barely move, but he heard every word Annie said. He managed to stroke her blonde hair just a little. He turned his head slightly to look at Annie and said, "**I'm sorry our wedding was ruined**. His voice broke. "**I love you so much; forgive me. Annie, remember these words: you found me once, you will find me again.**" Annie kissed Brandon on his lips for the last time.

"His pulse is dropping!" the tech shouted. "He's starting to flat line!" They pounded on his heart; they did all that they could do.

The tech shook his head. "We lost him." He held Annie's hand. "I'm sorry."

Annie refused to let go of Brandon's hand. She looked up to Heaven and cried, "Why?"

Within moments, Brandon floated out of his body toward the shimmering light, onward to Heaven.

Heaven was blue and misty. And out of the mist I, Gabriel, emerged and greeted Brandon. "Hello, Brandon, I'm Gabriel."

Brandon was confused. "Am I dead?" he asked.

"Yes."

Brandon was in shock; he was bewildered and obviously afraid. He stuttered, "I…uh…I am? Why did this happen? Who did you say you are?"

"Gabriel."

Brandon shook his head. "Annie was right; you really do exist."

I said calmly, "Have a seat; I will explain everything to you."

I had Brandon sit down and right before his eyes I rewound Brandon's past so he could observe his whole life as in a movie. He saw himself as a young boy trying to make it in show business. He saw the first television show he was on. The review of his past life was happy and joyful and also painful for Brandon. He could feel all the pain that had been inflicted on him, as well as the happiness he gave to the world.

He watched himself ice skating at Central Park and colliding into Annie. Brandon smiled and pointed. "That's my Annie," he said.

"That's my Annie, too," I said proudly. "I am her father."

Brandon gasped with surprise. "I didn't know."

"Brandon, I want to show you something; watch and observe." I flicked my fingers and parted the clouds from Heaven, and we both peered down at Earth to observe what was going on.

We watched as John, Rob, Kate, Rose and Pat made their way back to the van. They sat in silence; Rob absently turned on the radio. They all gasped at the 'breaking news' blaring from the radio:

This is a FOX NEWS NETWORK bulletin. Brandon Turner, the star of the Late Evening show, was shot at Central Park today at the ice skating rink. It was his wedding day.

A vagrant named Lenny, who was passing by, allegedly pulled out a gun and shot Turner. He died in the ambulance on the way to the hospital. Tune in at 6 o'clock for an up-date on this story.

Everyone in the van reacted with shock. Kate and Rose sobbed; Pat shook his head; Rob was too stunned to say anything. Rob snapped out of it briefly and looked at John. "Lenny… that name sounds familiar."

200 • Dayle Schear

John's grip on the steering wheel tightened. He answered Rob's unspoken question. "It should, Rob. When I tackled Lenny, I asked him why he did what he did. He told me he was aiming the gun to kill you."

"Why me?" Rob asked in disbelief.

"Do you remember the **1000ᵗʰ** caller on Annie's last radio show?"

"Yes, it was some person—woman, I think; I really didn't pay that much attention. Why?"

"Well, it turns out that Lenny was the guy I had on hold, waiting to speak to Annie that morning. He was the one who had a pressing issue. I had to let the call go, since you had ended the morning show thinking she had helped her 1000ᵗʰ caller."

John glanced at Rob before pressing his point angrily. "That was the morning you and I had that huge fight about the counter. I told you she had only reached 999 souls; you screamed at me, telling me not to worry about it, that it was no big thing. Well, Rob, I guess it was a big thing, because Lenny is the one who was aiming to kill you for not letting him speak to Annie. And lucky you, you bent down and the bullet hit Brandon."

Rob exclaimed, "Oh, my God, this is my entire fault! Why didn't I listen? What did I do?"

Pat, who was sitting in the back of the van listening to this whole conversation, interrupted. "Rob, everybody, LISTEN to me; let me interject something here… this is my line of work; I am a psychic channel. Rob, this really was no one's fault; it was all meant to be. I am guilty as well. When I was with Brandon last night, I wondered why I couldn't see his future—well, I know now. I wasn't meant to stop any of this; I wasn't allowed to interfere in Brandon's karma.

"Now, the way I see it, this is one big KARMIC lesson for everyone concerned here. Let's go back in time… Annie found Rob so she could help 1000 souls on the radio, which would hook her up with Brandon. Correct?"

"Yes," they said in unison.

Pat continued. "She reached **999 souls**; she never knew the counter was off till after the fact. Yet her angel, Gabriel, allowed Annie to meet up with Brandon anyway."

Pat looked around at the others. "Why?" he asked.

They all wondered aloud, "Yeah, why?"

"I'll tell you why. You see, the men upstairs are famous for making a point to us; they send us signs all the time with the hope that we will listen and learn. Sometimes we do, and sometimes we don't. There are many futures for us—if we follow one path, there is a future; if we follow another path, there is another future. The way I see it, Annie wasn't the one being tested here; it was Rob."

"Me?" Rob pointed to himself.

"Yes, you. You see, Rob, apparently John pointed out to you your mistake while you were having the party on the radio. And even after all that hoopla, you could have made an announcement to your audience that there was one phone call hanging and that you were going to let Annie answer that last call.

"If, in fact, you had let Annie talk to Lenny, none of this MIGHT have happened. But Rob, being the hard-headed person that you are, you chose not to. That created an alternate future for everyone concerned." Pat paused. "Are you guys following me?"

"We think so," John said. "Please continue; this is getting interesting." John pulled the car over so he could focus his whole attention on what Pat was saying.

Pat continued. "You see, every person in this world counts, and there is a reason for everything. It's called the RIPPLE EFFECT. Everyone affects everyone else in the circle of truth and life upstairs. No matter how minute and inconsequential we think we are, we are all here to learn and serve and assist one another to make the world a better place. It elevates our KARMA.

"So you see, Rob, ONE single soul, REALLY does count. Lenny has affected all of our lives forever. That's your big learning lesson. To be brief, Lenny called your show; you didn't allow him to speak to Annie. He was mentally ill; he held a grudge toward you after that. And when the opportunity arose, such as his passing by just at the time of Brandon's wedding and noticing your logo on the van, he stopped and spotted you. That was a sign in his mind to kill you. But you bent down for some reason and he shot Brandon instead."

Rob was dumbfounded. "I get it. I more than get it. I only wish I could take what I learned from you today, stop all action, and go back in time to that one day at the radio station. Maybe if I had let Lenny talk to Annie, Brandon would still be alive."

Pat interjected, "And maybe NOT. We never know what they have planned upstairs. It could be that it wasn't Brandon's time to go; he could have died prematurely before his time. Someone might have goofed up there; to spare him the pain, they might have taken him out too soon—we'll never know. Whatever the case, Brandon's dead."

Rob's cell phone rang, startling everyone.

The voice on the other end was screaming and crying. "Rob, it's Annie. Please come get me; I'm at the Hospital at Cedars. Brandon's dead and there's press all around."

"We'll be right there, Annie." Rob nudged John. "John, step on it. Annie is alone with the press at Cedars."

John screeched out of there.

Up in Heaven, Brandon turned to me and asked, "Is it true what Pat just said, Gabriel—that I might have been taken out before my time?"

"It could be, Brandon," I answered. "Almost everything that Pat said is true. Especially, that One Person Makes a Huge Difference in the grand scheme of things. Why don't people on Earth get it? Pat is a very gifted soul; when it's his time, I will make sure that he gets his wings."

Brandon thought he may have stumbled onto a loophole. "Gabriel, if it wasn't my time, can I go back to Earth and find Annie?"

"Let's not rush things for now; just keep watching. I'll check on what happened to you and see if we took you out before your time."

While I was checking, Brandon made himself comfortable and watched the rest of his life unfold. It was like watching a first-run movie; he couldn't believe this was happening. He felt sad; he wished he were back on Earth with Annie. I knew he would try to bargain with me later.

The group on Earth arrived at Cedars in the nick of time. Chaos had set in. The press had surrounded Annie; they were firing questions at her left and right. Rob and John rushed to her side. John held up his hand and covered the cameras, then covered Annie with his jacket. "Sorry, no more questions." The press didn't let up; they followed everyone as they tried to walk away. The press screamed and shouted, "Are you Mrs. Brandon Turner? Did you know the guy who killed your husband? When is the funeral?"

Rob stepped in at that point. "Hey, Guys, you know me—**Roll-over-with-Rob-in-the-Morning.** Give the lady a break; she just lost her husband. We all know that Brandon Turner was famous, but there's a time and a place for everything," he said.

One of the reporters called out, "How do you fit into this mess, Rob?"

"Annie works for me."

Someone shouted, "Annie? She's that psychic angel on your show." Rob never denied it. The reporters were now having a field day; they chattered among themselves; one by one they picked up their cell phones and called the story into their home base.

Rob decided he'd better stay with the reporters to appease them. He waved off John and told him to get Annie home.

"Okay, boys, fire away," he told the reporters.

Kate consoled Annie in the van all the way to their apartment. "Annie, come with me; we need to get you all cleaned up," Kate said, leading her gently by the arm to the bathroom. The rest of the gang sat glued to the television in the living room. Brandon's face was plastered all over every news channel. **Brandon Turner, dead at age 44; shot by a vagrant.** Every channel, every station, they sat there in awe.

Kate helped Annie take a quick shower to wash the blood off. "Annie, I don't know what to say. I don't understand why this happened."

When Annie came out of the shower, she was no longer crying; now she was angry. "I think I understand why this happened," she said. "But Kate, what I don't understand is why I've been calling for Gabriel non-stop—he has all the answers—but I can't get through to him. Gabriel has never done this to me before. It's like I'm stuck here on Earth. I just want to go back to Heaven and find out what really happened."

"I hear you, girl. This is really messed up," Kate said. "Annie, Pat seems to have a lot of the answers; why don't you ask him?"

Annie rushed to the living room where Pat, Rose, and John were watching television non-stop. Annie grabbed the remote and turned off the television. "Enough," she said. "Pat, I need answers." Annie got everyone's attention.

Pat nodded. "Yes, Annie, I'll tell you what I know and we can go from there." There was silence in the room when Pat spoke and tried to make sense of the day's event.

"Annie, it all started when you were on the radio. You thought you had reached 1000 souls and, for that matter, so did Rob. John informed Rob you had only reached 999—you remember Rob and John went over this with you a while back."

"Yes, I remember. But why did Gabriel allow me to meet Brandon at the ice skating rink, when I had only reached 999 souls?"

"Good question. Annie, this is what I feel happened; this all revolves around the word 'trust.' Annie, you trusted Rob when he said you helped 1000 souls; you never confirmed it."

"Why would I? We had a counter that kept track for us."

"Yes, you did. But did it ever occur to you that your counter might have been broken?"

"Why would the counter break at the last soul?" Annie asked in bewilderment.

Pat replied, "One reason could be that all this was meant to be. Because these are life's lessons we all have to go through; and, apparently, you're not exempt. Annie, only Gabriel can tell you for sure, but I believe there is a very special reason why all this happened. Give it time. I know it's hard, but please be a little patient. I'm sure the answer will reveal itself."

Just then, Rob came storming through the door. "Whoa, I can't believe what I just went through with the press. Annie, are you okay?" Rob plopped down next to her.

"Rob, I'm okay. I'm so angry and hurt. I don't know what to think or believe."

Rose joined in the conversation. "Sorry, guys, I have to get back to the studio. You're not the only ones who will be given the third degree. My boss has called me at least ten times on my cell. I mean, he has a television show and no host. We have to make funeral arrangements. This is not easy. Annie, I feel for you; but please understand that I have a job—at least, what's left of it—and whether I like it or not, I have to continue moving forward, for Brandon's sake."

Pat stood up. "Annie, I've got to go, too. I'll be at your service if you need anything; call me." Pat escorted Rose downstairs.

That was the longest night in Annie's life...without Brandon. She was overwhelmed with grief; her only solace was in Rob, Kate, and John. She was angry. For the first time in her life, she didn't have all the answers. She wondered why she couldn't reach me, Gabriel. So many questions ran through her mind, questions that would remain unanswered for now. She knew she had to be brave and put up a front; she had to save herself for the funeral.

The Funeral and More

Chapter 18

It was a very dreary day; the sun was no longer shining. It was the day of Brandon's funeral. People had lined the streets of New York City to watch the funeral procession go by.

Brandon was so loved. Rose did such a wonderful job; she managed to pull everything together in such a short period of time. People from all over the world had bid their farewells; the flowers and telegrams came non-stop.

The news coverage was clearly remarkable. There wasn't a magazine stand in all of New York City that one could pass by without seeing Brandon's face plastered all over it.

The private memorial was just that—Kate, Pat, John, Rose, Annie and Rob attended. Many movie and television stars paid their respects briefly. They were shocked and dismayed, yet secretly fighting for the position of next host for his show.

Brandon would be cremated—that was his wish—and his funeral ceremony would be short and sweet. He loved the stage; but when it came to his private life, virtually no one was allowed in.

Rob held Annie up as the others gathered around to hear the brief eulogy:

BRANDON TURNER WAS LOVED BY MANY. HIS DEATH WAS A HORRIBLE, UNSPEAKABLE ATROCITY. HE WAS A MAN WHO GAVE LIFE AND COMEDY TO A WORLD THAT WAS IN DIRE NEED OF HIS TALENT.

BRANDON WILL BE MISSED BY MANY, ESPECIALLY HIS NEW BRIDE ANNIE. BRANDON DIED KNOWING HE SAVED THE LIFE OF HIS BEAUTIFUL BRIDE.

THIS IS A TIME FOR CELEBRATION; SO I SAY TO YOU THIS EVENING, CELEBRATE! DRINK AND BE MERRY! BRANDON WOULDN'T HAVE WANTED IT ANY OTHER WAY.

Annie lost it; she fell into Rob's arms and cried uncontrollably.

Brandon, who was peering down from heaven, also cried. His tears, his emotions, his love managed to reach Annie in a flash at that very moment in time. She felt him.

Six Months Later.

It was back to work as usual for Annie. Oh, those wonderful radio days. Annie worked her heart out helping so many people on the radio. There would never be a doubt in any one's mind again, for Annie had hit well over her 1000th caller mark.

With each day that passed, Annie felt just a little bit more alive. She had Rob to thank for that. He kept her so busy day and night, she didn't have time to think.

Kate was busy with John almost every evening, and Pat had a HUGE following left over from Brandon Turner's television show.

Brandon had been replaced with an unknown comedian; the station wanted to appeal to a younger demographic in television land. All was falling into place slowly. Annie wasn't badgered anymore by the press; they moved on to other sensational stories in the news. And as for Lenny, he ended up in a mental institution for life.

Meanwhile, up in Heaven, six months of Earth time was just a fragment of a second of Heavenly time. Brandon had been educated on the inner workings of Heaven. He was sitting in a chair reading the same book Annie had read, *The Book of Life*, when I, Gabriel, approached him.

"Good Morning, Brandon; did you enjoy watching your life's review?" I asked.

Brandon put down his book. "It made me sad. I felt so bad for Annie." Brandon looked up at me. "I have a lot of questions and I need answers. Will you help me?"

"Fire away."

"I really want to know if I was taken out before my time," he said.

I pulled out a sheet of paper, "I'll try to explain to you what happened. You see, in heaven we have a set of rules we must follow. It turns out that Raphael, one of my best angels, was assigned to your case.

"Now, Raphael is an archangel known as the Healer of God; he is known to have special healing relationships that transcend the idea that angels work as mere messengers. His territory covers more than just physical healing. It includes more fixing of things within Earth/Human people. He repairs and strengthens and pacifies when it is necessary."

Brandon was glued to every word that I was saying. I continued, "Raphael's idea of life is to restore a person to his original state of being, to heal the heart and the soul. From what I gather, when Raphael saw you shot on Earth, protecting our Annie, his heart was filled with joy."

"I don't get it," Brandon said.

"Raphael felt you did the most honorable thing; you protected our Annie and you were willing to give up your life for hers. Raphael knew you would be in a vegetative state for the rest of your life if you lived. He telepathically whispered in your ear his findings; he asked you if you wanted to stay on Earth in this condition.

"Apparently, telepathically, you told him NO, you didn't want to burden Annie or anyone else. So you were allowed to leave Earth, because you sacrificed your life for her. That is what we call a slight version of *free will*. You chose to come back home to Heaven. Brandon, it was you who made the decision. Raphael couldn't bear the thought of you in pain, so he took you out."

A feeling of acceptance came over Brandon. He believed every word I told him. He knew in his heart what I was saying was true.

Brandon bent his head down. "So what happens to me now?"

"Well, after much discussion, we have decided to send you back to Earth."

For the first time in a long time Brandon was speechless—at least, momentarily. "Gabriel, are you joking? Will Annie and I be together again?"

"Yes, with just one condition."

Brandon got excited. "What are the conditions? You know, Gabriel, I will do anything to be with her."

"We know," I said solemnly. "Brandon, I can send you back to Earth; but you will no longer be Brandon Turner the television star—

you will be just an average person. You will have no remembrance of Annie whatsoever."

"How will we find each other?" he asked.

"Brandon, you have to believe; you have to have faith that all things will work out. Trust in the Universe. Have faith in me; I know how much you love Annie."

I rubbed my chin. "I'll send you back to Earth, if you find a way of helping mankind. We are facing many Earth changes; many souls will pass; there will be an outcry such as no other. We need you to help people deal with everyday matters on earth and to adjust to the Earth changes. If you agree to all this, you will be back on Earth in a mere flash."

A smile came over Brandon. "I agree," he said.

"Brandon, I think I have found just the right person whose body you will take over." I pointed through the heavenly mist. "Do you see that man lying in his hospital bed? He's sort of lifeless." Brandon nodded.

"His name is Brad, and he reminds me of you in so many ways, Brandon. He's a little younger, about 38; he's handsome, intelligent, and kind. He is instrumental in helping so many of the homeless people in New York City. He has given them shelter from the cold, found them jobs, and makes sure they have warm food whenever he can. I really don't know how he does it. He also has set up a nonprofit organization that helps with national disasters. He's known all over the world as a savior of mankind.

"Recently, a very dear friend of his, a man named George, passed away. He had taken George off the streets, cleaned him up, and fed him. Little did he know that man was testing people; George wanted to know to whom he could leave his millions. He picked Brad, with the condition that Brad would always carry on his work of helping the world.

"Brad was about to embark on buying a few world-wide radio stations so people can communicate from all over the world when a national disaster hits. He was well on his way to success." I shook my head at the wonder of one man doing so much for others.

"What's wrong with him?" Brandon asked.

"He caught a very bad cold last week. He never cared about himself; he only cared for others, and he never went to the doctor. He has a high fever—106, now; it looks like the cold developed into pneumonia." I checked my watch. "In about five minutes from now, Brad is going to cross over."

"Why?"

I lowered my eyes. "Brandon, it's his time. And besides, we need him up here; he could organize many things for us."

Brandon asked me, "Is he married? Does he have kids?"

"He never married. He fell in love once, but she ended up with someone else. Brad never got over her; and all these years he's been waiting for someone else to come along, someone to love him and his work. What can I say—it never happened," I said.

I checked my watch again. "Okay, you have less than two minutes to decide if you want to take over his body and live his life."

Brandon made up his mind really quick. "Yes, I will."

"Okay, Brandon, you have a seat while I give you your memory shot. You will have no memory of being here with me. You never met Annie before. You are now Brad Cummings, and you must fight for your life down on Earth."

With a flick of my fingers, Brandon was now Brad Cummings, lying in a hospital bed in New York City, fighting for his life.

Brad coughed uncontrollably; the nurse ran to his aid. "Call the doctor!" she shouted.

The doctor arrived immediately and checked Brad's condition. "Looks like he's going into convulsions. Put some Phenobarbital in his IV, nurse. Pack him in ice to bring down his fever." The doctor worked all through the night to keep Brad alive.

When Brad awoke in the morning, his temperature had dropped and he was almost back to normal.

Brandon had a new lease on life. He now was Brad, highly respected in the community of New York City and some parts of the world. He was noted for helping the homeless.

Gordon, Brad's best friend and buddy, never left his side at the hospital. Brad had saved his life many times in the past; if it weren't for Brad, Gordon would be dead.

Seeing Brad stir and open his eyes, Gordon said cheerfully, "Hey, buddy, looks like you're going to make it. We were all praying for you. I guess it worked."

Brad looked at Gordon. "Hey, buddy, were you here all night?"

Gordon smiled. "Yes, where else would I be? You gave us a scare for a while. The doctor said he didn't think you were going to make it."

"Who, me? It's not my time yet; I have so many people to help. And Gordon, you are my buddy; thank you for being by my side."

Brad motioned to Gordon to come closer. "You know, I had the weirdest dream last night. I was floating among the clouds and I could see a bright light and a tunnel; I could see my dad who passed and also my mom; they were waving me on. When I reached them, I saw my younger sister who died some years ago when she fell through the ice while skating. She told me I had to go back. I didn't want to. She told me I would help many people; my work wasn't finished. She told me I wouldn't be lonely anymore. She pointed her finger away from the light and almost ordered me to go back. The next thing I knew, I woke up and... well, there you are, my friend Gordon."

Gordon was concerned. "It was just a dream," he said.

Brad, however, was spiritual; he believed he was given a second chance on life. He knew he had pushed it before, but now he would take care of himself a little more; he had many people to help.

Gordon consoled him. "Hey, buddy, rest; get better. We have so much work to do. We have a list a mile long of people to help, and we need to get some more donations for our homeless program."

"Gordon, what about my dog, Pete? Where is he?"

"Don't worry about him; he's with me in my apartment. The moment you took ill, I went and grabbed Pete; I know how much he means to you."

Brad smiled. "I love that dog; he's the best golden retriever I have ever had, thank God. I can take him to work with me every morning. I swear, Gordon that dog has a sixth sense. He knows when people are trying to take us for a ride——he barks and barks; but when the person is good inside, he gives them lots of kisses. By the way, did you water my plants?"

Gordon looked at Brad and said, "You're back. Yes, I watered the plants." He playfully hit Brad on his shoulder. "Man, you care for everyone and everything more than you care for yourself. It just amazes me."

Gordon smiled. "You know, Brad; you're good looking, somewhat young yet, tall, built nice; you have big brown eyes and hair that falls in your face all the time. For the life of me, I just don't understand why you haven't found the right one yet. I mean, if anyone deserves it, you do."

Brad laughed. "She'll come along when I least expect it." Brad knew this was true, yet he looked off in the distance almost feeling sad.

Brad slowly got better and by week's end he and Gordon were back at work helping the homeless people.

Meanwhile, on the other side of town, Annie was getting ready to go to the radio station.

Kate interrupted her. "Annie, John asked me out to dinner tonight; he says he has something he wants to ask me. What do you think?"

Annie replied, "I don't want to spoil the surprise, Kate. You know what I think and I more than approve."

Kate smiled. "What are you going to do tonight?"

"Rob has asked me out to dinner; I think I will go this time. I really need to get out of this house. Kate, his birthday is next week; I found something great I want to get him."

"What's that?" she asked.

"A small puppy, Kate. He's so lonely; I really think this would solve all his problems."

"Annie, YOU'RE the one that will solve all his problems, can't you see? Rob is crazy about you. What are you going to do about it?"

Annie cringed. "I'm going to buy him a puppy." She giggled, just like her old self.

Kate shook her head. "What am I going to do with you? Do you need a ride to the radio station?"

"As a matter of fact, I do," Annie said.

Off they went. They just happened to pass by a pet store on the way to the radio station. "Kate, pull over," Annie ordered.

Kate moaned. "Oh, no, Annie, I thought you were kidding; I guess you're not."

Annie shouted as she ran into the store, "Wait here, Kate; I won't be long!" Annie managed to find the cutest black female Labrador puppy and promptly bought the puppy for Rob. Back in the car, she held the puppy in her arms and nuzzled its face. "Isn't she cute? I want to give the puppy to Rob at the radio station."

Kate sighed. "Annie, you know who's going to take care of this puppy? We are."

"Don't worry, Kate; I have it all under control." Annie smiled. She held the puppy carefully in her arms all the way to the radio station.

When they finally arrived at the station, Kate couldn't wait to hear what John had to say about all this.

John looked up. "What in the name of…is that?" John asked, pointing to the furry black object.

"Rob, I think you'd better come out here!" he shouted.

Rob walked out in a huff. "What do you want? I was in pre-production; Annie's come to help me cut some commercials. What is it?" he said irritably.

Rob saw the little puppy running around the radio station; she had a pink bow tied to her neck. "Annie, what a cute puppy," Rob said. "Whose is it?"

Annie acted coy. "It's yours; I just bought it for you. It's an early birthday present."

Rob got down on the floor with the puppy and played and played with her. "What shall I name her?" He looked up at Annie's big blue eyes, then at the puppy. "Wait! I know." He looked at Annie and smiled. "Her name is Angel; she was brought to me by an angel." Rob kissed Annie on her cheek. "I guess we have a baby now."

Rob and Annie spent the rest of the day playing with the puppy. They forgot about work and cutting commercials. It took weeks for Rob and Annie to train Angel; she was always getting into everything. One thing was perfectly clear—Rob fell madly in love with the puppy. He wasn't lonely any more. Annie was right.

The puppy brought Annie and Rob closer together. Rob invited Annie to his apartment for dinner. Annie didn't mind going; she didn't want to be alone and she loved Angel the puppy.

She arrived at Rob's apartment with a huge bottle of red wine. Rob was famous for his spaghetti and his moonlight dinners on his heated patio.

Angel, the puppy, galloped and tugged on Rob's shoe. She followed Rob everywhere he went.

Rob stopped cooking for the moment and grabbed Annie's hand and the bottle of wine. "Come with me out on the patio," he said. "Let's look out at the stars and city lights, at our beautiful city of New York." Annie followed.

Rob poured the wine very generously. They both toasted New York.

"Annie, I wonder what Kate and John are up to. John's been telling me how much he is in love with Kate. I really wonder if he'll pop the question."

Annie smiled and whispered in Rob's ear, "I know he will."

Meanwhile, in a different part of town, Kate and John were high above the city, in the Empire State Building. Looking out over the city, John held Kate close to him. "Isn't she beautiful?" he asked, sweeping his hand over the panorama of the city. Kate whispered, "Yes."

John looked at his watch. "Kate, it's getting late; the Empire State Building is on its last run. We'd better be going," he said.

Kate stared at John. She didn't want to go; she never wanted to leave his side. As they headed for the elevator, John stopped abruptly. "Wait, Kate, I forgot something; come with me." They ended up back at the City View Telescope.

The elevator door opened. "Sorry, Folks, this is my last run and we have to go now," the elevator operator said.

John ran over to the man and handed him $50. "Please wait just a moment for us," he said. The man did.

John put his arm around Kate and kissed her powerfully. He pulled out a black ring box from his jacket and opened it, revealing a beautiful diamond ring. As the elevator man watched, John got down on one knee, as is traditional, and said, "Kate, I never thought I would ever say these words again. I love you and want to spend the rest of my life with you. Will you marry me?"

The elevator man rolled his eyes; since that movie, *An Affair to Remember*, came out, the Empire State Building has never been the same. Along with John, he waited for Kate's answer.

Kate cried for the first time in a long time. "Yes!" She wrapped her arms around John and kissed him.

John slipped the ring on her finger. He looked up and said, "I think our ride is waiting." They walked slowly hand in hand to the elevator.

"Going down," the operator called out. "Congratulations. You both look very happy."

They smiled and looked at each other. "We are."

Kate and John made their way back to his apartment; they spent the rest of the evening making love.

Meanwhile Rob and Annie were having dinner at Rob's apartment.

Chapter 19

New York City was lit up in all its glory. The different colored lights, how they sparkled; it made one proud to be a New Yorker. The evening was beautiful outside; the air was crisp, winter was winding down, and soon it would be spring.

Rob and Annie were in deep conversation when the phone rang. It was John. "Hey, pal, I wanted you and Annie to be the first to know. Rob, put on the speaker so Annie can hear this."

Annie put her head on Rob's shoulder; he bent down so Annie could hear the phone conversation right along with him.

"Kate and I are getting married!" John shouted.

Rob and Annie could hear Kate laughing with joy in the background. Kate called out, "Annie, wait till you see my ring—it's beautiful! And you both are invited to our wedding."

Rob and Annie simultaneously said, "Congratulations, you two."

Annie said, "We were just discussing whether John was going to pop the question, and you called. Kate, I'm so happy for you and John." Yet Annie was somewhat sad, remembering what she once had with Brandon. "You guys have a good one; I'll talk to you tomorrow."

Rob hung up the phone. He turned to Annie and said, "It couldn't have happened to a nicer couple." Rob stood in silence, looking at the city.

He held onto Annie for dear life; he couldn't contain his emotions any longer. He bent down and kissed Annie slowly; his hot tongue intertwined with hers.

Annie wasn't fighting him any longer. She longed to be touched; she longed to be held. The wine had brought out her sensuality.

Rob picked her up and carried her to the bedroom. He had waited so many lifetimes for this one single moment. He was relieved to see their puppy, Angel, was tucked away in her own little bed.

Rob slowly undressed Annie, kissing and caressing her. He couldn't stop loving her, even if he tried. Annie's blouse was open, and he fondled her breasts and kissed them gently, then her neck and mouth. Annie kissed him back. This time I, Gabriel wasn't there to stop her.

Rob was on top of her, undressing himself as fast as he could. He was just about to…when Annie sat up on the bed.

"Did I do something wrong, Annie?" he asked.

Annie spoke quietly; she didn't want to hurt his feelings. "Rob, I can't do this." She moved just a little farther away from him. She bent her head down. "It's not that I don't desire you—I do." Tears ran down her cheeks.

He held her tightly and rocked her in his arms. "Annie, please don't cry," he said.

"Rob, I forgot myself. Just for a moment I thought you were Brandon. I really wanted to be making love to you. It's too soon. I still can't get Brandon out of my mind. Please understand, it's not you, It's me."

Rob understood. "Annie, it's okay," he assured her. Let me hold you; I promise I won't do anything to hurt you."

Annie laid her head back down on the pillow. She closed her eyes and they fell fast asleep in each other's arms.

The next morning when Annie awoke, Rob was already in the kitchen making coffee. Annie joined him. "Rob, I'm sorry," she said quietly. "I really thought I was over Brandon, but I still have very deep memories."

Rob turned around and sat at the kitchen table with her. He handed her a cup of coffee and reached for her hand. "Annie, I've waited this long for you; I can wait longer. I'm a patient man. I want you to want me as much as I wanted you last night, and I'm willing to wait till you're ready."

Annie felt a little bit better about the situation. She said, "Rob, what if it never happens until another lifetime?"

Annoyed, Rob pulled his hand back. "Annie, I have my work; I have you on the radio; I have Angel, our dog. I think I have a lot on my plate right now and, if it never happens, that's the way my luck goes. I will continue on."

Seeing Annie get teary again, he said, "Hey, don't be so sad. Besides, you're not the ONLY girl in the world; I'll get over you eventually. Now, mind you, it might take several lifetimes, but, that's the way it goes."

Annie and Rob smiled at each other. His light-hearted tone broke the ice; he didn't want to lose her at any cost.

He glanced at his clock. "Holy smokes! Get dressed, Annie. We're on the radio in less than an hour; we've got to go."

They both scrambled, and they barely made it to the radio station. As they both ran in the door, there was John; he had everything under control.

He chuckled when he saw them. "Well, this is a first—Rob being late for his show. What were the two of you doing?"

Rob motioned to John, "Hand me my earphones."

John counted down, "3,2,1."

"**Good morning, New York City… This Is Roll-over-with-Rob-in-the-Morning.** I have my partner here with me, our lovely angel, Annie. And our new puppy, which is running around this morning, eating our radio wires. Just a moment, folks. John, get Angel, will you?" John scrambled.

"I'm back, folks. Well, I do believe we have a caller on the line."

John said, "Rob, we have Mike on the line waiting to talk to Annie."

"Good morning, Mike, how can we help you?"

"I need to speak to Annie." His voice was trembling just a little.

Annie squirmed when she heard his voice; she didn't like what she was going to hear.

"Hello, Annie." Mike paused.

Annie took control of the conversation. "Mike, are you all right?"

Mike couldn't believe that anyone could read his voice over the phone. "Not really," he said.

Annie was touched; there was something in his voice that reminded her of Lenny. "Mike, I want to help you. Tell me what I can do to help you," she pleaded.

"Annie, it's too late, I think," Mike said softly and sadly.

Annie refused to accept that. "Mike, it's never too late, unless you're dead—and even that is questionable."

Mike's story came rambling out of his mouth. "Annie, my wife left me for another man. I have two kids that she won't let me see. I lost all my money in the stock market. What can I say? Can you help me? I have nothing left to live for. Everything I've worked so hard for has fallen apart. My life is in shambles. Annie, is there hope for me?"

Rob cut in. "Mike, hold for a moment; we have to take a quick commercial break." The commercials ran while Rob questioned Mike just a little bit further. Rob sensed something bad. "Mike, where are you calling from?" he asked suspiciously.

"I'm on my cell." Mike stumbled over his words. He looked up and noticed the lettering. "I am… at the George Washington Bridge."

Rob quickly put Mike on hold and turned to Annie. "Annie, please be careful with this one," Rob pleaded. "Maybe we should call the police. John, call 911."

Annie raised her hand. She shouted across the room at John. "No, John, put down the phone. I can handle him. He's despondent."

Annie got up from her chair; she put on her jacket and grabbed her purse. She switched to another phone in the back and said, "Mike, where are you exactly?"

He explained.

Annie made a point of telling Mike that she was on her way down there. "Please wait till I get to the bridge. I can help you," she said.

Rob and John both raised their voices. "Annie, this is far too dangerous. Just call 911."

Annie was annoyed. "Rob, John, there are times when you have to take a stand. I have to do this. I know what I'm doing, so please let me do my work. Remember Lenny. For God's sake, I'm an angel; I can handle him."

Annie raised her voice in defense. "Look, I have a cell phone; I'll call you and let you know what happens. Please don't worry about me; I can take care of myself."

Annie bolted out of the radio station. She ran down the stairs as fast as she could and hailed a taxi. "George Washington Bridge—and hurry!"

"Lady, I can't let you out there; it's against the law," the driver said.

Annie was insistent. "I understand. Drop me off as close to the bridge as you can. Please, driver, it's a matter of life or death."

Meanwhile, Rob returned to the air. "Well, folks, we're having some technical difficulties; sorry. We'll be playing some music till we fix our problem."

He turned to John. "What do you think? Should I follow her?"

"No, Rob; I think she knows what she's doing. Let it be."

"John, this is the first time Annie has left the studio to help someone. I'm worried."

"Well, don't be. This might be the first time, but it won't be her last. Trust me on this." John seemed to know what he was talking about.

At that moment Rob's cell phone rang. The caller sounded desperate.

"Rob, I need to talk to you. I broke up with my boyfriend. Can you meet me for lunch at noon, please?"

"Yes! See you at our usual place."

"Who was that?" John asked.

"It was my ex-wife, Jan. She broke up with her boyfriend and she wants to talk to me. I told her I would meet her for lunch. As Annie would say, 'there must be something going on with the planets today.' It's really weird out there today, John."

"What are you going to do, Rob, when you see her? I mean, do you think it's wise to meet your ex-wife after all she's done to you?" John frowned. He was very concerned for Rob; he knew how vulnerable Rob was.

"Don't worry, John; this is something I have do. She's the mother of my children; I want to be there for her." Rob nodded. "It's okay; I can handle her."

While Rob and John were deep in conversation, Annie's taxi approached one end of the George Washington Bridge. Annie spotted Mike leaning over the side, waiting for her. She asked the driver to pull over to a safe place just to the left of the bridge and to please wait; she paid him to do so. "I won't be long," she said as she got out of the cab.

Annie quickened her pace. She waved and shouted, "Mike, it's me, Annie; I'm here to help you."

Mike walked toward her and they both met at the beginning of the bridge. Annie pulled Mike away and said, "Come sit down with me over here where it's safe."

Annie could see that Mike was a very defeated man. His head hung low. She noticed he wasn't a bad-looking man—about 40ish, brown hair, green eyes, medium build. She could tell he was not your usual vagrant.

Annie sat by his side. "Mike, life is so very precious. So you made some mistakes; we all do. That's how we learn. Trust me; it's not the end of the world."

"Annie, I hate to say this, but I was just about to jump. I felt hopeless; no money, no job; I don't even have food to eat. How can I help anyone? I'm useless." Mike looked away in disgust.

Annie gave Mike an encouraging speech. She put her arm around him. "It's not the end of the world," she repeated. She turned and stared directly into his eyes. "Mike, so many people have been in your situation. You'll be able to get back on your feet again, Mike. I promise you; I see it. And when you do, you will go on to help many people just like yourself. You just have to give yourself a little bit of time.

"Killing yourself is not the answer. Your children would grieve and their lives would be destroyed. Mike, life is so precious. I know your family loves you. Trust me, Mike; we can straighten this all out.

"Right now, I know of a place that can help you and get you back on your feet. You'll have a bed and food, and they're famous for rebuilding people's lives."

Mike looked up; there was a ray of hope. "I prayed for help, and you came. I guess there is a little light at the end of the tunnel. Annie, I'm so down I'll do anything at this point. What do you want me to do?"

Annie helped Mike up from the curb. "Follow me." She was relieved.

Annie held Mike's hand as they made their way to the cab. She thanked the driver for waiting and said, "Take us to the homeless compound, West 23rd Street." Mike was famished. He could care less where he was at this point. The drive-through traffic was slow going. Annie picked up her cell and called Rob.

"Rob, it's Annie. I called to tell you I have Mike in the cab with me. Everything is going to be all right. I don't want you to worry. I have to take care of him. We're headed to the homeless kitchen. I'll be fine. I'll get back to you WAY later. Don't worry about me, Rob, no matter what happens. Trust me. I will always be there for you." Annie had a feeling that this might be a long journey that she had undertaken.

"Annie, what do you mean? Trust you, and you will always be there for me? Are you going somewhere else?" Rob was concerned.

John overheard Rob's conversation. He interrupted him. "Rob, let it be. Annie knows what she's doing."

Within moments after her conversation with Rob, Annie arrived at the homeless compound. She and Mike walked through the doors together. Mike was dragging his feet; he was weak from hunger. Two young men came rushing to Annie's side to help her; they knew Mike was in bad shape.

"Don't worry, lady; we can take it from here," they said.

Annie was worried about Mike. "Yes, help him, please. He needs to eat. And maybe a doctor could see him?"

The two gentlemen were gracious. "Yes, we'll take good care of him." They held Mike up and walked with him so he could get a hot meal.

"What's his name?" they asked.

"Mike."

Annie felt strange leaving Mike, but she knew he would be in good hands. She would call the homeless compound later and see how he was doing.

Annie was about to head out the door and catch a cab back to the radio station. She thought her mission was over. At that very same moment, Brad, who was dishing out food to the homeless, spotted Annie out of the corner of his eye. He couldn't take his eyes off her. She was glowing. Her bright light blinded him. He put his utensils down and rushed over to Annie just before she got to the door.

"Excuse me, my name is Brad," he said. "I'm the director of this homeless compound. Can I help you?"

"My name is Annie. Thank you, Brad." Annie looked up. There was a familiar light glowing in his eyes. "I think those young gentlemen have been more than gracious. I can't thank you enough."

"Annie, would you like to tell me the story behind the man you brought in? We really like to get to know our people before we help them, you know; we want to make them comfortable," Brad said.

He had a suggestion. "I have an idea. How would you like to have a warm, delicious cup of coffee with me? We could sit down and talk; and besides, you look a little bit tired yourself. Why don't you let me take care of you now?"

Annie liked that. She smiled and closed her eyes for a moment. "Yes, Brad, I would love a cup of coffee right now."

Brad took off his apron, brushed his wavy hair back and said, "Follow me, young lady."

Annie paused. "Where are we going?"

"I know this great place; it's a patisserie called Serendipity. Have you ever been there? It's on East 60th Street. They make lush frozen coffee and hot chocolate. It's simply wonderful."

Annie stopped dead in her tracks. He reminded her of Brandon. Could it be? Was it him? Annie shook her head. "NO," she told herself. She had to play this one out.

They arrived at Serendipity and were seated in the corner by the window looking out over the trees outside with their white twinkling lights that flashed on and off. Their round table had a big red candle as a centerpiece. A waiter approached them. "May I take your order?"

Brad spoke the very same words that Brandon once said. "We'll have that delightful coffee for two—you know, the one in the huge champagne glass—the frozen hot chocolate, with iced cocoa. And waiter, please, a splash of coffee on the side."

"Thank you, sir," the waiter said and left.

Brad couldn't help himself. He stared at Annie. "You're beautiful," he said.

Annie was taken aback. She peered deeply into Brad's eyes. He was so handsome, and his eyes were so gentle and comforting. There was something so familiar about him.

The waiter brought their frozen cocoa, with two straws. Annie sipped the drink at the same time Brad did. She looked up and smiled.

They spent hours getting to know each other. Annie explained in detail all about Rob and John and the radio station and how she managed to get to the homeless kitchen.

Brad told her about his philanthropic works and dreams of a better world.

Annie squirmed. She could hardly contain her emotions. She had the SAME feeling for Brad as she once had for Brandon.

Annie took the gum that she had been chewing while listening to Brad, rolled it into a ball with her finger tips, then stuck the wadded up gum under the tabletop. That old quirk of hers was back.

Brad observed what she did and gave a gasp. "What did you just do?" he asked.

Without thinking, Annie said, "Oh, I'm sorry; it's a weird quirk of mine—this gum thing." She shook her head. "I won't do it again. I promise." Brad's eyes lit up, as if her gum was a familiar memory. "I don't know what possessed me to ask about your gum; I didn't mean to be impolite. Annie, it's cute; it's okay."

At that moment an intense wave of emotion overpowered Annie. She felt love tingle all over her body, the same love she once felt for Brandon. She was experiencing it all over again with Brad.

"Brad, excuse me for a minute," she said and got up quickly. She went to the ladies' room to gather her thoughts. She washed her face and when she looked up, she saw me, Gabriel, smiling at her in the mirror. Annie smiled back. That's when she realized it was indeed Brandon.

She picked up her cell and called Rob and John at the station.

"Hello, this is John."

"John, it's Annie. Is Rob there?"

"Yes," John said, waving Rob over to the phone.

"John, put me on speaker so Rob can hear me." John did. "Please, you guys, listen to me; I don't have much time. I'm at Serendipity with Brad; he's the head guy from the homeless compound. Please understand what I'm about to tell you…I think Brandon kept his promise."

In unison they both asked, "What promise, Annie?"

Annie explained, "In the ambulance, just before Brandon died, he held my hand and told me I would find him. Rob, John, I think I found Brandon."

There was silence on the phone.

"I'll be a while. I have to find out if it's him," Annie said.

Rob and John looked at each other, dumbfounded. They shook their heads. John said, "Don't look at me; I don't understand her either." The phone went dead; Annie had hung up.

Annie composed herself and returned to her seat where Brad had been waiting patiently.

"Is everything okay, Annie?" he asked.

Annie smiled and nodded. Before Brad could say another word, Annie reached across the table and gently squeezed his hand. She gazed into his eyes with deep longing. She whispered softly and with intensity the very same words she longed to say to Brandon. **"Brad… Brandon, Remember Me?"**

Time stood still. The world around them faded out and the veil came down for Annie. From the very heart of her soul she knew it was Brandon.

The heavens parted and I, Gabriel, gazed down from Heaven. I smiled a long, broad smile. "They finally got it right." I turned and walked away amid the white puffy clouds.

Epilogue

Our story doesn't quite stop here. **Kate and John** ended up having a small wedding in New York City. Kate helped John form his own Rock Band, something he always wanted from the bottom of his heart. He appeared in small gigs, all over New York, and he still maintained his position with Rob on the radio. Kate was his number one fan. She never told him she was once an angel; for, you see, she was given the choice to go back to Heaven or remain on Earth. Kate chose to remain on Earth with John.

Pat, the Psychic Channel, became world famous. He appeared on talk show after talk show. He landed his own television show shortly thereafter. Pat went on to help thousands of souls. He loved his life and his travels.

Rose, Brandon's confidant, went on to produce several quality television shows. She's now working on producing her first psychic television show which includes Pat, the Psychic Channel.

Rob had his work to keep him busy. Annie continued to work with Rob on the radio for many years thereafter; they remained the best of friends. Several years later he was given the opportunity to buy the radio station, and he did. Rob spent a lot of time with his puppy, Angel...and, he went back with his wife; they were giving it one more try.

Rob still thinks of Annie now and then and wonders what might have been.

Annie and Brad/Brandon. The love Annie had for Brad/Brandon was beyond any lifetime she ever experienced. They spent the

226

rest of their days together, till the end of time. They died in each other's arms by the sea at a very old age.

Gabriel. When Annie and Brandon reached Heaven's gates, I was there to greet them. I was proud of my angel child. Brandon helped so many souls that he evolved to a higher level. And as for Annie, she sits by my side in Heaven, always trying to find a loophole and a way back to Earth so she can re-live her future life with Brandon once again—and maybe, someday I'll let her.

The End

**Coming soon, more adventures with Annie in
Somewhere
Between Heaven and Earth**

PSYCHIC DAYLE SCHEAR

TELEVISION APPEARANCES
Hard Copy Magazine (9 Stories, International Telecast)
Extra (National Telecast)
Beyond Chance (Lifetime, National Telecast)
Sally Jesse Raphael (National Telecast)
Gordon Elliot Show (National Telecast)
Sightings FOX (National Telecast)
Hour Magazine CBS (National Telecast)
The Late Show FOX (National Telecast)
Alive & Wellness Show, America's Talking (National Telecast)
New Year TV Special (FUJI-TV Tokyo, Japan-National)
AM San Francisco KGO-ABC (Regular 1 Year)
2 At Noon KTVU (Oakland)
ESP & You One Hour Specials
(KGMB-CBS & KITV-ABC, Hawaii, 14 Yrs)
Your Future One Hour Special (KGMB-CBS Hawaii)
Hawaiian Moving Company (KGMB-CBS Hawaii)
Anchorage Live, Good Morning Alaska (KIMO-ABC Alaska)
ESP & You One Hour Special (KIMO-ABC Alaska), **Tahoe Today KMTN**
Mystical Healing (Cable 22, Hawaii),
Daytime Show (KOLO-ABC Reno)
KHON News (NBC Hawaii), **KITV News** (ABC Hawaii)
KGMB News (CBS Hawaii), **KOLO News** (ABC Reno),
KMTN (Lake Tahoe)
KHBC (Hilo, Hawaii), **Numerous Telethons** (Charities)

NIGHTCLUBS
Sunset Station Casino (Las Vegas, Nevada**) 2005**
Westin Casuarina Las Vegas 2005
Harrah's Casino (Bill's Casino) (Lake Tahoe, Nevada)
Horizon Casino Resort (Lake Tahoe, Nevada)
Harrah's (Lake Tahoe & Reno, Nevada)
American Hawaii Cruise (Cruise Ship)
Holiday Inn (Waikiki, Hawaii), **23rd Step** (Hawaii)

RADIO SHOWS
21st Century Radio (Syndicated Nationally);
KGO, K101, KEST, KALX (San Francisco);
**KSSK (K59), KGU, KULA, KKUA, KIKI, KCCN,
I-94, KISA, KMVI, KKON, KPUA, KAUI, KBIG** (Hawaii);
KOWL, KTHO, KPTL, KLKT, (Lake Tahoe & Reno);
KENI (Alaska); **WWDB** (Philadelphia); **WCBM** (Baltimore); **KTAR**
(Arizona), **KTVB** (Texas), **KOOL, The Point 97 FM** (Las Vegas)

ARTICLES/OTHERS
What's On LV, Las Vegas Review Journal, (Nevada)
Washington Times (Washington DC)
Honolulu Advertiser, Honolulu Star Bulletin
Honolulu Magazine, Honolulu Weekly, Pets & People (Hawaii)
Tahoe Tribune, Reno Gazette, Nevada Appeal, (Nevada)
The Psychic Reader (CA), **The Spectator** (Mass.)
National Enquirer, Fate Magazine (National)

Books Published/Others
Dare To Be Different (Autobiography)
The Psychic Within (True Psychic Stories)
Believe (Spiritual Fable)
Tarot For Beginners (Book & Video)
Top 100 Psychics of America (Simon & Schuster)
Who's Who of America

For More Information visit Dayle's website;
www.dayleschear.com

To contact Dayle or to respond about the Book

Write to: *Dayle Schear*
            P. O. Box 172
            Zephyr Cove, Nevada 89448
            Website: dayleschear.com
            Email ESP555555@aol.com

About the Author

Psychic Dayle Schear was born in Newark, New Jersey, but Dayle's parents soon moved the family to Los Angeles.

Inevitably, the world-famed Psychic, Peter Hurkos, discovered Dayle's talent. Following their encounter, she underwent six years of rigorous training with Peter until his death. Dayle is his "only living protégé."

In December of 1988 Dayle married a local boy from the Hawaiian Islands, Blythe Arakawa. Together with their prized German shepherd, they divide their time between Honolulu, Hawaii, and Lake Tahoe, Nevada.

Dayle is also the author of **Dare To Be Different!**, which describes the eventful, spiritual journey of a Psychic; **The Psychic Within, True Psychic Stories; Tarot for the Beginner** (Blue Dolphin Publishing, 1994, now in its fourth printing); **Believe, a spiritual fable.**

Dayle appears in nightclubs in Las Vegas and Lake Tahoe. In her new show she is able to cross over to the other side.

She had an on-going television talk show called "ESP & YOU" on CBS and ABC affiliates in Honolulu for fourteen years. She has been a guest on numerous national television talk shows as well as radio talk shows throughout the nation.

Dayle and Blythe enjoy traveling and playing with their German shepherd, as well as boating and golfing in Lake Tahoe and around the Hawaiian Islands.

If you want to address the author, write to Dayle Schear, P.O. Box 172, Zephyr Cove, NV 89448, or call 775-588-3337 or Honolulu, Hawaii, 808-395-2327, where Dayle spends most of her time now.

Please let us know how you like this book,

An Angel over the Airwaves.

You can reach Dayle at www.dayleschear.com
or e-mail to ESP555555@aol.com